MY LIFE

BLOODY BUSINESS

BOOK 2

AJ WOLF

Cover Image/Book Design & Formatting by AJ Wolf
Editing by Sisters Get Lit(erary) Author Services

Don't fight
for the love
that doesn't
fight for you —
respect yourself.

— Juansen Dizon

IT'S A BLOODY
Eun Affare

BUSINESS
Insanguinato

Back in Euphoria

"**O**kay! mercy… mercy! Yelling through my giggles I try to roll away, but Donatello has me in a firm grip, tickling my sides as I kick and squirm in an attempt to escape his punishment.

Laughing at my struggles, he easily pulls me up and onto his lap, grabbing one of my wrists in each of his large hands to keep me in place as I straddle his hips. "Now tell me the truth, you rotten woman." He's smirking at me as my giggles trail off, and I lean forward to steal a quick kiss, smiling against his lips before sitting back.

My belly fills with fireflies as his russet eyes dance across my face, and his thumbs brush the inside of my wrists; he's trying to keep a serious face, lips pressed tightly together, waiting for my answer. "Fine, since you have to know sooo badly…" I trail off, and he raises a brow in warning, a smile trying to fight its way out, making the corner of his lips tick. "I have a tournament with Grizzle this weekend. That's why I won't be here…not because I'm spending time with my other secret boyfriend."

Placing a kiss on each wrist, he releases his grip, eyes flicking between my own as he wraps his arms around my lower back and pulls me close. His fingers brush along the sliver of skin showing between my jeans and tee, causing goosebumps to bloom along my skin as he tilts his head back to rest on the couch. "Where is it? I can probably come watch you compete on Sunday."

"Nassau Coliseum. It's close enough I could come home every day but it's easier to stay there…" Now that my hands are free, I run my fingers through his dark hair, pushing loose strands from his forehead, tracing a finger from his hairline, down his nose and over his lips. I laugh when he crosses his eyes, following the path of my finger before my hand drops between us. "And if I'm lucky I'll get to see the stars without all the giant buildings and bright lights all over."

Pushing some of my own hair over my shoulder he runs his fingertips along my neck and up to skim my cheek, giving me a lopsided grin when an involuntary shiver zips along my spine. "You want to see the stars?"

"Yes. They're beautiful." I nip at his finger as it traces over my lips, mimicking my earlier touch and his smile grows. "Why? You don't like looking at the stars?" I ask it with playful annoyance, knitting my brows as I fight a smile of my own.

"I don't need to look at the stars." He sits forward and presses his lips to mine, his hand pushing into my hair as he pulls back just far enough to speak, his breath feathering along my lips while the fireflies in my belly start buzzing again. "Sei più bella di tutte le stelle nel cielo." *You are more beautiful than all the stars in the sky.*

Chapter One

I should be doing the mountain of laundry I dumped in my living room or, at the very least, buying groceries instead of grinding against the blond haired, blue-eyed playboy I'm currently dancing with. But here I am anyway, putting off the inevitable. At some point, I'll need to deal with all the feelings I ran away from when I stormed off to Auburn University; face the person I left behind.

I knew I needed to leave the minute I stepped foot back into my apartment; put all that on hold just a little longer and allow myself a few more hours of freedom from the regret and bitterness that's staining the sheetrock and filling the space like a cloying fog. There are too many memories hidden in the walls to deal with right now, whispering ugly lies and half-truths like poltergeist intent on making me go mad.

The perfect way for me to let loose is to do exactly what I'm doing now, losing myself in the thrum of loud music and copious amounts of alcohol. I'm fairly underdressed compared to the other girls parading around in their short skirts and flashy dresses; my cropped black tank, high waisted shorts, and wedge

Converse are more appropriate for somewhere less swanky, but I hadn't felt like taking the time to dig through my clothes. I had taken the time to straighten my naturally wavy hair this morning, though, so it helps dress the outfit up, hanging to mid-back in a glossy black sheet. Judging on the number of free drinks I've been able to swindle so far, I don't think my outfit is an issue anyway.

Spinning to face my unsuspecting partner in crime, I lean forward to speak into his ear over the music. "I'll be right back. I'm going to get a refill." I hold my empty beer up as I pull back, and he smiles with a nod, giving my hips a soft squeeze before letting me shimmy by. Resting my chin on my fist as I wait at the bar, I can't help but eavesdrop on the pair of girls giggling behind me. From what I can tell, they're swooning over some mystery man… pass; I'm content to just dance tonight. I have my own mystery man to worry about, one I shouldn't even be thinking of right now. Shifting my gaze back to my dance partner, I watch as he glides towards a leggy brunette, forcing himself into her group of dancers with a few calculated moves; what a traitor. That must be my cue to leave.

Sighing dejectedly, I wave towards the bartender, making sure she sees the tip I place under my bottle while I reach over the counter to grab the bag that she was kind enough to watch for me. Pushing through the exit, I pause on the sidewalk to dig out my phone to get an Uber, the music from inside growing loud as someone opens the door after me.

"Not going home with blondie back there?"

His voice invades my space like a physical being, wrapping me up in its smoky mist, bringing with it a tumble of emotions that makes my breath catch in my lungs and my spine involuntarily stiffen. I try to hide my reaction and ignore him, keeping my eyes trained on the app screen as my fingers pinch around my phone.

I'm not really all that surprised he found me; Beverly's been talking about me coming home for weeks now. If anything, I'm actually surprised he waited this long to approach me; I almost expected him to bombard me the moment I landed back in the city. I should have known he'd come sneaking along to snatch my short-lived peace out from under me like a dirty rug instead of allowing myself to think I'd be safe from him for the night.

The stupid fireflies in my belly are swarming like a group of hornets, stinging my gut almost painfully as I avoid looking over at him; just knowing he's in such close proximity sends an unwanted buzzing up my spine and along my limbs. If I were a junkie, he'd be my fix, and my body is having some serious withdrawals after spending so much time apart. His presence is burning into my side as I force my face to remain passive, pretending to mess with my phone even after I've finished requesting my ride. Knowing he won't leave without a response, I grit out through tight lips, "My boyfriend wouldn't like that." I don't actually have a boyfriend, but he doesn't need to know that.

Finally, allowing my gaze to rise to his face, my heart beats like a caged animal against my ribs, breath squeezing through a throat tight with nerves. Nine months and he's still the only one that gets those damn fireflies buzzing, and believe me, I tried finding a replacement, tried damn hard to forget everything about his man.

He isn't even trying to hide the skepticism from his face as his russet eyes trail along my exposed skin, a single dark brow arched as a thumb brushes along his full lower lip. "You're not dating." It's said like concrete fact instead of an assumption, and it makes me bristle with annoyance even as his appraisal blooms an unsolicited warmth beneath my skin.

"You don't know anything about me anymore, Donatello." I say it once his dark eyes meet mine, letting him know he was caught peeping; he just shrugs, a smirk ticking the corner of his mouth. "I have a boyfriend," I say it definitively, letting my eyes coast over his form while feigning a look of distaste; there's absolutely nothing distasteful about him though, and he knows it if his confident grin is anything to go off of. Despite his lack of emotion, I know the idea bothers him, based on how his tattooed thumb is spinning a ring on his forefinger. Good.

"Sure you do…" He steps closer, invading my space, and I turn away to look out at the busy street; he's close enough that his chest brushes against my bare arm, and I take a slight step to the side to break the contact. "Are you going home? I'll bring you."

Flashing an insincere smile, I hold my phone up then cross my arms over my chest, looking back towards the street. "I got an Uber… you can leave now." His following chuckle sends those damn fireflies fluttering again, and I frown over at him, my lips twisting into a sneer. "Seriously, Donatello, leave. I'm more than capable of getting myself home."

His eyes are trained on my burgundy painted lips as I speak, lifting to mine for the barest of seconds before I turn my face away. "Beverly's orders. Unless you want to call her and risk waking up the babies… I'm taking you home."

Resisting the urge to roll my eyes, I continue to stare at the street. Of course, Beverly would be mother henning me right now. I can see his smirk from the corner of my eye; he knows I'm not going to take the risk of dealing with Beverly's wrath. Eyes narrowing on Donatello, I mockingly hold an arm out, gesturing for him to go ahead. "Fine. Lead the way."

"How were you drinking? You're not twenty-one." Donatello asks as we get closer to my apartment, breaking the silence we've been riding in. His voice is such a contradiction; it's smoky and coarse, but it runs over you like thick, smooth honey. Every word from his mouth sticks to my skin as a messy reminder of what used to be, and I resist the urge to physically scrub my hands over myself to shake off the feeling.

Keeping my gaze trained on the passing lights out the window, I almost ignore his question, pretending like I don't notice the goosebumps creeping along my skin. "I let the bouncer grab my tits." At his scoff, I flick my eyes to him with a crude smile.

"You have a fake ID, yea?" He briefly meets my gaze before I look back at the road; he's not even slightly convinced by my explanation. I find it incredibly annoying how unphased he's been around me. I didn't expect him to grovel at my feet, he ended things with us, but I also didn't expect him to act like everything is right as rain.

I wait a long enough time to answer that it seems like I'm not going to, eyes shifting to study his profile as he drives. "If you knew the answer, then why did you ask." It's a rhetorical question, so I'm not expecting an answer, but I use it as an excuse to stare at him for a minute. He looks really damn good. His dark chocolate hair is artfully disheveled in that way only guys seem to manage, the longer pieces on top starting to fall across his forehead; my fingers itch to reach out and brush it aside, so I clench them in my lap, squeezing hard enough I can feel my nails leaving crescents in my palms.

His skin is a golden tan that I know brings out the red in his eyes without having to look at them, and he has his usual outfit on, black tee, dark jeans, and boots; fingers still wrapped in several rings. The three arrows pointing towards his knuckle on his left thumb is the only tattoo that I can see and assume is still his only one.

Noticing my lingering gaze, he gives me a crooked grin. The kind of grin that used to make my heart clench. The kind that should have absolutely zero effect on me now because I am so over Donatello that I shouldn't even question the fireflies tickling my gut or the loud beating of my heart in my ears. Inconspicuously running my sweaty palms across the denim of my shorts, I don't return his smile; he can take his hospitality and shove it up his ass.

Brows knitting into another frown, I look back out the front window. I catch myself rubbing a thumb along my left ring finger, over the small tattoo that pairs with his and stuff my hands between my thighs. He doesn't know about the two small arrows I got inked into my skin when I naively thought he was my everything and he can't see it either; thanks to the henna design that wraps around my fingers, across my hand, and up to my wrist that I had done before coming home. I hate the tattoo. It's a constant reminder of how stupid this man made me; how stupid I was for thinking he could ever love me the same as I did him. I can feel his eyes on me, and my pulse flutters with the attention. Ugh, I'm so ready for this ride to be over.

As soon as he pulls up to the curb, I'm jerking the car door open and speed walking up to the glass paned security door. It takes me a minute to remember the new code, and I huff, feeling Donatello at my back as I finally punch the correct sequence in and unlock the door. "What are you doing? I'm not letting you up." I spit out over my shoulder as I open the door, spinning to face him with my back against the glass. It's cool against my overheated skin, an effect of all the feelings I've been riding since Donatello showed up. He surprises me by stepping even closer than he was already standing, putting my scowling face inches from his smiling one.

After a fleeting, almost awkward silence, he reaches up and skims his fingers across my cheek to push a strand of hair from my face; my breath catches at his touch, and he uses the distraction to push his way through the door and into the stairwell, ignoring my protesting scoff while shooting a smirk over his shoulder at me. "Hurry up, Delaney. It's late, and I'm tired."

What the hell? "What do you think you're doing?! Get out!" I yell at his retreating back as I let the door slam shut and stomp up after him. He's taking the steps two at a time, so I'm forced to run up the stairs or be left behind. He's chuckling at my labored breaths once I catch up, and I'm half tempted to shove him down the stairs as I grab onto the back of his shirt to slow his pace. I shoulder past him as we hit my landing, forcing myself in front of him in the hall, which makes him laugh even more. "I'm not letting you in."

"You said that about letting me up… yet, here I am."

I shoot a glare over my shoulder as I'm unlocking the door, extremely aware of his gaze on my back the entire time. "Go home." He doesn't respond so I quickly try to slip inside and shut the door before he can get past. He must have anticipated it because his large hand smacks against the door, easily keeping it open as I attempt to push it shut.

My feet are skidding and sliding back on the floor as he pushes back using a single arm, and I can't help the growl of annoyance that sneaks out of me. What has he been bench pressing, fucking elephants? "Donatello, knock it off! Go home!" I'm trying to be quiet and not wake up the other residents on my floor, so it starts as a loud whisper but escalates into an actual yell as it becomes increasingly more obvious that I'm not going to be able to keep him out.

He brushes past me once the door is open enough, letting go of it on his way in which causes me to fall forward and unintentionally slam the door obnoxiously loud, my face nearly smacking against it before I catch myself. Great, I'm going to get written up my first night back here.

Ripping at the laces of my wedges, I throw my shoes off one by one, letting them smack against the wall dramatically while he stands at the end of the small entryway, arms crossed over his chest watching me. I notice his boots are already off, set neatly by the wall, and I open my mouth to tell him to fuck all the way off, but he cuts me off before I even begin. "It's two AM. I'm staying... do you have any clean blankets? Because that pile of laundry says otherwise."

I feel my cheeks heat with both embarrassment and annoyance at his observation and grit my teeth; how rude. "Yes, I have clean blankets." I snap it at him while tossing my bag onto the console table and send him a look that shows just how stupid I think he is. "Those are from my dorm...I just haven't taken care of them yet." I don't know why I feel the need to explain that to him, but I do it anyway, smacking the thumb he used to gesture toward the pile out of my way. Now that I'm not in heels my eyes are level with his chin, and I have to tilt my face back to glare at him while I push him out of my way and stomp, quietly because I'm not trying to get any more possible complaints, to my room to change. He can wait for his damn blankets.

I change into a loose tank, and sleep shorts then wash my face before I even bother grabbing an extra comforter and pillow from my closet. I should demand Donatello leave; I don't have to put up with him anymore. I definitely shouldn't feel any kind of relief that I don't have to stay here alone, especially since the entire reason I don't want to be here is because of the same man who forced his way in. I shouldn't, but I kind of do, feel relieved that is. I'm not necessarily thrilled Donatello is the one here, but it is nice. Chewing on my lip I take a big breath and then head out of my room, it's been a while since I came back to change, maybe he decided to go home anyway.

His long, lean form is stretched out on my sectional as I exit the hall, flipping through channels on my TV; didn't leave then. "If you have a boyfriend, why hasn't Beverly said anything?" His eyes are on the TV when he asks, and I throw the blanket on his head, putting some extra oomph into it instead of answering. He's seriously still on this? I thought we ended this conversation forever ago. As soon as he pulls it off his face, I smack him with the pillow, smiling at his muffled grunt.

"Probably because it's none of your business."

His eyes track me as I walk to the pile of clothes and attempt to lift it all into a basket and push it out of the way. "What's his name?"

Scowling over my shoulder at him, I pick up a few stray clothes that fell from the basket and toss them into the corner with the rest, trying to ignore the tingles brushing along my skin as his eyes roam over me in obvious approval of my clothing choice. "Why would I tell you that? So, you and Ollie can find him and scare him off? No thanks. Drop it, Donatello." Straightening, I put my hands on my hips and face him fully. "Why the hell do you even care? We aren't a thing and barely were before."

The sting I was hoping to deliver with my remark doesn't seem to hit as I watch him slowly stand from the couch, the look he's leveling me with making my heart thump in my chest and setting off those pesky fireflies again. Hooded eyes track my movements as my back bumps up against the kitchen island in a pitiful and albeit, halfhearted attempt to keep distance between us. He pushes into my space, bracing his arms on the counter on each side of me as his spicy, sweet scent fills my airways, rich and warm like spice cake. I fight the urge to breathe him in, his scent alone like a balm for my aching soul. Instead, I force shallow breaths that leave my chest in small shaky exhales, pretending I don't notice how his nostrils flare just the slightest bit as he allows himself to do the very thing I fought not to do.

His big hard body is tugging at mine by the loose strings of my heart, and I have to fight the need to lean into him, run my hands along his toned chest and pull him to me. Russet eyes dance over my face, catching on my lips as he finally breaks the silence. "I will always care where you're concerned." He brings a hand up to run his fingertips along my jaw in a whisper of a touch, tracing over my cheekbone, and pushing hair behind my ear while he looks between my own coffee colored eyes. "Ti meriti il mondo." *You deserve the world.*

His soft words, paired with the yearning look on his face, makes my heart squeeze in my chest with a longing of its own. No. Nope. I'm not going back down that trail of heartbreak… I can't.

I dip under his arm despite the protesting of my body and take a few steps away to create some much-needed space, heart crawling into my throat like it would jump out to him if it could. "What are you doing? We tried this, remember. It didn't work out…and now I have a boyfriend." His head is hanging, big body arched over where I previously stood, an arm still resting on the counter. "A really handsome one who is probably going to be a doctor or something equally prestigious… So back off, Donatello."

Standing up straight, he slowly crosses his arms over his chest, a lopsided grin creeping along his lips as his eyes lazily trail along my form once again, like he's unconsciously reassuring himself I'm actually here. Or maybe that's just wishful thinking on my part that he missed me as much as I missed him. "Probably going to be? You don't know what your boyfriend is majoring in?"

I point at him from my place across the room, hands shaking the slightest bit from the turmoil of emotions that have been bubbling since he showed up at the club. I narrow my eyes on him in a frown and hope he doesn't notice my inability to hold still. "Stop doing that."

"Stop what? I'm not doing anything." He laughs as he says it, and I cross my own arms, copying his posture while hiding my trembling hands.

"You know what you're doing... Stop trying to find ways to make my VERY REAL boyfriend seem fake."

A dark look flashes over his features, and he marches over to me before I have time to react, gripping the back of my head in his large palm and yanking my lips to his. It's a brutal clash of lips, our teeth clinking almost painfully, lips pressed together roughly. But it only takes a fraction of a second to change into something so much sweeter as he cups my face with his other hand, thumb stroking my jaw as his tongue dances with mine. I'm responding to his touch like a love drunk moron, lifting onto my toes to press against him, clutching his shirt in my hands. He tastes like Big Red gum with a hint of bourbon, and my hand reaches up to pull his face even closer, gripping the back of his nape, to run my fingers along the short hair there of its own accord.

Goosebumps pebble my skin as his kiss hits me with a kind of euphoria I only find with him, my heart banging so roughly against my chest I can hear the echo in my ears, those loose strings aching to wrap around his. Being in his arms feels so damn good, his touch burning across my skin as a hand slides up under my tank to push up my back. It's enough to bring some of my attention back into focus, breaking the spell he cast with his lips. What the fuck am I doing?

I hastily drop my hand from his hair, pressing my palms to his chest to push back from him. He only lets me pull a fraction away, though, our lips still brushing. He's smiling against my lips, slowly opening those russet eyes to stare into my own. "How real is that boyfriend now?"

He lets me shove out of his arms, as I make a big show of wiping my mouth off, scowling over at his crooked grin. "Keep your hands off me, Donatello... you're disgusting."

"Hmmm. You sure didn't seem disgusted when you were sticking your tongue down my throat." He uses his thumb to wipe the corner of his mouth, and I can't help but be drawn to the movement. My body unintentionally leaning towards him.

Feigning nonchalance, I pull myself straight and scoff loudly, praying he didn't notice while brushing imaginary lint off my tank to avoid eye contact. "That was me gagging. You're lucky I held in my vomit."

He lets out a loud guffaw, and I glare over at him as he speaks. "You're a terrible liar."

"And you're an awful person. Who purposefully kisses someone that's in a relationship?"

He's still smiling as he moves back to the couch to lay down, propping his pillow up behind his head, then folding his arms behind his neck before his gaze finds mine again, the warmth pooling in my belly turning into an inferno as his tongue runs over his lower lip. "You're not in a relationship."

God, he's stupidly annoying. "You're delusional, and I'm going to bed... turn off all the lights." I wave a hand around in a vague gesture towards the lights as I turn away from him, purposefully flicking on a few that were already off as I give him a rude kind of smile.

"Why don't you? You're already up." I can hear the smile in his voice as he says it to my retreating back, and I ignore him, quietly stomping to my room.

My skin is buzzing from his touch; my heart still banging an uneven rhythm against my ribs. Turning to shut my door, I stare down the hallway for a moment; it's almost tempting to march back out there and demand he finish what I stubbornly ended. But that would just end in disaster for me, I know it.

Clenching my jaw, I yell out to him. "I hope you sleep terribly!" His laugh leaks through the door as I push it shut and climb into my own bed. It's going to be a long summer.

Back in Euphoria

"**O**KAY, ONE MORE... you got it this time." Aiming my piece of popcorn for Donatello's mouth across the couch, I laugh when it bounces off his forehead and onto the floor.

"I feel like most of this is your fault." He says, waving towards the popcorn all over the couch and floor as he sits up, loose pieces falling from his shirt to land with the rest.

"How? You're the one who missed them." I drop my head into his lap, smiling up at him when he looks down at me.

"You have terrible aim." I scoff as he grabs a handful of popcorn from the bowl on my stomach, purposefully dropping pieces onto my face as he shoves it into his mouth.

"You're a mess."

He chuckles, grabbing the bowl off of my stomach and leaning forward to set it on the floor. His hands come to the back of my head, lifting me to his lips as he bends over, kissing me in his lap. "Maybe…" He brushes his nose along mine, making me giggle before he sits again, pulling me up with him. I straddle his waist, tucking my feet behind his back, so I'm wrapped around him. "Rock, paper, scissors to see who has to clean it up."

"No… you always find a way to cheat." He presses a kiss to my chin as I wrap my arms around his neck, a smirk tipping the corner of his lips at my response.

"I don't cheat. You're just not very good."

"That's rude." I laugh when he tickles my sides, wiggling in his lap. "Stop! Fine, I'll play your dumb game." I shift back far enough to bring my hand forward, making a face at Donatello when he brings his hand in front of me.

"Rock, paper, scissors." We say in unison, his hand forming scissors while mine stays rock.

"Yeeees!" I throw my hands up in cheer, doing a winning jig in his lap as he sits back against the cushions in defeat.

"Damn… guess I'll have to leave it for the cleaners tomorrow."

"That's cheating! You have to clean it!" I smack his chest, and he laughs, palming my cheeks and forcing me down for a kiss.

"There were no rules on how we had to clean it." He says once he lets me back, another laugh coming out of him when he sees my expression.

"You are seriously the worst… no wonder Ollie refuses to make bets with you." I let my arms go back around his neck, running my fingers through the hair at his nape.

He hums and shrugs his shoulders, his arms wrapping around my waist. "Work smarter, not harder, Vita Mia."

"Parole di saggezza dal vecchio." *Words of wisdom from the old.*

"Divertente. Dimmi di nuovo perché mi piaci?" *Funny. Tell me again why I like you?* Raising a brow, I pull my hands from his hair and fold my arms over my chest, earning a chuckle from him. "Oh, I remember..." He says, pushing his hands into my hair to pull my face towards his. "You're smart and funny..." he brushes his nose along mine again, making me smile, "you smell like leather and coconut, and you look amazing in those tight pants you wear riding..." He smiles at my snort, his russet reds shifting between my eyes and lips. "E tu sei la donna più bella che abbia mai visto." *And you are the most beautiful woman I have ever seen.*

"Those are pretty good reasons." I manage to squeeze out before his lips land on mine, my smile bleeding into his kiss.

Chapter Two

I'm bouncing a slobbery Amalia in my lap as Beverly attempts to wrangle Carmella into a clean onesie, something that took her almost ten minutes to do with Amalia. "I never said that." Beverly says after finally getting Carmella's arm through the correct hole, only took fifty tries. In her defense, though, the girls tried their best to stay naked.

"What do you mean, you never said that?" Snapping the onesie in place, Bev frowns over at me like my question was the dumbest thing she's ever heard, and Carmella takes the opportunity to roll out of her grip, chunky little arms, and legs crawling in the opposite direction at what I can only assume she considers breakneck speed.

"I mean exactly what I said…" She hurries and snatches up the stray baby, grabbing a little leg to push into a pair of floral print pants. "I didn't tell Donatello to get you."

"Are you freaking kidding me?!" Amalia starts squealing and waving her arms about happily, clearly misinterpreting my yell for one of excitement than the annoyed disbelief that it actually was. I can't help but smile down at her wiggly little body in my lap, even though I'm brimming with irritation. I forced Bev to FaceTime me every Sunday since they were born, but getting to hold and cuddle them in person is so much better. They're almost the spitting image of Beverly with their dark hair, freckles, and hazel eyes, just as feisty, too. "He just made that up?"

"Obviously." Carmella starts kicking wildly, squealing with her sister, and yanks a leg from the pants Beverly was just about done fighting to get on. Throwing the pants across the room, Beverly lets Carmella scoot away. "What the fuck ever…You don't need fucking pants." She stands and scoops up the girls' dirty clothes while yelling to Gretchen in the kitchen, "Gretchen? Can you watch the girls for a few? They're just in the living area."

Gretchen pops out from the doorway almost immediately, wiping her plump hands down the front of her apron before slipping it over her grey head to lay across the back of the couch. "Si. Lascia quei bambini con me, hai bisogno di una pausa comunque." *Yes. Leave those children with me, you need a break anyway.* At Beverly's blank stare, she frowns and begins waving her arms in a very obvious get lost motion. "Yes… Go."

"Okay, I'm just going to take care of this laundry and check on Dylan real fast."

Gretchen is still shooing her as she moves to sit on the floor by the girls, her cooing at direct odds with the frown she sends towards Beverly when she sees her still in the room and not sprinting away at her command. I nudge Beverly with my elbow, and she starts towards the laundry room with a slight shake of her head, her newly shortened hair swinging around her shoulders with the movement. "I can't believe that ass lied to me. He even forced his way up and slept on the couch." I fold my arms over my chest as I watch Beverly spray an ungodly amount of stain remover onto the girls' clothes. "I don't think you need that much, Bev…And when did you start doing laundry? Don't you have a cleaner?"

She ignores me and sprays even more, the fabric soggy and dripping over the washing machine. "Yes, I do, or it will stain. They stain everything unless I douse it in this shit." Shutting the machine door, she turns to face me, looking rather aggressive, considering the conversation is about clothing. "We have someone who does laundry, but those stains would set into the fabric before they got washed. I like to spray them first."

"That's really dramatic. They're stains… and have you read the directions on that bottle? Because I'm positive, that was way too much."

Leaving the room as I trail her, she heads towards the backyard. "What would you know? I heard you don't even do your laundry."

I gasp at her back. She's rather snippy today, I see. Gretchen is right. She does need a break. "Have you been talking to Donatello behind my back?!" She laughs at me, moving out the door to stand in the lawn to whistle for Dylan. "And I had just gotten back from my dorm… I've done those clothes now." She gives me a disbelieving side-eye as Dylan trots over to us, carrying a pinecone. "Fine… I've washed most of them." Reaching down to grab the pinecone Dylan dropped at my feet, I toss it for him before leveling Beverly with a look. "Why are you talking to

Donatello about me? That has to break some kind of best friend code."

"He brought you up." She takes the pinecone this time, throwing it ridiculously far for someone her size. "I got the impression he was weeding for information about your fake boyfriend."

"Why do you think he's fake? He's not fake. Why is it so hard for you people to believe I have a boyfriend?"

Rolling her eyes, she crosses her arms over her chest. "You're telling me that you somehow kept this boyfriend of yours a secret? You can't keep secrets. And you're a terrible liar."

Crossing my own arms, we stare at each other. She raises one of her dark brows in a sassy challenge as I struggle to keep my defiant stance. Her hazel eyes narrow further, and I concede, slapping my arms down at my sides as she smiles over her victory. "Fine… I made my boyfriend up." Dylan drops a stick at Bev's feet this time, and she chucks it across the lawn. "I knew it'd bother Donatello and it's kind of a buffer to keep him at bay…Well, it's supposed to be." He clearly isn't wildly intimidated about my mystery man, curious but not worried, based on his actions last time I saw him. Yanking on my hoodie strings, I frown towards the tree line as Dylan disappears to find something else to play with. "What did you tell him?"

"That you had a boyfriend, and if he wanted more details, he had to ask you himself."

I feel the muscles in my shoulders loosen at her answer, some of the tension dissipating with the knowledge that she kept my secret. "Good." I'm not sure why I even care, but it somehow feels important to keep the lie going.

Flicking her eyes over to me, she scans me for a moment, a look of contemplation on her face. "You ready to talk about…" She waves her hand in a circle, gesturing at me vaguely, "all that Donatello bullshit that had you sprinting off to school a week early?" I open my mouth to deny any such situation, but she cuts me off. "Don't even start with me. We both know you and Donatello were more serious than you let on. You took off for school, and he sulked around here for weeks, even Remy noticed."

"Hmmm." I hum while anxiously adjusting my ponytail. The mention of Remy causes a rush of annoyance to prickle at my skin. Donatello never said it, but I know Remy is one of the main reasons he refused to be anything more than closet fuck buddies. I also have a suspicion he's the reason Donatello ended things so abruptly before I left for school. "No. I'm not ready to talk about anything." My voice sounded more bitter than I meant it too, so I try to soften the words with a smile sent Bev's way. "Thank you, though…you'll be the first to know if I ever decide to rip that band-aid off."

She nods and lets out a loud breath. I wouldn't be surprised if she knew more about my situation then she lets on, she's just considerate enough to keep her unwanted opinions to herself. One of the many things I love about her. She knows when to leave shit be and when to push me into talking. "Remy is going to want to see you soon."

Her passive aggressive statement hits its mark, and I shove my hands in my sweatshirt pocket. So, she definitely knows I've been avoiding him. "I know. I can stay for dinner sometime this week."

That seems to placate her because she turns to go back inside without another word, Dylan trailing behind her with a crunched-up tennis ball he must have found in the bushes. "Rico should be here soon... I'm sure he's tired of having to be your stand in since you left."

"Rico loves listening to your gossip, don't let him fool you. He and Marcus play poker every Thursday night at Uncle Theo's and spread all the tea like it's their own." I reach down and lightly tug Dylan's ear as we walk, and he playfully flashes his teeth while wagging his tail; if I were anyone else, he probably would have bitten me like the rude butt he is. "If you stopped talking to him, he'd have nothing to report, and they'd kick him out of the group."

"How do you know that?"

"I was eavesdropping on Andrea and heard him telling one of the made men to watch what they say around Rico because he's a gossip. Then, the made man brought up poker." Gretchen is still on the floor playing with the girls as we walk into the living area, and she barely spares us a look as we both sit down. Coaxing Dylan up onto the sofa next to me with a few exaggerated pats on the seat, he hops up next to me, flipping onto his back for a belly rub.

"Smetti di incoraggiare quell cane! È già viziato marcio dia Beverly." *Stop encouraging that dog! He's already spoiled rotten by Beverly.* Gretchen scowls up at me while making grabby hands at Amalia, who's giggling at her.

"What did you say? Are you talking about me?" Beverly pipes up from the other couch, frowning at Gretchen while reaching down to scoop up Carmella.

I ignore her and roll my eyes at Gretchen. "Come se non aessi risparmiato cibo extra ad ogni pasto solo per lui." *As if you don't save extra food at every meal just for him.*

She huffs at me but doesn't say anything, and Beverly reaches over to pinch my arm. "What the fuck are you guys saying? You know I hate that."

"Ow!" I frown over at her while rubbing my arm, speaking to Dylan instead of answering Bev. "You have a mean mommy, Dylan." Beverly is holding her hand up like she might smack me this time, so I push up out of my seat and out of reach. "Gretchen said Dylan was spoiled and to get him off the couch."

This earns a gasp from the ever-dramatic Beverly who turns to Gretchen. I hurry and skirt out of the room to avoid the ensuing bickering and head towards the kitchen to sneak some candy from Bev's jar. Stepping through the door, I run straight into Rico, who makes a loud 'oof' sound as I bounce off his chest and grab the door frame to keep myself up.

"Oh, shit!" He grabs one of my arms to make sure I'm steady, a small smile tugging at the corner of his lips as his cheeks start turning a light pink. "Sorry, Laney."

Properly righting myself, I smile up at him, the curls flopping across his forehead, hiding most of his umber gaze from me. "Bev said you missed me while I was gone." She never said that, but I know me saying it will make him squirm, which is kind of a favorite pastime for me. I know it's one of Bev's, too; the poor guy is never going to get a break, it seems. He could request a different job, but Remy probably wouldn't let him leave anyway, Bev likes him, and Bev gets what she wants where Remy is concerned.

That pink hue is creeping along his neck now as he dips his head to avoid my gaze completely, stuffing his hands into his front pockets. "I... Yea, I guess I did miss having you around."

I laugh at his nervousness, lightly pushing his chest, so he knows I'm only teasing him. We are still pretty close; neither one of us has really moved from our initial contact, making our interaction appear way more intimate than it actually is. "It's okay, Rico. Everyone missed me. You don't have to be embarrassed about it."

"Yea, Enrico... everyone missed her." My smile quickly turns into a frown at Donatello's voice, and I briefly close my eyes, gathering some composure before looking over Rico's shoulder to see the devil himself leaning against the pantry door frame. He isn't even supposed to be here today. I specifically asked Beverly.

"Some people know how to ruin the mood, don't they Rico?" Rico shifts uncomfortably in front of me, throwing a quick look over his shoulder at Donatello. He can probably feel the daggers being eyed into his back by the latter.

"Uh... I'll probably see you later, Laney." Rico gives a tentative smile and edges around me, giving an awkward slight nod to Donatello before hurrying out of the room.

Leveling a glare on Donatello, I stomp towards the pantry. "Why are you here? I specifically came today because Beverly said you'd be gone."

"You were asking Beverly about me? How sweet." He shifts to block the pantry doorway, effectively blocking my path before I can get by him. "Your boyfriend know how close you and Enrico are?"

"What are you even talking about? Rico and I aren't anything." I shake my head at him in annoyance, choosing to ignore the hint of jealousy woven into his words. Gesturing towards his large mass taking up the doorway, I narrow my eyes at him once more. "Get out of my way."

"What's the password?"

My throat squeezes at his question, the sweet playfulness too much for me to handle with our current situation and far too reminiscent of memories I'd rather stay buried. "Are you serious? Move."

"What's the password, Delaney?" He's taken a fraction of a step closer to me, still blocking the door but now assaulting my space with his warmth. His thick voice low, dripping over my skin as my heart beats a marathon behind my ribs.

"I'm not doing this." I force it past my tight throat, hands shaking with the effort to not let him see how much his simple game has affected me. I start to spin away, giving up on getting that candy, but he snatches my arm, stopping my progress and turning me back to face him. He's closer now, his chest brushing along mine with each quick breath I fight into my lungs.

He bends down and puts his mouth close to my ear, and I can feel his breath dancing along my skin, feel the phantom touch of his lips as he whispers, "What's the password?"

His thumb is stroking my inner arm, where he still has his fingers wrapped around my bicep. His other hand is heavy against my hip as I try my best to keep my own hands to myself. I know it's intentional, crowding my space with his spice cake scent and soft touches to manipulate me into playing his wicked game. He's a wolf in sheep's clothing. A smooth-talking Casanova bound to suck me in just to spit me out, broken and sad like a favorite childhood toy that's been outgrown.

I tighten my hands into fists to try and gain back some of my inner control, my nose just brushing his skin as he leans close. I can feel myself losing my already weak grip on my restraint, the brush of his lips scraping away at my paper walls. "Nutter Butter." It escapes my lips almost unbidden, barely loud enough to be heard. I hadn't meant to say it, but it fought its way out as I was unable to deny the pull between us.

A puff of air hits my ear as Donatello quietly chuckles, I can feel his smile as he rewards my participation with a soft kiss pressed to my temple, a quiet "Good girl" whispered against my hair. He straightens to look between my eyes. "I wasn't supposed to be here. I had some business that I ended up not needing to be part of."

I'm confused for a moment, forgetting about the earlier conversation. Pushing his hands off of me, I move to step around him, and he lets me this time, leaning his shoulder against the doorway to watch me grab the candy jar out from its hiding spot. I'm not sure why it even gets hidden anymore; everyone knows where it is. "Okay?" I snap at him while pulling out a handful of candy, shoving it in my hoodie pocket before putting the jar away, not bothering to ask Donatello if he wants any. I take a moment longer than necessary, shifting things into place to try and calm my racing heart, force my breaths to slow.

He continues to watch me as I pull out a little strawberry hard candy, making my skin heat when his dark eyes catch on my lips as I stick it in my mouth. "You're not going to ask if I want any? That's rude."

"No. I don't care about what you want." He hums as he pushes off the door frame, a hand snaking behind him to pull the pantry door mostly shut, blanketing the small space in almost complete darkness; the only light a small streak coming from the crack in the door. I bump up against the shelving as he creeps closer, his face a dark mask I can barely make out with the lack of light.

"Since you're not offering, I'll just have to take it then." His breath feathers across my mouth a second before his lips take its place, his body pressing flush against mine and pinning me against the shelves at my back.

I lose the battle to his dark lure, any common sense I might have had disappearing down the rabbit hole I seem to fall in whenever he's around. He uses a hand on my throat to tilt my head back, fingers lightly pinching each side of my jaw to give him better access to my mouth as I rise up on my toes and run a hand over one of his toned shoulders. My other hand is sliding into his hair, gripping it tightly to keep him in place. I feel drunk off his kisses, the taste of Big Red numbing my senses as his tongue slides over mine. I can barely hear anything past the whooshing of my heart in my ears; all my senses honed on the man sucking my bottom lip into his mouth. His hands are running over every inch of my body that they can reach, shamelessly grabbing my ass, fingers biting into any exposed flesh.

There are so many reasons I should end this now, stop it before things can progress, but I don't want to. For just this moment, I want to pretend he's the man I want him to be; that we were able to make things work. The hair raises along my arms as Donatello trails his lips down my chin to bite at my throat, sucking the skin at my pulse point as I drop my head back with a low groan. With a hand gripping the back of my head, he comes back to my lips. His breath puffing out as he skims his lips along my own, keeping far enough back that it's barely even a kiss. I lean up to deepen it once more, and he shifts back, smiling as he keeps his lips out of reach. "Beverly's looking for you."

His words barely register through my lusted-up brain, and I frown as he pulls back from my attempted kiss again. "What?" I can barely make out her voice calling for me in the background now that he's brought my attention to it. "Who cares?"

He bites my lip gently at my next attempt to kiss him, squeezing my ass in one of his hands before pulling back from me completely, slowly backing towards the door with a lopsided grin I can barely see. "You should go find her before she sends a search party."

I blink as the pantry floods with light and then scowl at Donatello as he laughs at my expression. "Are you serious right now?" Although his behavior is far from unexpected, it's irritating and jabs at my heart nonetheless.

"Thanks for the candy." His next smile shows off my strawberry hard candy pinched between his teeth, and he laughs as I stomp out of the pantry towards him. He easily dodges my wild grab and shuffles backward towards the door. "I'll see you around, Delaney."

The heat in his gaze and promise underlying his words cause an involuntary shiver to shake up my spine, and I grind my teeth together in annoyance as I watch him escape out the door. He turns just before he's out of sight, yelling to where I'm still standing in the kitchen, "You'll say hi to that boyfriend for me, yea?"

I scoff at his trailing laughter and run a hand over my lips in an attempt to wipe the taste of him away. I need to get a grip, or this summer will end just like the last one, with my heart broken.

Back in Euphoria

I slide the black and gold half skull mask onto my face, adjusting the strap, so it's hidden under the thick braids looping the top of my head. I've already put on my dress, a floor length sheer gold lace that loops around my neck with a black collar. I've put a black bandage style dress on underneath that crosses over my breasts, stomach, and butt; it covers just enough to be considered more than lingerie and leaves everything else visible through the lace. I went with simple black stilettos, not wanting to distract from the rest of the outfit.

Grabbing a clutch to stick my phone and essentials, I head downstairs for my ride. It's dark but warm, the city vibrating with summer energy. The venue is busy when my ride gets there, and it takes a good five minutes just for him to be able to get me to the front. Thanking him, I climb out, seamlessly blending into the other masked faces attending the party. I wasn't going to come; I didn't want to risk being seen, but that fear underweighted the one of having Donatello come with someone else. I can see now that my fears of being seen were mute, the lights are all dimmed inside, and there are so many people you can barely move without brushing into someone. There's no way someone will notice me unless I remove my mask.

I head for where I know most of the Famiglia attendees will be, intent on finding Donatello. I never confirmed I was coming, but he knew it was a possibility; hopefully, he was smart with that information. I put a lot of effort into my look. I'd hate for it to be wasted because he didn't want to dance alone, brought someone other than me.

My eyes find Donatello almost immediately, his dark head standing on the edges of everyone else. He rarely wears a suit, but he has one on now, all black but for a silver mask. His arms are crossed over his chest, and I can practically see his frown through the mask; he's never been a fan of parties.

My heart is pounding with both excitement and nerves as I move to walk behind him, trailing my fingertips along his back. He throws a look over his shoulder at me, head swinging the other way when I turn to stand in front of him. I step into his space, and he steps back. "Not interested."

His response makes me smile, bringing out my dimples. "Not even for a night?" I walk my fingers up his chest, watching as his eyes narrow inside of his mask, realizing who I am.

My smile grows when I see him grin, grabbing my hand from his chest to kiss my wrist. He pulls me closer to him so he can whisper in my ear. "Vieni a ballare con il diavolo la mia bella ragazza?" *Come to dance with the devil my beautiful girl?*

Chapter Three

In an attempt to create some kind of normalcy in my current schedule, I dragged my ass out of bed, spent an hour doing the yoga routine I've been slacking on since coming home, showered, and got dressed for the day all before eight AM. Besides all that, I have zero plans for the rest of the day; at least I can say that I did something besides sleep until eleven and binge Netflix. Grizzle, my dapple-grey Hanoverian gelding, isn't scheduled to be trailered to the stables until next week. He's the main reason I decided to go to Auburn University to begin with. They have an amazing equestrian team, and I didn't want him sitting in a stall while I went off to school. I already showed him competitively in show jumping and dressage, so it made sense to join the team and continue to do so. I'll be at the stables almost every day once he gets here, but until then, I don't have a lot planned.

Grabbing a black bag from my closet, I pull it over my head, so it lays across my chest and adjust the loose, messy bun I have my hair in. Slipping into a pair of worn black sneakers, I head out the door. I'm dressed casually today; pastel blue tee tucked into a black distressed denim skirt. Maybe I can convince Beverly to go shopping with me, she needs to get out of the house, and I have nothing better to do.

The sun is warm on my skin as I walk the few blocks to the corner coffee shop, deciding that I deserve a full fat grande latte after getting up so early. My apartment is in West Brighton, which gives me access to the beach and Coney Island whenever I want, but it also means lots of tourists, especially this time of year. I don't usually mind sharing my little neighborhood though, I've always been a socialite.

The line for coffee is nearly out the doorway, so I plop onto a bench further down the sidewalk to wait for it to die down. Scrolling through my phone, I almost don't notice the shadow looming over me. The sudden chill from the loss of sun is what actually draws my attention. "Can I help yo…" My voice trails off as I lift my gaze and see exactly who is standing next to my bench. "Are you freaking kidding me?"

Donatello laughs at my reaction, choosing to wedge himself between me and the iron armrest, effectively forcing me to scoot over or be sat on, instead of walking around to the other side of the bench. He leans back, slinging his tan arm onto the back of the bench behind my shoulders, ignoring my scoff as I flick his fingers off of me. "It's nice out today, yea?"

I give him my best 'what the fuck' face and scoot further down the bench, so our thighs are no longer pressed together. My heart is thumping happily in my chest at his appearance, but I don't share the same feelings; I'm pretty sure I don't anyway. "Are you really trying to talk about the weather right now? What the hell are you doing here, Donatello?" He doesn't live anywhere near this neighborhood, so I know him showing up and 'finding' me was very much intentional.

His gaze shifts over to me, starting at the tips of my toes and sliding up to meet my own narrowed gaze at a leisurely pace. The attention makes me want to squirm, but I tamp the urge down, not wanting to give him the satisfaction of knowing how he affects me. His russet eyes are a deep mahogany in the sun, red pools soaking up every inch of my face as he takes his time answering my question. "Spend the day with me."

I shake my head in disbelief, clicking the lock screen on my phone before sliding it into my bag. The weight of his gaze settles heavily on my shoulders, my body overly aware of him. I must have heard him incorrectly because there is no way this man thinks I will spend the day with him. "I'm sorry... what?" He's still watching me when I look back at him, a smirk ticking up the left side of his mouth.

"You heard me, Delaney." He shifts, so his elbows are resting on his knees, intentionally dragging his fingers along the back of my neck, before propping his cheek on a closed fist, eyes never leaving mine. "Spend the day with me."

Besides our two impromptus make out sessions, we haven't spent any time with each other since I got back, nor have we had any serious conversations. What the hell is he up to? It can't be anything good, and his motives are highly suspect. I have already proven I can't be trusted around him, and he appears to be going out of his way to torture me at this point. "Why would I do that, Donatello?"

He shrugs, finally shifting his eyes off of me, and I barely stop myself from fidgeting at the loss of their phantom heat. "Why not?" His chin is still propped on his fist, and his words come out slightly mumbled. After a pause, and my non-response, he turns his face towards me again, russet eyes heating my body once more with their warmth. "We have fun together, yea?" He must see the 'hell no' written all over my face because he adds, "I'll do whatever you want to do."

I scoff and look down at my nails as I ponder his suggestion. I'm not seriously considering this, am I? Absolutely not. We aren't friends. He broke my heart, nothing good could possibly come with us spending time together. I raise my head, fully intending to tell him to fuck off with his bullshit, but that damn lopsided grin stops me mid-frown.

While I was concentrating on my hand I failed to notice him close the distance between us, and now he's all up in my bubble; close enough I can see the two crooked teeth that he got in an alley fight behind his full bottom lip and smell the Big Red on his breath. He reaches out and tucks a bit of loose hair behind my ear, making the fireflies dance in my belly. "Okay." It shoots from my mouth like verbal vomit and I press my lips together tightly to prevent any other moronic things from spilling out.

His grin turns into a full-blown smile that makes my breath catch in my throat as he claps his hands loudly, rubbing his ringed knuckles together as he stands and shifts to face me. "What are we doing then?"

"Absolutely fucking not." Donatello says the minute he realizes we're headed towards Deno's Wonder Wheel Amusement Park. I roll my eyes, stopping when I realize he's not walking anymore. "I don't do rides, Delaney." He looks extremely serious, a deep crease in his brow as he stares at me.

I cross my arms and raise a brow in return at his ridiculousness. I may have picked this activity because I knew he'd hate it. The rest of our morning has gone smoothly enough during breakfast, and I found it irritatingly pleasant; so, I decided to switch things up a bit. "You said, and I quote, 'we'll do whatever you want to do'... did you not?" I lower my voice, trying to imitate him as I repeat what he told me earlier, sounding more like a croaky old man than Donatello.

He's still frowning at me, clearly not finding my imitation of him very humorous, upper lip curled in distaste as he shakes his head and starts walking towards me. "You knew what I meant, anything that I also want to do... and I don't sound like that."

I laugh as he gets to me, spinning on my heel to continue towards the gate. "That's not what you said, though... and yes, it is." I shoot a cheerful little smile up at him as he sneers down at me, hands shoved into the pockets of his dark jeans as we pass through the gates. I stroll right up to the wonder wheel line after we pay for our tickets, biting back my smile at Donatello's obvious discomfort. Now, this is the kind of pleasantness I can get on board with; he honestly deserves it for what he did to me.

"I'm not getting on that." He's staring up at the giant Ferris wheel, hands clenched tightly at his sides. Flicking his gaze to me and back, he gives a slight shake of his head, the longer pieces of his hair falling across his forehead. "I don't care that I paid for it already. I can watch you from down here."

I scoff at him, turning my own gaze to the wheel as he runs his hands through his hair to push it back in place. "You can't make me ride that by myself! You were the one who said we should spend the day together." His arm brushing against mine brings my attention back to him; he's still looking at the wheel like it's the worst thing he's ever encountered. "You routinely get in dangerous fights, get shot at, and kill people, but you can't ride a freaking Ferris wheel?" I whisper the last part, but clearly not quietly enough because the man in front of me looks rather worried as he peeks at me over his shoulder. I smile politely, and he turns back to face forward.

"Those things aren't scary. This shit is." Donatello grumbles out, his gravelly voice barely audible over the rest of the happy crowd.

"I honestly don't even know how to respond to that." I twist to tap the man in front of me on the shoulder, the one who was looking at me just a few moments ago and give him my most charming smile when he turns to look at me. Apparently, I'll need to take matters into my own hands to get what I want. "Would you mind riding with me? It seems my…" I throw a quick look Donatello's way, I'm not completely sure what he even is to me. "friend here is having some issues, and I don't want to ride alone."

He looks pretty hesitant, so I peek around him to make sure I'm not crashing his own date, but it looks like he's with a group of other guys. Meeting his green gaze, I run my fingers playfully down his arm, making sure to flash my dimples with my next smile. "Please? I would really appreciate it." My voice is as sweet as syrup, and I hear Donatello huff at my back.

Green eyes shares a quick look with one of his friends before turning back to me with a nod and a bright smile. "Okay. Wouldn't want you getting scared by yourself up there."

"Perfect." I flutter my lashes at him, then turn to scowl up at Donatello. "You can leave. I've found a replacement."

Donatello isn't looking at me, though. His dark eyes are on the hand currently resting against the inside of my forearm. "Fine."

I tilt my ear towards him, pretending I didn't hear that sweet little word he gritted through clenched teeth. "What was that? I didn't hear you."

His red gaze snaps up to my face as he steps closer, smacking the hand off of me and ignoring the yell that comes from green eyes. "I'm riding with you."

Green eyes clearly has some big balls because he steps forward then, too, frowning at Donatello. "Hey man, she said you can leave. She's riding with me." His chest is puffed out like a prize turkey, and Donatello barely spares him a glance, eyes on me when he addresses him.

"She also said I kill people..." He runs a ringed knuckle under his chin before pulling his eyes from me and onto the other man. "Want to test it?"

Green eyes blanches, deflating like a balloon as his eyes nervously shift between myself and Donatello. "Uh... No... You can ride with her."

"Then shut the fuck up and turn back around."

The line has shifted during the confrontation, just in time for Green eyes to spin around and hop onto a bench with one of his buddies, not looking back at us once.

I smile up at Donatello, as we step up next to be loaded, bouncing on my toes with barely contained excitement. I love it when things go my way. "Well, that worked out better than I could have imagined."

He's frowning again; bottom lip stuck between his teeth as he stares at me. The ride attendant calls us forward, drawing my attention away, and I happily hop up onto the swinging bench, smiling at the attendant as he clips the bar in place and murmurs his safety spiel. We coast forward and up as I swing my legs, bench swaying with the movement.

"Can you please not do that?"

A quick look over shows a very clammy Donatello, ringed fingers white knuckling the safety bar, spine rigid. "Do what? Are you okay?" I reach forward and wave a hand in front of his face when he continues to stare forward, still as stone. His jaw flexes, but he remains facing forward.

"Swinging your legs. Stop it." I hadn't realized I was still doing it, but stop immediately because of his tone alone, scooting closer to Donatello, who throws a quick, wary look my way pausing my movements.

"Okay, I stopped... better?"

He barely moves his head with a nod, side eyeing me as I shift around, trying to get comfortable without shaking our bench too much. "Delaney... Stop. Fucking. Moving."

Rolling my eyes at him, I pretend to move in slow motion, over exaggerating my movements as I scoot even closer to his side again to be more in the center of the bench. He huffs but otherwise stays silent at my little show. Finally settled, I look over at him. He's still gripping the bar like he thinks he'll slip out of the bench at any moment, still sitting like he's got a stick up his ass, which he honestly might. "You're kind of a baby for someone who's supposed to be a badass."

This earns me a glare and a flexed jaw as he grinds his teeth. "I'm not a baby." He spits out at me like that was the worst insult he's ever heard. "Being scared of heights is a normal thing. This shit isn't normal, who the fuck willingly gets on some rickety ass bench to swing around a hundred feet above the ground? You can't even see shit up here. It's all tiny as fuck."

"You willingly got on here." He turns his face to look at me with that statement, and I can barely contain my laugh at his expression, pressing my lips together to keep a straight face. "Is it really only a hundred feet? It feels taller than that."

"I have no fucking idea." Our bench swings as the ride shifts us towards the top of the wheel, and Donatello wheezes in a breath with the motion. The tiny sound is enough to make me lose the battle between my giggles, and they spill out of me.

"Could you not?" He grumbles out as we pause at the top, the last few people loading up.

We start forward once more, moving into our first loop, and Donatello's grip tightens on the bar, hands squeaking against the metal with the action. He is clearly not having a great time, and even though that was my intention, I didn't anticipate him hating it this much. "Donatello, you need to calm down, it's just a ride. Nothing is going to happen... Look how pretty it is!"

"Yea, okay." It's said with some extreme sass, and I can't help but laugh. Leaning forward to draw his attention, I look at his face until his dark eyes shift to me. "What the hell are you doing? Sit back, or you'll fall out."

Rolling my eyes yet again, I sit back, but reach forward to peel one of his hands off of the bar. "Hold my hand... you squeeze that any tighter and you'll break it in half." He barely cooperates, fingertips hanging on for dear life before I'm able to rip them off. I link our fingers, tugging his hand to get him to look at me. He ignores me, jaw ticking as he stays facing forward, so I force his gaze; palming his cheek, I physically turn his head to face me. His lips are pressed into a thin line when his russet eyes finally find mine, and I smile at him. "Hey."

He frowns at me, dark eyes flicking to our hands and back. "I hate this."

I hum to avoid laughing at him again, looking out towards the ocean as we get nearer to the top. One more loop, and we're done. "It's almost over..." Returning my gaze to his, I choose to ignore how close we are. "You'll just have to find something to distract yourself for a few more minutes."

"Distract myself? How exactly do you suggest I do that?" His thumb brushes along my own in a soft caress as he asks, and I pretend I don't notice, keeping my eyes on his. Smiling, I shrug, opening my mouth to answer when he stops me, his other hand raising to run his thumb along my bottom lip as he closes the distance between us, "I have an idea."

The words barely escape his lips before they meet mine, almost swallowed up by the press of our lips. I don't even hesitate to respond, turning to press myself into Donatello as we enter the last loop of our ride. It's almost impossible to resist him, to resist the dark pull he has over me. I didn't want us to end. A fact that becomes more evident with every interaction we have since I've gotten back. I told myself I'd get over him, move on, never let him hurt me like he did before, but I underestimated just how deeply he had me woven in his wicked web. I know this is bound to come back to bite me in the ass, but I'm willing to risk it for moments like this. Moments I can look back on when he pushes me away again because I know he will.

I'm vaguely aware that our fingers are still linked in my lap, that his other hand is wrapped in my hair while I do my best to distract him just like he wants. I'm overly aware that we are close to getting off, though, that our little moment is about to end almost as quickly as it began. I feel him start to pull back, clearly keeping tabs on our ride as much as I am, and I push forward, locking his lips to mine for one more bittersweet, almost desperate kiss. As soon as this is over, reality will come crashing back in; a tidal wave of could have been and never will be, to taunt and tease me.

My attempt to prolong the inevitable is shot to the wind when Donatello uses his strength against me, lightly pushing us apart with his fingertips against my jaw. I reluctantly sit back, casting my gaze towards the ocean to avoid looking at him. He started this mess, yet I'm going to be the one dealing with the repercussions.

Neither one of us says a word as our bench slowly comes to a stop, but the way he withdraws his hand from my own and purposefully puts space between us before we get to the operator, before anyone but the other riders can see us as more than just friendly acquaintances, speaks volumes. I quickly exit the ride, angrily leaving Donatello behind. Once again, I let myself get pulled into his bullshit, let him take advantage of the situation like he always does. What's more irritating is that I know I'd do it again, too. No, that I will be doing it again because I highly doubt this will be the last time. I feel him come up next to me and clench my fists around the strap of my bag over my chest.

"So where to next?"

He's unbelievable. "Nowhere. I'm done spending time with you, Donatello."

Grabbing my arm to stop me, he shifts us off to the side as I roll my eyes with annoyance. "Sei arrabbiato?" *Are you angry?* He's frowning in what I can only guess is confusion as he crosses his arms, waiting for a response.

"Sei serio? Sì, sono arrabbiato." *Are you serious? Yes, I'm angry.* Wiping some stray hairs from my face, I level my gaze on him. "We can't do this, Donatello." I raise my hand to point at him. "You. You can't do this. We clearly can't be normal friends, and I don't know that I even want to be." I start to turn away but stop to yell at him some more. "Anche io ho un Ragazzo. Ricorda?" *I have a boyfriend, too. Remember?* I don't know why I'm continuing this farce, but I'll be damned if I let it die now.

He lets out a bitter laugh, eyeing my scowl with a smile. It's hardly a smile though, more of an angry twist of lips. "Fingendo ancora di avere un Ragazzo? È tempo di lasciarlo andare, Piccola." *Still pretending to have a boyfriend? It's time to let that go, Baby.*

I grit my teeth to keep myself from continuing this ridiculous argument, spinning on my heel to stomp away instead.

"Aw, come on, Delaney! Don't act like that."

Flipping him the bird over my shoulder, I keep walking. "Stay away from me, Donatello!"

He just laughs at me in typical Donatello fashion, shouting over the crowd just loud enough for me to hear as I stomp away. "Ci vediamo presto Mia Vita." *I'll see you soon, My Life.*

My steps falter at his term of endearment, but I clench my bag and continue forward. Not today, Satan. Not. Today.

Back in Euphoria

"What?!" Reaching over, I snatch the Queen Frostine Candyland card from Donatello's fingers, needing to see it for myself. "How do you keep getting this card!" He laughs at my outburst, smugly lifting his little green man to the queen's part of the board game. Shooting him a dirty look, I flick his player over as soon as he sets it up, making him laugh again.

"I'm clearly a Candyland master." He plucks the card from my hand to lay on the top of the discarded card pile, his crooked grin lacking its normal appeal due to my hate for losing. He's basically at the end of the path now. There's no way I can catch up. I eye my yellow game piece stuck on a 'draw red card' spot next to Lord Licorice. What are the chances there's a red in the last three cards in the stack? With how my luck has been so far, zero.

I snatch the last three cards and roll my eyes so hard it feels like they might get stuck in the back of my head. Two yellows and an orange. I toss my cards at Donatello, smirking when one hits him in the forehead. "Reshuffle the deck so I can draw another fifty just to lose anyway." He chuckles at my antics, picking up the cards scattered around the bed to shuffle the discarded pile.

"You're quite the sore loser."

Ignoring him, I adjust to sit criss cross applesauce, eyeing Donatello across the board. I watch as he carefully tucks a card in a specific spot of the stack and gasp loudly, pointing at him. "You're cheating!"

He throws his head back with a loud guffaw, setting the stack down. "I never."

"Yes, you are!" I grab the cards and flip the top of the stack, seeing the perfect set of cards for him to win stuck strategically for each of his next few turns. "You've been setting it up so you'd get Frostine this whole time! You Cheater!" I smack his player off the board again as he roars. "Have you been making sure I get stupid Gloppy too?!"

He grabs my arm, pulling me to him across the bed, smiling at me as I glower at him. "I didn't plan for that actually, that was just really bad luck on your part."

Pushing at his chest, I try to get out of his arms, but he doesn't let me, keeping me trapped against his chest as he lays back on the bed. "Let me go, you cheater... Cheater, cheater, pumpkin eater, hang you from a telephone line, and beat you with a pole!"

He rolls over, so I'm pinned below him, his forearms boxing in my head as his heavy body keeps me in place. "That is definitely not how that goes." He kisses my nose, and I scrunch my face at him, a crooked grin splitting his lips. "Want to play a different game?"

"Why so you can cheat again? No, thanks." I can feel his smile against my cheek as he starts to trail kisses along my skin. "And I'm a Luciano. That's how we deal with cheaters."

Chuckling, he nods in what I assume is agreement. "You'll like this one." He comes back to my lips, lightly tugging at my lip with his teeth. "I promise."

Letting out a loud sigh, I raise a brow. "Fine. What is it?"

"X marks the spot... think of a spot on your body and tell me if I'm hot or cold until I find it." His lips are already skimming along my skin, fingertips pushing my shirt farther up my stomach.

"As if I want to fool around with a cheater pants like you." In direct contradiction to my words, I arch my back and raise my arms to help him remove my shirt, ignoring his smug grin. His teeth nip along my lower belly, and I clutch the bed sheet at my sides. "Cold." He continues lower, thumbs hooking into the waistband of my cotton shorts. "That's cold... like super cold." Ignoring me, he proceeds lower, pulling my shorts with him. "Donatello! You're cold!"

Sitting up on my elbows, I frown at him as he pushes my legs apart with his shoulders, pulling me closer to his face by my hips. "I heard you... I think you're wrong."

"You suck at playing games."

He laughs at this, pressing a kiss to the inside of one thigh before moving to the other. "Do I? Because I know exactly what's hot for me."

My response dies on the tip of my tongue as Donatello moves higher, proving how true his statement is. He might suck at playing games, but he definitely does not suck at this.

Chapter Four

"You're sure you can handle watching them by yourself?" Beverly asks for the five hundredth time as I try to usher her towards the door. Remy hasn't shown up yet, but he should be here soon, and I'm more than ready for Bev to leave.

"Yes, Beverly, I am sure. Just as sure as I was the first hundred times you asked." She huffs at this, chewing on her bottom lip as she looks past me and up the stairs, no doubt trying to use some imaginary x-ray vision to see into the girls' nursery. "Honestly, you need to have some faith in me. Everything will be fine, and they're already sleeping… you're paying me to watch TV at this point."

"I'm not paying you." She says it almost absent-mindedly, still staring up the stairs.

"What do you mean you're not paying me? I told Ollie thirty an hour, or I wasn't doing it." She finally looks at me, eyes narrowing on me as I smile at her. She knows I'm joking, but at least her attention is on me now.

Remy steps through the front door then, honey eyes barely skimming over me before landing on Beverly. If I could find someone to look at me with even half the love and devotion he looks at her with, I'd be happy; hell, I'd be happy with a fraction of that.

"Come on, Cuore Mio, Delaney will be fine." He holds his hand out for hers, kissing her palm before linking their fingers and lightly tugging her towards the door. His eyes find me again just before he closes the door. "Call me if you have any trouble."

The look he's giving me would make paint peel off the wall just to get out of his line of sight, drastically different from the adoration that was just on his face. Obviously, I'm not the only one with an ax to grind, though I fail to see how he thinks now is the appropriate time for his antics. His scowl makes me want to squirm, but I hold his gaze, steeling my own face to appear tough, a farce I'm sure he can easily see through.

Despite the urge to be petty and ignore him, I nod at his unspoken command; don't message Beverly. Looking over his shoulder, I give a little wave to Bev through the crack in the door. "Bye! Have fun doing whatever you're doing!" She returns my smile and lifts her fingers in a wave right before Remy closes the door, murmuring something to her that I can't hear, but has her beaming up at him.

Walking to the window, I watch them climb into their car and leave, drumming my fingers along my arm. They didn't say how long they'd be gone, but it's only eight P.M. now. According to the extremely detailed schedule Bev left me, the girls will wake up around eleven for a bottle; until then, I guess I'll just watch TV. Snatching the baby monitor off the side table, I carry it to the kitchen with me. Beverly was very adamant I keep it with me at all times, because God forbid the girls cry for longer than thirty seconds should I not hear them immediately. However ridiculous I find it, I'm not risking getting caught without it and having to deal with all the crazy that Beverly can be.

Pulling out some jerky, I whistle for Dylan, who comes through the open doorway with a lazy stretch. Tossing him a few pieces, I stick one in my own mouth before sealing the bag and throwing it back onto the counter; we'll probably want more later. "What looks good, Dylan?" I look over my shoulder as I stand in the pantry doorway, holding up a container of cheese balls to get his opinion, but find myself alone in the kitchen. "Huh, must have gone back to bed… lazy mutt." Putting the cheese balls away, I push some crackers out of the way and grab a bag of pretzels instead, backing out of the pantry to set them on the counter.

"Are the girls sleeping?"

I scream, jumping as I spin to see a laughing Donatello. He's smirking at me; a hand held up in mock apology at my reaction. "What the hell are you doing here?" I yell, heart beating wildly in my chest, whether from being scared or from his presence alone, I'm unsure.

"Knock it off, or you're going to get Dylan all worked up," he says, eyeing the kitchen like he's looking for the pup to spring from the shadows as he leans against the counter.

"Donatello." I cross my arms and glare at him. "Why are you here?"

He grabs the bag of jerky I left on the counter and pulls out a piece for himself before answering. "I figured you'd need help with the girls and thought I'd lend a hand." He gives me a lopsided grin when I scoff. "Also, Remy asked me to stop by and check on things."

I narrow my gaze on him as he shoves the rest of the jerky into his mouth. "Are you lying?" I find it hard to believe Remy would ask him of all people to stop by, especially considering they just left.

He shrugs and grabs the bag of pretzels, turning to leave. "Maybe."

Grabbing the baby monitor, I hurry to follow him out of the room, frowning at his back as he walks us out to the backyard. "What do you mean, maybe? It's a yes or no question."

He plops down on the lawn, looking up at me expectantly. Rolling my eyes, I sit down, setting the monitor next to me. "Well?"

Smirking at me once again, he shoves a handful of pretzels into his mouth, taking his sweet time answering. "Yes."

Shaking my head at him when he doesn't elaborate, he just laughs and eats more pretzels, the plastic bag crinkling obnoxiously loud in the quiet yard.

Chuckling at my glare and annoyed huff, he finally sets the bag to the side, wiping his hands on his jeans. "Remy didn't ask me to stop by."

"Okay, great. Now that we got that settled, you can leave." I flash a crude smile his way, picking at the edge of my skirt and turning to look towards the dark tree line when he doesn't respond.

"Come here, Delaney."

My head snaps sideways at his tone, the sticky tendrils of his honey voice running down my back, sending a shiver I barely contain up my spine. "What? No."

After a moment, he stands, dropping himself behind me in the grass so he can tug me between his long legs. I start to push up to stand, but he pulls me back down by one of my wrists, gathering my loose hair in his hands, to kiss the back of my neck. "Just sit with me."

Everything about this is so wrong. My brain is screaming at me to get up and go in the house, but all I can focus on is the soft pull on my scalp as Donatello brushes his fingers through my waves, weaving the thick strands into a loose braid to lay over my shoulder once he's finished. Scooting even closer, he spreads a palm over my breastbone, lightly pushing me back into him, so my head rests on his shoulder. "Donatello…"

"Shh, Vita Mia. Just look up."

I roll my eyes but give in, shifting my gaze towards the sky. "What am I looking at Donatello?"

He chuckles in my ear, running his fingers along the backs of my arms, causing goosebumps to spread along my skin. "The stars, Delaney. You're looking at the stars."

Letting out the breath I didn't realize I was holding, I bring my focus to the sky instead of his fingers dancing along the edge of my shirt. He's right though, the sky is clear but for a few lone straggling clouds, and you can see all the stars bright against the dark canvas. The sight brings a smile to my lips and I shift farther back to rest my head more comfortably on him. I love the stars; they've always been a passion of mine.

I decide to give in for a bit, letting Donatello wrap his arms around me as I stare up at them.

Pointing to a constellation right above us, I tilt my head to the side, eyeing him before looking back at the sky. "Do you know what that is?"

"No… tell me." It's said low and gravelly, his breath warm along my ear.

"That's Cassiopeia. It's named after the vain queen who boasted of her unrivaled beauty."

"Hmmm. She sounds delightful." He mumbles against the side of my head, and I laugh, dropping my arm.

We sit in comfortable silence for a bit, me watching the stars while pretending I don't notice Donatello watching me. I start to shift like I'm going to stand, and the arms around me tighten, keeping me in place. "Do you really have a boyfriend?"

The question is so quiet I almost miss it, so I turn my face to look back into the dark gaze scanning my face. "Yes."

After a moment, Donatello laughs, leaning forward to kiss my forehead. "Why are you so stubborn?"

"Why did you bring me out here?"

He gives a questioning side-eye before tilting his head back to look up at the sky. "To see the stars, obviously."

"Yes, but why." He doesn't answer me, so I twist in his arms, so I'm facing him, sitting on my knees between his legs. When he still avoids my gaze, face still tilted towards the sky, I lightly push his chest to get his attention.

"Because you love the stars." He says after a pause, head dropping so that his dark eyes are on mine once more.

It's my turn to scan his face, my eyes coasting over his every feature trying to weed out the answer I'm looking for. "Why?" I don't need to elaborate; I know that he knows exactly what I'm asking. Why does he care, why is he so determined to spend time with me, why does he keep kissing me, and more importantly, why did he leave me to begin with.

Instead of answering the questions, I desperately need the answers to, he shifts forward and palms my cheeks, pulling my lips to his in a soft whisper of a kiss. His kiss is a question all in itself, asking for my permission to continue, asking if I want him to care, if I want to be his. He won't answer my questions, but I'll answer his.

I press into his lips, deepening our kiss in answer, heart sighing with content as his chest bumps up against mine. He won't answer me, but I'll throw my answers at his face like a flashing billboard, smother him with them until he sees them for what they truly are, sees me for what I could be if he let me. Pushing forward, I straddle his hips, his hands dropping from my face to grab my thighs as I sit in his lap while bunching his shirt in my hands. That initial whisper of a kiss turned into a savage all-consuming one as our tongues and teeth fight to taste and savor each other.

My hair is hanging in a half-braided tangle of waves down my back as I tilt my head back, allowing Donatello to trail his lips along my throat. One of his hands has left my thigh, and his fingers are skimming along the edges of my pleated skirt, sliding under the fabric without hesitation to run them along the growing wet spot on my panties. Sinking my fingers into his hair, I adjust my legs so he has better access as his teeth nip a path along my skin, his fingers hooking into the side of my panties to pull them out of his way.

Donatello is a wildfire of a man, this scorching, unstoppable, and all-consuming mixture of relentless passion and agony. Every time I'm near him, I get pulled into the vortex of flames, burned by his sugar-coated words and molten touch. I'd be lying if I said I didn't enjoy the burn though, didn't crave the sweet lies he has branded behind his russet eyes. No, I want to be devoured by this man. I want his touch to melt my skin to the bone, his lips to scar my flesh with their heat. If I'm going to be destroyed, either way, I might as well go all in and let him wreck me for good.

I suck in a sharp intake of breath when he pushes his fingers into my heated slick core without preamble, shamelessly encouraging me to ride his hand as a low groan leaves my lips. Using his other hand to bring my face back to his, he growls against my mouth, his teeth sinking into my bottom lip. "Shh, Baby or the men on guard will hear you…" Shifting back slightly, his dark eyes drop to watch my chest bounce. Reaching down, he yanks my t-shirt up and over my boobs, bunching the fabric up under my chin so he can see them better. His eyes flick to mine as he pulls the cups of my bra down, causing my already aching nipples to tighten with anticipation once they hit the cool night air. Pinching a nipple between his fingers, he sucks the other into his hot mouth, pulling back with a pop to nip at the skin below my ear. "Quindi chiudi la tua bella bocca e scopami la mano come la ragazza sporca che so che sei." *So, close your beautiful mouth and fuck my hand like the dirty girl I know you are.*

His dirty words, combined with the pumping of his fingers, sends a warm prickling along my skin, a deep ache pooling in my gut as a sense of euphoria crashes along my soul like a tidal wave. Sure, I've slept with other men, several actually in the past months alone just to try and forget this one in particular, but no matter how hard I tried, this feeling couldn't be replaced, Donatello couldn't be replaced. My heart had staked its claim on him that first stolen kiss we shared, and despite my efforts, it refuses to change its mind or see reason. We are destined to end in disaster, to have our paradise invaded and picked apart by those who don't understand our love. Unfortunately for me, our biggest critic just so happens to be the one who owns my soul; we will always fail because Donatello won't ever let us win. But in this particular moment, this brief escape to euphoria, we can pretend things are how they should be, and I've become quite the master of pretending.

Leaning down, I pull Donatello from my chest, sinking my lips into his, dipping in to taste the Big Red on his tongue. My soft moan gets swallowed up between our lips as he hooks his fingers in a way that makes my belly clench. His rough palm rubs my clit with each thrust of my hips, and I can feel my orgasm blooming, a hot spark gathering in my belly that grows stronger with each brush of my nipples on his shirt. Donatello's fingers are pinching into the skin of my waist as I chase my orgasm, grinding into his hand as he marks my neck with his teeth.

My release knocks into me with full force, and I curl around him, throwing my arms around his neck and shoulders, squeeze his waist with my legs as he yanks my face to his to muffle my sounds with his lips. Once I've come back down from my high, he slowly withdraws his fingers, peppering soft kisses along the edges of my lips as he cups my face in both hands and pushes stray strands of wild hair behind my ears. He's looking at me like he has something to say, eyes flickering between my own as he tries to sort out the words he wants to use while his fingers caress my cheek.

Not wanting to spoil the moment, I keep my own mouth sealed, waiting for him to break the silence we've fallen into. When nothing comes out, I adjust my bra and shirt, then lean forward and rest my forehead against his shoulder, turning my face to bury it into his neck. My breaths are more steady now, but my pulse is still fluttering, a nervousness slowly creeping in to ruin my bliss. I don't want him to ruin this moment just yet. I feel his chest rise, feel his words before they are even said, but before he can get them out a loud crackling cry breaks the silence.

Sitting up abruptly, I reach and grab the baby monitor laying in the grass next to us and turn the volume down, rising from Donatello's lap while adjusting my underwear without meeting his gaze. I stand next to him for a moment, watching him from the corner of my eye, not really sure what to say.

When neither of us can come up with words, I start for the house, but Donatello reaches out and snags my ankle, stopping my progress. His thumb strokes my skin as he tilts his face to look up at me. "I need to leave, but I'm not running away…" I keep my face neutral as I look down at him, watching as he leans forward to place a soft kiss on my leg. "We're not done, Delaney. I know it was ugly how we split, but we aren't over. Not yet."

My breath catches at his statement, and I watch motionlessly as he releases my leg, russet eyes returning to my face. He tilts his chin towards the house, indicating that I better go inside, and I turn wordlessly, unable to form a coherent thought in my head fast enough to answer him. As I enter the house, I look over my shoulder to find Donatello gone, no longer sitting in the grass; the pretzels are gone too, I note. Shaking my head, I close the door and hustle up the stairs towards the nursery. There isn't any fussing coming through the monitor anymore, but I need to check on the girls anyway.

Amalia is standing in her bed when I open the door, Dylan sprawled in front of her bed, sound asleep; he must have come to do some investigating of his own. I scoop the baby up, taking her out of the room before she wakes up Carmella, and go into the adjoining sitting room. Settling into an oversized glider, I wrap us up in a blanket and start rocking, gaze drifting to look out the windows.

Now that I'm not caught up in the moment with Donatello, his words are playing on a loop in my brain. I agree we aren't over, we clearly have unfinished business, but I'm not the same girl that left here nine months ago. I'm not willing to slink around in the background this time around. If he wants us to be together, he has to prove to me that he is willing to have me without the shadows, without the secrets. I'm done being his closet pet.

Amalia coos in my arms, and I smile down at her, adjusting her in my arms to see her face better. "You should be sleeping." I whisper to her. She gives a loud shout in response, wiggling her legs to kick off the blanket I have over us. Chuckling, I shake my head at her playfully, pulling the blanket back in place. "Don't get mad at me. I didn't make up the rules... your mama did."

At the mention of her mom, she starts blowing bubbles, chanting "Ma ma ma ma ma." Over and over again. Smiling to myself, I look out the window again and continue to rock us. Despite the small noises coming from the chatterbox in my arms, I can feel myself getting tired. It couldn't have been more than two hours since Bev left, so it's not like it's late. Snuggling Amalia closer, I whisper against her head, "If I'm not careful, I might fall asleep with you."

I jump, hearing Dylan's bark, and blink several times to shake away the grogginess clouding my vision as I take in the dark room. Amalia is sound asleep against my chest, and we're still in the glider; I must have fallen asleep. I can hear Bev speaking in hushed tones in the adjoining room and straighten in the chair, trying to appear more awake. Remy glides in through the open doorway, hands in the pockets of his joggers as his dark eyes take in the scene before him. They've clearly been home for a while if he's already changed. Despite that knowledge, I'm going to pretend I wasn't just sleeping. "Oh, back so soon? I just got this little bug back to sleep... been up most of the night, actually."

The corner of his lip ticks slightly in a Remy version of a smirk as he hums in response, walking towards me to take the baby from my arms. "Is that why we could hear you snoring all the way out in the hall for the last twenty minutes?"

I huff and stand, folding the blanket we'd been using and tossing it on the arm of the glider. "That's a lie." I follow him out of the room, watching as he kisses Amalia's forehead before laying her in her bed, then as he walks to Carmella's bed to kiss her forehead also. I notice that it's just the two of us in the room besides the sleeping babies. "Where'd Bev go?"

Remy motions for me to follow him with a tilt of his head, closing the nursery door quietly behind him when we step out into the hall. "Probably downstairs…" he grumbles out, staring at me like I have the plague… or something worse. What the hell?

"What?" I frown at him, bristling at his expression. Crossing my arms over my chest, I shift uncomfortably under his gaze, gesturing for him to say something. "Why are you looking at me like that?"

"Have company over, Delaney?" His narrowed eyes quickly flick to my neck and back as he waits for a response.

My hand comes up to cover my neck as realization hits. I must have marks on my neck from Donatello. Fuuuck. Adjusting the collar of my t-shirt anxiously, I frown over at him. "If you're insinuating that I invited someone over while you were gone, then you're wrong." Even though it's not a lie, I still feel prickly about saying it, and I shift to start walking away.

"For your sake, I hope it wasn't my Consigliere."

I stop mid-step at his threat and spin to face him, immediately going on defense. "Or what?" At his nonresponse, I take a step forward, letting my annoyance lead my actions and give me false bravery. "Or what, Capo Famiglia? You going to teach me a lesson like one of your soldiers?" Emphasizing my words with air quotes, I step into my brother's space, ignoring the slight twitch of his hands clenched at his sides. Remy is many things, but a woman hitter is not one of them; that doesn't mean he doesn't want to hit me, though. "You don't get to boss me around, Ollie. I'm an adult who can do whatever the fuck I want… and last time I checked, so is Donatello."

Besides the flexing of his jaw, Remy doesn't respond immediately, staring down at me with a hard mask. When he finally speaks, he leans into my space with the smallest of gestures, his voice hard and low. "You are a child." He pauses for a brief second and I open my mouth to speak but he cuts me off with an angry twist of his lips. "A stupid child at that."

Brushing past me he dismisses me along with any remark I may have had. I glare at his retreating back, fighting the tears stinging the back of my eyes. He barely said anything, yet it feels like he cut me down with a million words. His anger cutting straight to my heart as his disappointment sinks into my gut. That false bravery of mine sloughed off like the plastic armor it was; unable to handle the slice of his cold words.

"Oh, and Delaney?" Remy says over his shoulder, drawing my narrowed gaze back on him as he starts down the stairs. "You might not be part of the Famiglia… but Donatello is."

Resisting the urge to scream at his back I flip him off instead once his head is turned, silently raging as I watch him disappear. I'll take his threat at face value, an attempt to scare me off and put me in my place. Unfortunately for him, I've never been good at staying where I should.

Back in Euphoria

"You owe me a dollar." I yank my ice cream back as Donatello tries to take an obnoxiously large bite, laughing at his pout when he misses the cone.

"Why? I bought you ice cream…" He reaches for my waffle cone, arching a brow at me when I pull it back from his hand. "that you're not sharing."

"Because I beat you at air hockey. You bet me a dollar, not ice cream." I take a deliberately exaggerated lick of the cone, smiling at him when I'm done. "This is just a bonus prize."

Eyeing me with a playfully narrowed gaze, he snatches my free hand, linking our fingers as we start to walk the boardwalk. It's bustling with people despite the late hour, the darkness, and crowd blending us into the background and allowing us a night to pretend we are like every other couple here. I have no problem being seen together, but Donatello has made it perfectly clear that it isn't going to happen anytime soon; for now, I'm fine with it.

Sitting on an empty bench seat, he tugs me down onto his lap, wrapping his arms around my waist as he rests his chin on my shoulder. "I'll give you two dollars if you share your cone."

I squirm in his lap to get more comfortable, smirking over my shoulder at him when he pinches my hips to keep me still. "No… but I might give you a bite if you agree to go on some rides with me."

"What rides?" He sounds almost nervous about the suggestion, so I turn more fully to get a better look at him, careful to hold my cone out of reach.

"Which ones will you go on?" He uses his thumb to wipe the edge of my lips, clearing away a bit of ice cream, then leans forward for a kiss, smiling against them when a group of teens start hooting as they go by.

"None of the coasters and definitely not the wonder wheel." He murmurs into my neck when I shift to look back at the walkway. I feel him reaching for the cone and jab him softly in the ribs with my elbow, making him pull back slightly with a chuckle.

"That's literally all of the rides, Donatello." I say between eating my ice cream and giggles, wiggling around as he tickles my sides, trying to get me to give him the cone.

"Nah… they have a carousel, don't they? I'll go on that." He finally manages to grab my hand with the cone and bites almost all the ice cream off the top, giving me a sticky, full cheeked, lopsided grin when I spin in his lap to huff at him.

I fight my smile, feigning annoyance, forcing my lips to stay in a straight line and scrunching my nose at him when he palms my cheeks. "Sei arrabbiato?" *Are you angry?* His tongue darts out to lick the ice cream from his lips, smile still in place as he uses his thumbs to pull the corners of my mouth into a grimacing smile, similar to what I imagine a clown looks like, until I can't help but laugh. I shake my head, both in answer and trying to get out of his grip, but he keeps me in place, pulling my lips to his. "I'll buy you another cone, Baby."

Laughing when he pokes one of my dimples, I manage to slap his hands away, breaking out of his hold to sit up straight. "You can have the rest…" Handing him what's left of the cone, I bite my lip to keep in another giggle as he bites it almost in half, his eating etiquette that of a caveman's. "Why won't you go on the other rides?"

He shoves the rest of the ice cream into his mouth, tickling my sides again when I gesture for him to hurry up. "They're not my thing."

"Are you scared of heights, Donatello?"

He lightly pushes me up, humming a response that doesn't really answer my question, before tugging me to him for a sticky kiss. "How about I spend fifty dollars trying to win you one of those giant stuffed animals instead?"

Chapter Five

I'm dying. I'm one thousand percent positive of it.
Lying flat on my back along the side of the hiking
trail I'm on, I spread my limbs starfish style
trying to catch a breeze. My breath is wheezing
from my lungs as a shadow stretches over my form.
"Are you okay?"

Squinting up into the face of one of the other runners
in my group, I give her a thumbs up. "Probably. Just a
slight heart attack, maybe a mini stroke. I'll be fine." I
smile at her worried expression, letting my hand drop
back to the grass.

Her blonde ponytail sways as she casts an
apprehensive look at some of the other runners before
blinking back down at me. "Maybe you should call it
a day? We still have five miles to run…"

I scoff at her, shifting to my elbows. "Five miles?!
How? We've ran at least four already!"

She's frowning at me now, eyes shifting to the rest of
the group as they start to leave. "No… it's only been a

mile." Backing up she starts to shuffle down the trail, clearly concerned with being left behind.

"Just go... I'll catch up with you guys." I wave towards her general direction, laying back down to look up at the dark clouds starting to roll in.

"Are you sure?" I don't look over, but she sounds farther away, probably already back to jogging.

Tossing her another thumbs up, I listen to the crunching of her shoes as they get farther away then disappear. Why the hell did I even sign up for this? Oh, that's right, the Facebook event page said it would be a 'fun and engaging nature hike for all ages. Liars. I'd like to see a five-year-old do this shit.

Tugging my phone from the top of my leggings, I click the screen on to see the time; it's just after three in the afternoon. As if on cue, my stomach gurgles loudly, and I slap a hand over my midsection. In my hurry to get here on time, I missed lunch. I should call Bev and see if she can eat with me... and maybe pick me up.

Dialing her name, I put the phone on speaker and lay it in the grass.

"Aren't you supposed to be on some group hike right now?" She mumbles in greeting without a hello.

"Yes. Turns out their idea of a hike is actually running at top speeds endlessly. I gave up, and they left me."

She laughs through the phone, and I force myself into a sitting position, grabbing the phone to hold in my hand. "Well, why are you calling me? I'm not coming to search for you. I would never have signed up for that shit to begin with."

"Come get me, and then we can get food. I'm starving."

"Negative Usain Bolt, I can't leave the house right now. Just take a cab and eat at home for once. Do you even know how to cook?"

Huffing, I stand, brushing some grass and dirt from my clothes. "Asks the person who literally NEVER cooks. If it weren't for Gretchen and Ollie, you'd starve." She snorts through the line but doesn't comment. "You really won't come get me?"

"No. Just call a cab or something."

"You're lame." I grumble out, taking the phone off of speaker and bringing it to my ear as I start down the path towards the parking site.

"Not as lame as people who run for fun." I laugh as she continues. "Okay, I have to go. Don't get lost. I'd feel obligated to miss you."

"Ha ha. Bye then... love you, too."

Ending the call, I continue wandering down the path. I don't want to eat alone or pay for a cab. Bringing up my contacts, I scroll through searching for anyone tolerable enough to spend the afternoon with. My finger hovers over a contact labeled 'Loser', and I click call before I can second guess myself.

"Please don't tell me that you're being held hostage somewhere... that's the only logical explanation for you willingly calling me right now."

I roll my eyes even though no one can see, pulse pounding in my throat, and fireflies fill my belly as Donatello's smoky tone comes through the phone. "Does no one say hello anymore?" Speaking past his chuckle, I continue. "Come get me. I'm stranded at Salt March nature trail."

"Why are you there? And why did you call me?"

Good question, why did I call him again? The line is silent, but the faint echo of my breath in the phone as I avoid answering his question. He said we're not done, and I want some proof, starting now. "Can you pick me up or not?" Looking up at the sky, I can see the clouds rolling in before are now heavy in the sky, the deep earthy scent of rain filling the air. "It looks like it's going to rain, and I really don't want to be stuck out here forever."

A sigh comes through the phone, and I hear it being shuffled on the other end. "How close are you to the end of the trail? It'll take me at least twenty minutes to get there."

My heart lurches in my chest with the knowledge that he's actually coming to my rescue, and I smile to myself. "I'm slow, so it'll probably take me that long to get back to the end of the trail. Just hurry."

I hear him mumble to someone else on the line before responding. "Okay. See you soon."

I hang up without saying anything, mostly because I don't want to say anything that might make things awkward. There is a low rumble of thunder in the distance, and I look up at the sky, picking up my pace a bit. By the look of things, I'm not going to be able to avoid getting rained on; why does the thought that the group that left me behind is also going to get drenched make me happy?

My teeth are chattering, and my clothes are soaked through by the time Donatello gets to me. He actually got here in eighteen minutes instead of the twenty he thought. It just started pouring almost immediately after that first clap of thunder. Hugging my arms across myself, I bounce in place as I watch Donatello pull up alongside me. I can't see through the tinted windows of the SUV he's in, but I get a decent look at my own soggy self; my bun is saggy and wet, stray hairs plastered across my forehead as water drips off my face.

The door pushes open, and I'm greeted by his lopsided grin as I climb into the car, yanking the door shut as I get in the seat. "I have an extra pair of clothes in the back if you want to change." He says, eyeing my dripping, shivering form.

Rubbing my hands in front of the blasting heater, I nod in answer. "That'd be great… then I want some of those stuffed pretzel sticks from Benito's."

He chuckles as he opens his door. "Sure thing, Boss." I crawl over the center console as he shuts the door to plop onto the backseat; I'm definitely not changing in the front seat with Donatello. He opens the trunk and grabs a bag, smirking at me over the top of the seat as he pushes the door shut. Coming back around the side of the SUV, he pulls open the door to the back and climbs in with the bag.

"Get out of here. I came back here to change." I snatch the bag from his lap as he chuckles and uses a hand to shake the rain from his hair, sending cold droplets everywhere.

"Nah… should have had someone else come get you if you didn't want me perving on you."

I snort, pulling out a pair of drawstring sweats and a large black t-shirt. "So, you admit you're a pervert?"

Humming, he leans back against the door, watching as I peel off my soggy tank top and toss it into the back. I'm wearing an old plain sports bra, but the heat coming from his russet eyes says he finds it as appealing as something fancier. Leaning to remove my shoes and socks, I frown over at him, ignoring the warmth blooming under my skin as he runs his tongue over his bottom lip. "Stop watching me… it's making me uncomfortable."

He leans forward at this, the corner of his lips tipped into a half smile that screams trouble. "Play a game with me… you win, and I'll get back in the front and keep my eyes forward until you're done." He reaches out and sticks a finger down the front of my bra, pulling the fabric farther out to look down it. He chuckles when I frown and slap his hand away. "I win, and I get to stay back here and be a pervert." He does air quotes around the word pervert, settling back against the door again.

Licking my suddenly dry lips, I grip the clothes in my hands as I eye him. "What kind of game?"

A full smile blooms along his lips at my question. He looks very much like the cat who ate the canary despite the fact I haven't completely agreed, yet. "An easy one… thumb war."

I release a loud breath through my nose and place the clothes on top of the bag at my feet. That seems easy enough, and I don't see how he can cheat his way through it. "Fine." I bring my hand up between us, ignoring the heat that sears down my arm as his palm brushes against mine to grip hands.

"One, two, three, four… I declare a thumb war." We say it in unison, my heart thumping loudly in my ears as I try to keep my cool. It's a simple game, but I have the feeling I've made a huge mistake.

He uses our linked hands to pull me his way, jerking me forward quickly enough I don't have time to fight it. His lips meet mine in a hot, quick kiss that's over almost as quickly as it began, and I rear back with a glare as he smiles at me. "I win."

I scoff and try to rip my hand away from his, but he keeps me in place, his thumb pinning mine. "You cheated! You can't distract me to win!"

He shrugs but lets me go, purposefully dragging his eyes over my form as I scoot back to my original spot. "You didn't specify any rules… and you willingly participated already knowing I cheat." He scoots into the middle of the seat, reaching out to snag one of my legs. "I'll help you change because I'm a gracious winner."

I yank from his grip as he laughs. "I think not." Twisting to the side when he makes a grab for my arm, I glare at him and bend to grab the shirt off the top of the bag.

"You've always been a sore loser." Before I can sit up all the way, Donatello grips my arms and tugs my back to his front, keeping me in place with an arm banded over my bare waist. "Sii una brava ragazza e forse ti lascerò vincere la prossima volta." *Be a good girl and maybe I'll let you win next time.*

He's warm against my cool flesh and I wiggle against him in a weak attempt to loosen his hold. I know I won't be getting away unless he wants me to. I'm not even sure that I want to get away. The idea of playing his little game sends a shock of arousal straight to my core, the thrill of playing victim causing my breaths to quicken. "Let go of me you sick freak."

His hot breath fans along my neck as he chuckles at my insult, his lips just barely brushing along my skin. He pulls me the rest of the way onto his lap, my butt pressed firmly against the growing bulge in his denim. "Not until we get you changed." Moving his arm from my waist, he presses the palms of his hands up my sides, peeling the wet fabric of my sports bra up and over my breasts. He bites the back of my neck as I raise my arms, letting him pull the soggy fabric up and off of me. I hear it land in the back with a soggy plop. I cover my breasts with my hands, so Donatello has to fight me for access to them.

"You can give me my shirt now." I say over my shoulder, my eyes drawn to his lips only an inch from my own.

"I could." He states, cupping my own hands with his and squeezing my boobs through them. "But I'm not going to." He leans forward and nips my chin, lowering his hands to dig his thumbs into the waistband of my leggings. "I will be taking these off, though."

I use my hands on his thighs to boost myself higher, helping him tug them over my butt. Sliding me off his lap, he lays me on the seat next to him, twisting to face me as he pulls the wet fabric the rest of the way off. His russet eyes burn a path along my skin as they skate over my body, sending the fireflies in my belly into a full out frenzy. Wrapping a hand around my right ankle, he lightly tugs me towards him to grab the thin strap of my thong, sliding them off to drop them onto the floor.

"Thanks for the assistance, but I think I can handle dressing myself." My voice is quiet and rough from my arousal, something that I'm sure doesn't escape Donatello's notice.

When I sit up, he sits back, letting me grab the black tee once more. I watch him from the corner of my eye as I slide it over my head and arms, more than a little confused he's actually letting me get dressed. Before I can grab the sweats, though, he's grabbing me again, pulling me over to straddle his waist. An unbidden smile slips out at his action, I didn't want our game to end just yet, but I also didn't want him to know that. "Have you thought about what I said?"

I frown in confusion at him. His eyes aren't even on my face when he asks, but on my nipples showing through the thin fabric of his t-shirt. "When? What'd you say?"

I almost don't get the question out as he palms my breasts through the shirt, running his thumbs over my nipples. "The other night. Before I left." He flicks his gaze back to mine just as mine drops to his lips.

"Oh." He must be talking about us. About not being over. I take a deep breath, trying to ignore his touches and remember everything I want to say. "I'm not going to be your secret fuck buddy."

"But you will be my fuck buddy? Is that what you're saying?" He's smirking, like my use of fuck buddy is amusing to him. I don't think he's taking me very seriously, though, and I can feel my annoyance starting to bubble under the surface of my skin. He drops his head to suck my nipple through my tee, and I suck air in through my teeth, bringing my hands up to grip his hair. Sitting back up, my hands fall from his hair, and I rest them on his shoulders as he dips towards my lips. "Parliamo più tardi...Se non ti fotto nei prossimi dieci minuti, lo perderò." *Let's talk later... If I don't fuck you in the next ten minutes, I'll lose it.*

With that, he wraps an arm around my back, flipping us so that he's between my parted thighs, and my back is pressed into the leather seat. His tongue meets mine in the next breath, my hand going down to rub him through his jeans. He groans into my mouth before pulling back to sit up enough to undo his pants. Resisting the urge to clench my thighs in anticipation, I watch as he leans over the console to grab his wallet and pull out a condom, tossing it back into the front seat once he's got it. Tearing the packet open, he eye's me as he rolls the rubber down his shaft, tongue rolling across his lower lip. He grabs my legs when he's done, sliding a hand down my thigh and straight to my core, stroking his fingers up and down my slit before pushing the two digits knuckle deep.

Sitting up onto my elbows, I grab the back of his neck and pull him to me in a not so subtle cue to hurry the fuck up. I can feel his smile against my lips as he pushes me back and sinks into me, helping me wrap my legs around his waist with his hands before he drops a hand by my head to help support himself. His breath puffs along my lips as I arch into his first thrust, head falling back as pleasure courses through my limbs. Looking up, I can see the windows are fogged from our heavy breathing, and for just a moment, my mind is pulled from Donatello.

An accidental laugh escapes my mouth, and Donatello's kisses stop trailing my skin as he raises just enough to frown into my face, his hips moving at a slower pace. "Did you just laugh?"

Smiling at him, I shift my own hips to encourage him to keep moving. "It's nothing. Pretend it didn't happen."

He stares at me a moment but drops back down to press his chest to mine, propping my head up in his hand to kiss my neck. I bite my lip to keep my giggles in check, but one slips out, making him groan against my skin. "Can you please tell me what's so funny?" He kisses from my jaw to my mouth then nips at my lips. "Keep it up, and you might hurt my delicate pride with your chuckles."

This makes me laugh even more, and he narrows his gaze on me. "It's just… Titanic." I gesture towards the fogged windows with my hand, and Donatello shifts his dark eyes up then back to my face looking rather unamused. Easily one of my favorite movies, I used to fantasize about having my own sexy, steamy window moment. "You know? The car scene…"

"Yes, I've seen the movie." He's all but rolling his eyes at me when he says it. After a slight pause, he lets out a long breath. "Just fucking say it, Delaney, so I can fuck you properly."

I beam at him, then cup his face, pulling his lips close to mine so I can whisper across them. "Put your hands on me, Jack."

"Cazzo sei strano." *Fuck you're weird.* He pumps his hips a few more times before pulling out and sitting up, helping me straddle his hips. "Now stop fantasizing about Jack and ride my dick." His jaw flexes when I sink down on his shaft, hips thrusting up as he squeezes my hips in his hands to press me further onto him.

Grabbing the bottom of his shirt, I tug it up, and he pulls it off for me. I run my hands over his chest and shoulders, the skin hot under my palms. I go to pull my own off, and Donatello stops me, biting a nipple through the fabric as he squeezes my ass in his hands. Despite my earlier inattention, I can feel that familiar warmth pooling in my gut as I bounce on Donatello's lap, the car filled with the sounds of our panting and wet skin. Sucking his tongue into my mouth, my moans are muffled when he presses a thumb to my clit. It's just the small push I needed to lose it completely, and I arch into my orgasm, crying out into his mouth.

He keeps pumping through my release, taking control of my body by my hips when I start to go lax. With a few hard thrusts, he groans his release into my neck. The last pump is hard enough to throw me off balance, and I slap a palm against the window to stay upright. Pulling back my hand, I notice the handprint left and widen my eyes at Donatello, who rests his head against the seat with a loud sigh. "Don't even fucking start, Vita Mia."

Smiling at him, I press a kiss to his chest and push my nose into his skin to breathe in his spice cake aroma. Letting our breaths even out before trying to start a conversation, I lift off of his lap, flopping onto the seat next to him. "We really need to talk."

He turns his face to look at me, his hair a mess on his head, longer pieces falling into his face and sweaty on his forehead. "We do." He confirms before cupping my face with one hand and leaning in for a feather light kiss. "But I think there are other things we could be doing right now... don't you?"

I can't help but smile between our kisses, I know I should push the issue, but it feels good to be like this with him. So, I'm going to pretend it's not a big deal right now because that's what I excel at, pretending.

Back in Euphoria

"**I** have a crush on Donatello Genovese." Staring at my reflection in the mirror, I mumble the admission quietly to myself. Saying it out loud has the exact opposite effect I was going for. I just feel like an idiot and probably sound like one, too. I don't know why I thought hearing it would make it feel less wrong. I shouldn't think of my brother's consigliere like that. I'm clearly riding the crazy train too because I've even started convincing myself that Donatello might like me back. That our little conversations are more than just casual banter, that his casual touches have become something more flirty. But I should find his attention creepy, right? He's at least ten years older than me, if not older. That's weird, not attractive... not even a little.

Raising my hand to point at my reflection, I continue talking to myself. "You do not like Donatello. He is old... and his voice is all gravelly and deep, and he smells really good... like spice cake or something yummy." I catch myself losing my point and scrub my hands over my face. "Get your shit together, Delaney. You cannot like Donatello."

Adjusting the short tank dress I'm wearing, I step out of the bathroom. I definitely did not wear this particular dress because I know it makes my butt look really good or because it shows off how long my legs are. How could I have possibly known Donatello would be here... coincidence obviously. My pulse picks up as I get closer to Remy's office. I can hear Andrea grumbling about something through the open door but can't make out what he's saying. Gut fluttering with little fireflies, I feign inattention as I walk by the door. My eyes are drawn to Donatello like magnets when I flick my gaze into the room as I pass. He's leaning against Remy's desk facing the hall; a hand propped under his chin as he listens to whatever Andrea is saying. My heart stops in my chest when his eyes meet mine for the mere seconds it takes for me to move out of sight, cheeks warming at just the thought of him noticing me. I can't help the stupid grin that splits my lips as I continue downstairs.

"È un rossore che vedo? Con chi siamo infatuati adesso... Justin Bieber di nuovo?" *Is that a blush I see? Who are we infatuated with now... Justin Bieber again?*

Frowning at the back of Gretchen's grey head, I catch myself unconsciously, wiping at my cheeks like it'll get rid of the flush. How did she even see me? Her head is half buried in the oven as she checks the temperature of the roast sitting on the middle rack. "I'm not blushing." Ignoring her disbelieving hum, I continue. "And I haven't had a crush on Justin since I was twelve, thank you very much."

Chuckling as she shuts the oven and wipes her hands on her apron, she shakes her head at me. "Awfully dressed up for just visiting your brother, aren't we?"

I lean down to tug my sneakers on, straightening the short hemline of my dress when I'm done. "I always look like this."

The arching of her silver brow speaks for her as she starts to wipe down the counter. "You'll take that bag of cookies to Mario and Luca out front for me?"

"Sure." Grabbing the rolled paper bag, I head towards the sliding door. "Why don't you ever make me cookies?"

"Because you're a brat... now go." I roll my eyes as she shoos me out the door, peeking in the bag as I shut it. "Stay out of those, Piccolina!"

Rolling the bag back up, I hold it up to show her it's closed while sticking my tongue out, her chuckles leaking through the glass. Spinning on my heel, I start towards the front gates. It takes at least ten minutes to reach either gate from the house, longer if you take one of the wooded trails that line the fence surrounding the property. I know Remy had the trails added for Bev's benefit; she and Dylan walked it regularly when she was home. Choosing to stick to the gravel drive, I kick rocks as I walk, humming to myself. I wonder if I'll be able to see Donatello before he leaves; it seems like he's been sticking around to see me lately, but that could just be wishful thinking on my part.

Coming up on the front gates, Luca sees me coming and nods in greeting, eyeing the bag in my hand. "Move those legs a little faster, would ya? I've been daydreaming about those cookies for hours already." He smiles over at Mario, who just shakes his head at him. I'm sure he is thrilled to be paired with Luca, cue the sarcasm.

Luca and I are the same age, but he likes to pretend he's older and more mature simply because he's one of Remy's soldiers and a guard for the house. A job he only has because he's our first cousin. Holding the bag out to him, I flash a dimpled smile before pulling it out of his reach when he grabs for the bag, and hand it to Mario instead. Mario chuckles at me and pulls out two cookies, handing one to me while Luca huffs. "Hey! I'm the one who helped Gretchen move boxes last weekend, not her."

Rolling my eyes, I start to walk back to the house with my cookie, waving to Mario before I turn around. "I doubt you were much help with those chicken legs… bye, Mario."

My comment makes Mario roar with laughter. I smile to myself as I trudge back towards the house, stepping off the road to use one of the trails this time. I've just finished my cookie and am about halfway back when I hear approaching steps down the trail. My heart beating nervously in my chest when I recognize the dark head coming my way. Donatello is frowning at his phone, so I don't think he's noticed me yet. I subtly adjust my dress as we get closer together. Noticing he's not the only one walking, he glances up, a smirk pulling at his lips as he tucks his phone into his back pocket.

"Hey." It comes out awkwardly chipper and high pitched. I internally cringe, stopping on the path when Donatello stands in the way, arms crossed over his chest.

"Hey… what're you doing back here? I thought you left a while ago." He says in answer, his russet eyes leaving my face to skirt over my outfit.

It takes everything in me not to preen over his lingering gaze, and I link my fingers in front of me as nerves pinch up my gut. "Oh, you know…" I smile to hide my awkwardness, mentally berating myself; of course, he doesn't know, or he wouldn't have asked. "I brought cookies to Luca and Mario for Gretchen." I gesture behind me towards the direction I'm walking from, and he looks around me, taking a step closer.

"What's the chance they still have some left? I'm on my way to see Mario."

I shrug and run a hand up one of my arms. "I don't know. Luca was pretty excited about them. If it wasn't for Mario, I wouldn't have gotten

one."

He closes the rest of the space between us as he reaches out to swipe a thumb over the corner of my lip, making my breath catch in my chest as I drop my arms at my sides and look up at him. "You had some crumbs there…" He's looking down at me like he's expecting something, but I can't get any words out as my skin heats where his hand is now palming my cheek. He must see what he's looking for, because he brings his other hand up to palm my other cheek, as he lifts my face closer to his. "Tell me to fuck off now before I do something I really fucking shouldn't."

His breath feathers over my lips, and I finally gain some of the control over my nerves, bringing a hand up to grip the front of his shirt to yank him the rest of the way to my lips. I don't know how this is happening, but I'm sure as hell not going to let this moment slip through my fingers. My body is lighting up like a firecracker as he returns my kisses with the same intensity that's pouring from me. I know this should feel dirty and wrong, but damn if it doesn't feel euphoric. If someone weren't careful, they could become addicted to kisses like these.

Chapter Six

"**B**ring him into a collected canter before you ask for a flying lead change this time. It looks like he's confused about what you're asking him to do after the extended trot." Emily gives me a thumbs up from the middle of the arena, bringing her horse back to the beginning of the pattern she's working on. Resting my arms on the top bar of the polished wood fencing of the arena, I watch her complete the pattern once more, following my instructions. When her horse hits his flying lead change flawlessly this time, she hoots in celebration, turning a bright smile my way. Returning her smile, I reach out and pat her horse on the neck when they come over to me. "What did I tell you? It was an easy fix. Keep practicing it like that until he knows the pattern. Once he can do it without a hard cue, go straight into the lead change without bringing his speed down."

"I will. Thanks, Delaney."

Lightly thumbing her leg, I stand from the fence, brushing the dust from my riding pants. "No problem, now I need to go make sure Grizzle isn't being a terror for Meagan." Emily laughs, and I turn away from the outdoor arena to go to the main barn. Although usually well behaved, my gelding likes to get pushy with anyone that isn't me. Everyone here has been a part of these stables long enough that we're all familiar with each other's horses and their quirks. I've been here almost every day since Grizzle got trailered home. I don't mind it, though. The stables are my happy place. Grizzle is my happy place. I pull in a deep breath once I hit the barn entrance. The smell of leather, hay, and horse easily my favorite mixture; well besides the occasional spice cake.

Grizzle's grey head pops up, greeting me with a quiet nicker as I grab his rope halter and slide the stall door open. The rubber mat flooring is clean and fresh shavings have been raked out, thanks to Meagan, who smiles at me as I put the halter on. Her blonde hair is in its usual twin braids, and she's wearing a pair of denim cut offs paired with worn old cowboy boots, the classic Meagan look. She's a couple of years older than I am, and her daddy owns the hay company that supplies the stables. I've known her for years, and although I wouldn't consider her a close friend, she's nice, and I like her. We get along great but don't usually hang outside of the stables.

"Thank you for doing this." I gesture towards the stall, and she nods, pulling an apple treat from her pocket to give Grizzle. "He wasn't rude, was he?"

"No problem. I already did Bear's stall, and Emily needed the help this morning. She's been struggling with that pattern for days now." She slips past us and out the door, hanging a lead rope she had looped behind her neck by the stall nameplate. "But no, he didn't give me any trouble."

"Well, I owe you. I can help you with tomorrow's turnouts if you want?" Smiling again, she grabs the rake leaning on the wall as her light gray eyes make their way back to me. "Sure. I have the evening shift."

"I'll be here." I watch as she raises her hand in a silent goodbye, disappearing from sight. Attention back on Grizzle, I toss his lead over my shoulder and pull my hair into a ponytail while walking us towards the workout pens. "Time to work, Big Man." Dropping my arms, I keep his lead on my shoulder as he clops beside me. He snorts happily in response, and I pat his neck, if only every man were as easily pleased.

"She should be done soon, their warmups usually only last around half an hour." I hear Meagan saying as Grizzle, and I make our way back to the main barn for tack; she must be right outside the far doors, close enough that her voice is carrying through the building. Ignoring her, I continue to the tack room, clipping the built-in tie to Grizzle's halter to keep him in place while I get our gear. I drown out the rest of her conversation, and grab the tack I need, setting it off to the side while I quickly clean any remaining dirt from Grizzle's back with a soft brush. Meagan could be talking about anyone here at the stables, most of us show competitively and have similar routines.

Getting my saddle in place and cinched, I can't help but notice the obnoxious giggles coming from the other side of the barn, so very not Meagan like. It peaks my inner eavesdropper enough that I hustle to get the rest of the tack on, hoping to see who she's talking to before they leave. Not many people catch Meagan's eye, and none that I've met have ever made her giggle like that. As we get closer, the second voice gets clearer and very familiar. What the hell?

Picking up our pace, Grizzle and I come stomping out of doors in a semi aggressive huff that must startle Meagan because her giggle turns from laugh to half shout. Choosing to ignore the scowl I have plastered across my face, Donatello graces me with one of his full-mouthed grins before turning back to Meagan who is eyeing me like a mad woman.

"Delaney! I told Donatello you'd be out soon… guess I was right." The last bit she says to Donatello directly, another stupid little giggle bubbling out of her. Now that I know the source of her giggles, I find them a lot less intriguing and a hell of a lot more annoying.

Before I can unleash my inner green monster on her, I flick my attention back to Donatello as he nods in response, eyes on me as he speaks. "Guess so. Thanks for all your help, Meg."

Meg? Who the fuck? I snort loudly while Meagan smiles her stupid country bumpkin smile at him, oblivious to my annoyance. Logically I know that she probably has no idea who Donatello is to me, but I'm a naturally jealous person, and I'll be damned if Tractor Jane here thinks she can butt in on what's mine. Or should be mine. Whatever, she can't have him.

Speaking up before she can respond, I force what I hope is a genuine looking smile. "Do you two know each other or something?" I gesture between the two of them with my free hand, my lips trying to fight their way into a sneer as Meagan nods so enthusiastically she looks like a damn bobblehead. Grizzle must be feeding off of my irritation because he's started to shift in place beside me, quietly snorting.

"Oh, we met a while ago... last summer, was it?" She looks to Donatello for confirmation, sticking her hands into her back pockets in a way that props her chest up. I take back everything nice I thought about her earlier, she's a little skank, and I hate her.

Rubbing a hand over his lips to hide the laugh that starts to come out the same time my face twists into a disgusted sneer in Meagan's direction. Donatello finally takes his eyes from me to answer her. "Yea, around then."

After a slightly awkward stretch of silence, I loudly slap my hands down, drawing both of their attention. "Well, you were waiting for me, and now I'm here, so..." I say not so subtly, hinting for Meagan to leave.

She either takes the hint or decides on her own to quit looking at Donatello with stars in her eyes, because she turns her attention to me. "Okay well, I need to make a few rounds before I can leave still." Reaching past me, she pats Grizzle's neck on her way back in the barn before throwing a three fingered wave over her shoulder. She all but bats her eyelashes at Donatello, "Bye! It was good seeing you."

I'm staring so hard at her back, I'm sure she has burn marks from the lasers shooting out of my eyes. Once she disappears, my scowl snaps to Donatello. "Meg?" I practically spit it at him, while my little green monster coos in my ear.

Ignoring his loud laugh, I walk to a hitching rail and tie Grizzle off so my hands are free, might need to punch this idiot. Why is he even here? Sure, we've been talking the last few weeks, but nothing important has actually been said. We're riding a thin line between falling back into our old routine and becoming something new. I'm tugging one end of the rope while he's pulling the other; neither one of us willing to give the other any slack. I might be weak when it comes to him, but I won't let him make me a secret again.

"When are you done here? I have a surprise for you." Russet eyes meet mine when I turn back to him. He's either oblivious to the fact that I'm annoyed, or he doesn't care. Probably the latter.

"I don't know. Why don't you surprise Meg instead?" Flashing an extremely insincere smile, I cross my arms and prop a hip, eyes narrowing as he walks to me with a shake of his head.

"Geloso di non essere l'unica ragazza con un soprannome?" *Jealous of not being the only girl with a nickname?* His lopsided grin is in place as he says it, walking into my space to pull me against his chest. "Don't worry, Vita Mia, yours is the only one that matters."

Still frowning and arms pinned between us, I purse my lips. If he thinks his cute words are enough to distract me, he's very, very wrong; but I'll let him think this conversation is over for now and file it under my 'things to be bitter about' folder, subcategorized in the 'bring up during an argument' section. I could blow his eardrums with the number of things I already have stored away, ready arsenal for when I'm feeling snippy. "What is the surprise then?"

Sliding his palms up my upper arms, he cups my face, thumbs brushing along my cheeks. I can tell he's debating on whether he will tell me now or make me wait, his lips twitching slightly at my loud, impatient exhale. "We're going camping."

Camping? I almost shake my head at this, a disbelieving laugh slipping past my lips. Donatello doesn't camp. "Okay, funny. What is it really?"

Eyes on my lips, he repeats himself, dragging his russet reds to meet my gaze at my huff. "I have all of our stuff ready, so we can leave whenever you're done."

"You're serious? You planned a camping trip?" Some of my annoyance starts to slip away, little fireflies taking its place. I love camping. It's something I made sure to do every summer, usually able to sweet talk some of the other horse girls into coming with the promise of expensive wine and s'mores. I'm unfortunately the only one in my family and friends who got the outdoor bug. No one ever wanted to come out with me without bribery.

He chuckles at my disbelief, lips dropping to press a kiss onto my forehead before he answers. "I did. But I wouldn't call it a trip. It's only one night."

Pulling from him, his arms drop from around me, a full smile taking over his face when he sees the excitement on mine. "Where are we going? How are we getting there?"

Running a hand through his hair, he eyes Grizzle next to us who's kicking at a fly. "I don't actually know." Eyes coming back to me, he reaches out to push some loose hair from my ponytail behind my ear. "I was planning on letting you choose… since you'd know the best spots."

I can feel the burn of my cheeks, I'm smiling so hard. "We can camp here… Ollie bought the surrounding property for one of my birthdays, so I'd have a safe place to camp with Grizzle. There's a campsite and round pen that only takes about an hour to get to."

"Okay… how are we getting there?" He's eyeing Grizzle again like he already knows the answer but is hoping for a different one.

"We can ride. I can saddle Pete for you… he's super sweet, and you'll love him." I roll my lips between my teeth at his expression, trying not to laugh. He looks less than thrilled about that idea.

"You want me to get on one of those?" He points at Grizzle, shaking his head no at my own nod.

I smack his hand down. "Don't point, it's rude. And yes… we will be riding HORSES to the site." Patting his chest, I start walking back towards the barn. "Watch Grizzle for me? I'm going to get Pete."

"I'm not riding a horse, Delaney… that little rope is going to keep him from getting loose, right?" He looks incredibly unsure, taking a quick step back when Grizzle shifts in place. "What the hell am I supposed to do if he gets off… Delaney? I'm not riding one of these… Delaney!"

Smiling to myself, I wave a hand over my shoulder in dismissal. "Be right back."

"This shit is pinching my balls." Donatello is grumbling behind me, the leather of his saddle creaking as he shifts around. "Ow, damn it! Watch where the fuck we're going, yea?"

Turning in my saddle, I look back at him, chuckling as he rubs the red spot on his forehead left from the branch that just whacked him. "You realize you're steering him, right? You're literally running yourself into branches."

He huffs at me, frowning at the top of Pete's head. "He's definitely not listening to me." Pete drops his head then to grab a bite of grass, stopping abruptly enough that Donatello almost falls from the seat. "What the fuck!" Holding both arms up in the air in a 'do you see this shit?' kind of gesture, he looks at me while I laugh.

"Just pull his head up and quit being so dramatic. We're almost there anyway."

"Just pull his head up? He's strong as fuck and fights me…" I'm no longer looking, but I can hear the sounds of Donatello kicking Pete's sides to get him going again, and from the sounds of it, his efforts aren't very successful. "Hurry the fuck up, Pete. I'm as over this as you are… hyah, or what the fuck ever."

Most of our ride has consisted of Donatello either getting run into trees and bushes, almost falling from the seat, and bickering between him and Pete. All extremely entertaining and has made this impromptu trip one of my favorites so far. "Hyah? You really want him taking off with you, Cowboy?" Smiling over my shoulder again, I laugh when I see Pete walk right through another bush, the pair of them wandering off the trail. "Where are you going?"

"I don't fucking know..." Smacking the skinny branches away from his face, he aimlessly starts waving the loose reins around. "Cazzo, Pete! Seguire il maledetto sentiero!" *Fuck Pete! Follow the damn path!*

My belly hurts from laughing so hard, watching over my shoulder as they slowly make their way back onto the trail. Donatello is looking exasperated by the whole ordeal. "We'll be there in less than five minutes, Cowboy... think you can stay in that saddle that long?"

"I should have just walked behind you." Pete snorts in answer to him, and he huffs back, making me giggle again.

Grizzle is walking happily towards our destination, knowing he's close to getting some sweet cob at the campsite. I encourage the other riders to also use the property for trail rides, so the few campsites scattered about are always fully stocked for impromptu visits like these, extremely helpful for us now. The small shed and wooden round pen come into view first, and I twist in the seat to look at Donatello once more. "Want to race?"

He blanches at my suggestion, his fingers tightening on the reins that are draped uselessly around Pete's neck. No wonder he isn't listening, he's basically not even using them. "Absolutely fucking not."

Laughing, I turn back around and lightly nudge Grizzle into a collected trot. It's barely faster than what we were just going, but it's the push Pete needed to hustle up after us. I hear Donatello's shout and laugh into my hand. A glance behind me shows him bouncing precariously in the seat, arms and legs flopping around as Pete trots along behind us.

"What's happening?!" There's a genuine fear laced in his words, and I just can't.

I finally lose it, doubling over Grizzle's neck as I laugh. Wiping the tears from my cheeks, I slow back to a walk, Pete barreling by us towards the round pen while Donatello waves around his loose reins in an attempt to gain back some control. Pete comes to a stop at the hitching rail, impatiently tossing his head around when Donatello stays seated instead of getting off. Riding up next to them, I slide off of Grizzle, rubbing his jaw in a good job, before ducking under his head to grab Pete's reins that are now dragging along the ground.

"I knew you'd love riding... you don't even want to get down." Smiling up at Donatello, I pat his leg teasingly as he scowls down at me. Grizzle bumps my back with his nose in a silent reminder that he's ready to get his gear off, and I pat his side. "Hurry up so we can get the horses put away and the tent set up."

Tossing the reins over the rail, I turn to face Grizzle and do the same with his. They'll stay in place long enough for us that there's no need to tie them. I feel a boot tap against my back and look over to see Donatello struggling to get out of his seat. Sucking my lips between my teeth to keep from laughing. I watch as he drops from the saddle and hits the ground, legs buckling awkwardly as he stands hunched, facing Pete.

He finally turns to look at me, body still slightly hunched and uncomfortable looking. "Everything hurts."

My laugh breaking out, I uncinch my saddle before responding; Pete is starting to shuffle restlessly at the rail. "In that shed, there should be a tub of feed and some buckets... can you put a scoop in two and bring them here?"

He nods, walking away, and I watch his back as he goes. Although there's a slight limp from sore muscles, he still carries himself like a man with dignity. Apparently, his lack of equestrian skills isn't enough to tamper his self-esteem any. Smiling to myself, I quickly remove the horse's saddles, setting them on the rail as a temporary saddle tree, before tossing the few bags of supplies off to the side.

I have to admit it was a big feat getting Donatello out here, especially on a horse. I've been careful not to let myself get my hopes up, let myself think he might actually be trying to be something real, but it really feels like he is. I let my gaze wander towards the shed as I lead the horses to the corral, slipping their bridles off once we're there. He's good at that though, veiling the truth with extravagant displays and grand gestures. He's an expert at hiding his real feelings and making you believe what he wants. It'd be stupid to fall for his charade a second time around.

Donatello steps out with two buckets, eyes finding mine, he holds them up with a lopsided grin as he walks our way. "Took me a minute, but I got it." I return his smile, grabbing them to give to the horses before shutting the gate. The corral has grass and a gravity water trough that keeps itself full, but I'll probably throw them some hay later. Donatello catches me off guard, pulling me to him when I try to pass. Running a thumb along my cheek, he cups my jaw, russet reds scanning my face. "What's the matter? It looks like I lost you for a minute."

I must have not masked my thoughts enough if he was able to catch it. "Nothing." I smile to ease his worries, lightly pulling from his fingers. "How good are those fire skills of yours, Cowboy?"

He chuckles, following me towards our supplies. "I think that's something I can handle."

Turns out Donatello couldn't handle making the fire. After twenty minutes of failing at making one with the fire starter that he insisted on using to get what he called 'the full camping experience', he stomped into the shed and came back with a lighter. Although I assured him that using a lighter in no way hurt his masculinity, he definitely seems to be suffering a ding in his pride. Completely ridiculous, in my opinion, if he was going to be embarrassed by anything, you'd assume it would have been when he was flopping around like a beheaded chicken while riding Pete.

We're always able to swing right back into a comfortable place when we're like this. It's easy to forget all the ugly things that have happened when I'm giggling over the misshaped tent because Donatello set it up, and burning my lips on melty s'mores; easy to lose sight of all the reasons I put a barricade around my heart to begin with. Watching the fire dance across his features now as he makes up terrible jokes to keep me laughing has nostalgia pooling in my gut. We should have had a hundred nights like this already, a million little moments for me to cherish; instead, I was cast away like a pretty stone, skipped across a pond and left to sink.

"Why are you here, Donatello?" My question comes out louder than intended, unexpected by both of us. My own thoughts forcing their way out of my mouth.

Everything is quiet but for the crackling of the fire and the soft footfalls coming from the corral. It's hard to read his facial expression in the dark, his silence making me itchy. "Would you prefer to be here with someone else?"

My fingers dig into the grass beside my legs at his question. I should have known he wouldn't answer me properly. Getting up, I brush the dirt from my legs, staring at him as he watches me. "Don't do that. Don't deflect." Slapping my hands at my sides with growing annoyance, I watch as he stands. "Just answer my question, Donatello. I'm tired of pretending like you didn't send me off with a broken heart last summer."

He walks around the fire to stand in front of me, wrapping his arms around me in a tight hug that presses my face to his chest. I'm not returning his hug, but he ignores that, resting his cheek against my head. "I missed you, Vita Mia. I just want to spend time with you." He shifts so that I can look at him, a smirk on his face when my eyes finally find his. "I rode Pete for you... and even though the bastard goes out of his way to hit me with every branch along the way, I'd ride him every day if it meant I could spend ten minutes with you."

"You want to spend time with me, but you won't actually be with me…" I cover his mouth with my hand when he tries to speak, stopping his words. "I don't need any excuses or pretty words. You made yourself perfectly clear when I left… but what I don't understand is why. If you won't be with me then why torture us both, why not just let me move on?"

Removing my hand from his lips, he keeps my hand in his, linking our fingers. "Because I don't want you to move on."

Pulling from him, I run my hands down my face, rubbing my eyes roughly. "I don't know what you want from me Donatello… I won't be your secret again. I won't. So, if that's what you're hoping for, to have me at your beck and call like before, then leave now… I refuse to go through that again."

"You know we can't be a couple, Delaney… and you know why."

Closing my eyes to shut out the look on his face, I take a deep breath to calm my racing heart. "No, I don't. You know why we can't… I still fail to understand." I hear the crunching under his feet as he moves closer before I feel his hands on my arms.

"Let's make a deal, Vita Mia… one that will make us both happy." Opening my eyes, I scowl at him. That sounds like the worst idea. Donatello is a cheating, lying, selfish man who will undoubtedly spin whatever deal he wants in a way that will benefit him the most. "Get that look off of your face." He chuckles at me, running his palms up my arms to cup my cheeks. "You will get the final say… just listen to me."

"Fine." I blow out a long breath, my attempt to look at my hands, and not his face thwarted when he tightens his fingers. Everything is always a damn game with him.

"Spend time with me. Be my... friend, until you leave. Wherever you want, including in public." He wiggles his brows suggestively with the word 'friend', and I almost roll my eyes. "But we aren't a couple, Delaney. When school starts, we go our separate ways again."

He wants to be fuck buddies. Is that what I'm hearing? I feel like I should feel more offended by the suggestion, but we both know that's basically all I've ever been anyway, at least in his eyes. "I don't want that. I don't want to be together because of some deal, Donatello. I don't want our relationship... of any kind, to be based on some sick game you've made us play because you're too much of a big man to be seen with little ol' me." My chest feels tight with both irritation and tears, but I keep my face calm, I won't let him use my emotions against me. "I want to be a real couple. I want you to take me on dates where people will see how happy you make me. I want to be able to hold your hand without you pulling away from me the moment someone looks too long. I don't want to have to hide how I feel."

"Delaney..." I stop his low grumble with a raise of my hand, pausing whatever he was about to say.

"If you're so set on your deal, then hear my offer." At his nod, I lower my hand, my heart beating so roughly in my chest it feels like it might explode. "Date me... for real, for the remainder of the summer. You call me your Vita Mia, your life, so make me a part of yours in a way that means something. Let me prove to you how perfect we could be outside of this shadow prison you're so intent on keeping me in."

My hands are shaking with the effort it's taking to get my words out, the fear of rejection trying to poison my efforts. "If you still don't want me by the time I leave, then we end everything... including whatever so-called friendship we ever had."

"It's never been about not wanting you, Vita Mia." He reaches for me, but I pull back. I need to hear his decision before I lose my strength. I'm making a deal when I don't even want one. I can't see his face well, but I know his russet reds are brushing along my face and form, can almost feel their gaze like a physical weight.

"It's only six weeks, Donatello." It's whispered, more because I don't really want to say it. Six weeks is such a short amount of time. If he takes my deal, then it barely feels like enough guaranteed time with him. If he turns me down, then it's almost insulting that he couldn't even bother to try.

"Deal." That single word grumbled out in his honey voice drips along my skin, sinking into my pores to wrap around my erratic heart. He steps forward when I don't respond, pulling me to him with a palm on my nape. "Deal, Vita Mia."

His breath fans across my lips the next time he says it, and I suck in a quick, shaking breath. "You mean it? You're not joking or playing one of your own games?"

Pressing a soft kiss against my lips, I can feel the small smile on his. "No, Baby. I'm not trying to trick you... I even sealed it with a kiss."

Nervous, shaking laughter sneaks out of me, as I smile. "Well... what now?"

Bringing his hand forward to cup my cheek once more, he smiles against my lips, pressing his lips to mine for sweet soft kisses between his words. "I don't know about you…" kiss. "but I'm super…" kiss. "fucking sore…" kiss. "and tired."

He lets go of me and goes to the half-collapsed tent, and I watch as he pulls out our sleeping bags. I still feel shaky from our conversation, his casual switch of focus a welcome distraction from the heaviness before. "What, you don't want to sleep in the tent?"

Chuckling, he drops the bags in a fairly flat spot near the fire. "No…" He's looking down at the bags at his feet; arms crossed over his chest. "Fuck, this is going to be uncomfortable."

"It's camping. It's not supposed to be comfortable. That's part of the outdoor experience." Coming up beside him, I squat and start readjusting the bags. "Too bad we don't have pillows, though."

"We would have if we'd taken a car." It's mumbled above my head, and I look up while rolling my eyes. "I'm going to change… you sleeping in that?"

I frown at his back. "Did you pack me clothes?" I actually forgot about that since I was so excited about the whole thing.

"Yea… but I'm pretty sure that bag didn't make the cut when you were picking out what to bring." He disappears into the little tent, speaking through the open door. "You can wear my clean shirt. I'll keep this one on."

"Okay." Pulling my boots off, I set them off to the side. Donatello comes out, tossing me a tee that I barely catch. I quickly pull off my own shirt to pull on his clean one, then tug my riding pants off. I can feel his eyes on me, so I look over my shoulder, smiling as I watch him try to lay comfortably in his sleeping bag. Slipping my bra off under my shirt, I drop it onto my pile of clothes before standing awkwardly by our bags.

"Get in with me." Donatello says, lopsided grin on his face as he holds the bag open.

"We are not going to fit in that bag together." He pats his chest, and I laugh, climbing awkwardly on top of him, straddling his waist and laying my head on his shoulder. "This is not comfortable."

"I don't know... seems fine to me." He squeezes my butt when he says it, lightly thrusting his hips up.

"The bag is half open. We'll freeze." I sit up, pulling the bag with me, laughing at his frown.

"We will if you sit like that."

Reaching over, I grab my own bag and unzip it all the way to make a giant blanket, shifting off of Donatello. Pushing his side, I make him move over so I can squeeze in next to him, pulling my bag over the top of us. "There, that's better."

"There has to be a better way to do this... but I like having you all smashed up in here, so we'll leave it." He kisses my chin, reaching down to grab behind my knee to loop my leg over his waist.

"Switch me spots." He ignores me, starting to trail kisses down my neck. "Donatello, switch me spots."

Letting out an extremely dramatic sigh, he sits up on his forearm to look down at me. "Why."

"I don't want to be on the open side."

Smirking, he bends down to kiss me. "Well, I don't want to be."

"Donatello." He chuckles and nips at my jaw, rolling on top of me.

"We can stay like this for a minute, yea?" It's mumbled into my neck, his body pressing down on mine in a way that gets those fireflies going.

"I guess."

I can feel his smile against my skin as he trails his lips back to meet mine. One of his hands is pushing its way up my side, pulling my shirt along with it until my shirt is bunched above my chest. He palms one of my breasts, and I lift into his touch, bringing one of my own hands up to tug at his hair. "Can I fuck you, Vita Mia?"

His breath is hot on my lips as he leans over me, dark eyes on my lips as his erection grinds into me. "Am I your girlfriend now?"

His eyes flick to mine at the question. Our breaths mixing as we both stare defiantly at the other. Finally, he growls out, "A deal is a deal."

Not the exact answer I wanted, but I know it's the best I'm going to get. In answer to his question, I pull him back to me, sucking his tongue into my mouth in a way that has him pinching my skin with his fingers. Our movements are constricted in the sleeping bag, making it more difficult to properly explore each other, but it doesn't matter. If anything, it turns me on more, knowing he has to try harder to touch me the way he wants.

Reaching between us, I slip my hand under his joggers to stroke his erection, smiling at his groan. I run my thumb over the head of his dick, rubbing the precum on the tip. "I didn't grab a condom." He grunts into my neck, biting the skin when I roll my hand along his length.

"I'm on birth control... you don't need one."

"Fuck, why'd you make me use one last time?" He pulls from my reach, scooting down and hooking his fingers in my panties to pull them off. I have to move my legs to help him, both of us struggling to get them off in the tight space of the bag. Once they're off one leg, Donatello gives up, leaving them hooked around the calf of the other.

"I didn't think about it." I mumble out as his mouth drops between my legs. I don't know how he fits down there, but I'm not complaining. My back arches when he sucks my clit into his mouth, flicking along the tight bud with his tongue in quick motions that have my thighs tightening around his head.

He swipes his tongue slowly along my slit before peeling my thighs from his head, climbing up my body until we're face to face. "Put that on hold... it's hot as fuck down there. I'm about to pass out."

Laughing, I pull his lips to mine, hooking my ankles behind his butt to pull him closer. He reaches between us and adjusts himself, slipping inside my heat with a quick thrust that has us both groaning. Wrapping his arms around my neck and under my head, he buries his face at my throat, softly kissing the skin under my ear. Mimicking his gesture, I bring my arms around his neck, running my fingers through his hair.

Our movements are slow and deep; our bodies pressed tightly together. My legs drop to tangle with his as he continues to grind against me, pressing soft wet kisses along my neck as I arch against him. My skin is hot and sticky with sweat, my breath coming out in quick pants matching the ones I feel on my skin from Donatello. His lips finally meet mine, swallowing the moans that were previously echoing through the trees. That familiar warmth is pooling in my gut, zipping along my limbs as we keep our slow pace.

Pulling back slightly, Donatello whispers into my lips. "You need to come, Baby."

With a light chuckle, I suck his bottom lip into my mouth. "It doesn't work like that."

Adjusting, so his hands are now cupping my cheeks, he kisses me deeply, stroking his thumbs softly along my skin. The touch is sweet, the swipe of his tongue over mine, gentle and soft. His hips are still moving in slow, deep thrusts; his touch and actions saying more than any words could. Our last time was fast and unexpected. This is our real reunion, our true hello, welcome back. I know he's about to come, his hips thrusting a fraction faster than before while his fingers tighten on my face ever so slightly. I can feel that I'm also close, just a few steps away from that glorious edge.

Our lips separate just enough for his low groan to escape, one of his hands lowering to my jaw. The sound is enough to send me off the edge, strong enough to make my legs come up and curl around his legs, tighten my arms on his neck. He kisses me through my orgasm, running his thumb over my bottom lip when I'm done. Breathing hard, I pull his face down to my neck, running my fingers through his hair as he wraps his arms around me again.

My heart is just starting to calm when I feel his lips press against the bouncing rhythm in my throat, whispering against my skin. "Vita Mia." It's said like a prayer and coming from his lips, in this moment, I know it's more than just a simple nickname.

Back in Euphoria

I force a smile and raise a hand to the judges before exiting the arena, patting Grizzle's neck a little harder than necessary. "You're an ass." I grit it quietly through my teeth at him, his left ear twitching backward at my voice.

He snorts loudly, tossing his face around like a brat when I dismount and shoving my shoulder with his nose when I swap his bridle for a halter. I tie him to the trailer, whispering angrily over my shoulder at him. "Knock it off, or I'll smack your nose in front of everyone."

I hang his hay bag in front of him before moving to take off his saddle, the cinch swinging down as Donatello comes into view. I ignore him, ripping the saddle from Grizzle's back and dropping it onto the built-in tree of the trailer tack compartment.

I accidentally walk into Donatello, not noticing him behind me. He wraps his arms around me, keeping me against him. "Don't be upset. You got a thirteen... that seems pretty good to me."

I laugh through my irritation, appreciating his attempt to make me feel better. Resting my chin on his chest, I look up at his face. "We had two rail faults and a time penalty for being a second over because of Grizzle's refusal at point eight... where I almost fell off and looked like an idiot."

He kisses my forehead and then steps back. "You didn't look like an idiot. That girl who did the course all messed up did."

I give him a closed mouth smile, silently laughing as another rider walks by, scowling at Donatello's back for the comment. Maybe that was her. "You said that really loud."

He shrugs, lopsided grin in place as he steps out of my way, watching me start to brush Grizzle. He pauses my movements by wrapping his arms around my waist, kissing just below my ear. "What did the janitor say when he jumped out of the closet?"

I'm already smiling, starting to brush Grizzle again. "What?"

"Supplies!" He does jazz hands when he says it, dropping them to tickle my sides when I don't laugh as loud as he wants.

Slapping his hands away, I turn to look at him. "Mine's better..." He raises his brows in challenge, crossing his arms as he waits for it. "Why did the scarecrow get an award?"

"Why?"

"He was outstanding in his field."

He covers his laugh with his hand, trying to wipe his smile away and shrugging. "It was okay."

I scoff at his response, making him laugh at the annoyed look on my face. He steps forward, grabbing me to kiss my face and neck all over with obnoxious smacking kisses until I laugh and squirm in his arms. "Okay! Stop, I'm in a better mood now."

He smiles against my neck, placing one more kiss, softer this time. "Good." He stands straight, running his thumb along my jaw. "You'll have a better day tomorrow."

I nod, more to appease him than I agree. "Will you be here?"

He flashes a lopsided grin, dropping a kiss on my lips. "I'll be here."

Chapter Seven

"Shit." Noticing my hand in the mirror, I frown down at the two black lines that stand out from the faded tan of my henna design. I missed my last two appointments to get it redone because I was busy at the stables. I haven't seen Donatello all week, our schedules somehow clashing; the timing couldn't be more ironic really, it's not like we just decided to become official or anything. I finish brushing my teeth, wiping my mouth with the back of my hand once I'm done. I can't keep the tattoo a secret forever, but the idea of explaining it to him right now makes me nauseous.

Keeping the TV on in the living room for white noise, I head to my bedroom. It's only ten at night, but I have a hot date with my pillow. Pulling my blankets back there's a knock on my door making me pause; I have a feeling I know who it is. There's really only one person who repeatedly drops by unannounced or would bother coming here so late. Walking towards my door, I fling it open to expose a smirking Donatello. I'm not even surprised at this point. "You'd make a really good stalker... you already have the sneaking around and seemingly random drop ins down pat."

He laughs, stepping around me and into my apartment as I shut the door. "Maybe I am a stalker." Spinning, he catches me off guard to pin me against the door. "I like catching you off guard like this and I haven't been able to stop thinking about you all week."

"That was really sweet and creepy at the same time." I feel his chuckle in my own chest he's pressed so close, his sweet spice cake scent warming the air around us. "How'd you get in my building? It has a code."

Instead of answering, he presses his lips to mine, effectively shutting off my questions. Standing on my toes, I gesture for him to lift me up, and he does, grabbing the backs of my thighs as I wrap my legs around his waist. Despite my joking, I'm really happy to see him. Pulling his lips from mine, his eyes scan my dark apartment. "Why is it so dark in here?"

"You interrupted my bedtime." He hums, walking us towards my bedroom as I kiss along his jaw and neck. Stepping up to my bed, he drops me backward, giving me a lopsided grin when I look up at him frowning. Without a word, he takes off his shirt, tossing it onto the floor by his feet. He bends and unties his boots next, toeing them off before unzipping his black denim. They land beside his shirt as he comes up to the bed, gesturing for me to scoot over. "What are you doing?" It's asked as he crawls beside me, and I try not to ogle over how good he looks in just his boxers. I thought things were headed down a sexier direction than they currently are.

"Going to bed. Isn't that what you said you were doing?" He pulls my pillow from behind me to tuck under his head while I watch him in confusion. Once he's settled, I get under the covers also, scooting up next to him so I can share the pillow.

"You came over here to sleep?" I ask, needing to clarify what is happening right now.

"I came over to see you. If you're going to bed, then I guess so." He reaches out, running his hand over my hip and up the back of my tee, pulling me flush with him and tangling our legs together. "What're we doing tomorrow?"

My heart is beating happily in my chest at having him so near, thumping softly against my ribs, trying to match the beat of his own pressed close. "I don't know... don't have any plans?"

His fingertips are trailing along my back in a soft, tickling motion that's giving me goosebumps. He shakes his head no in answer, fingers continuing to dance a path along my skin. "I told Remy I was spending tomorrow with you."

My breath catches at his admission, drawing his eyes up to mine. "You told Ollie about us?"

"I did." It's said casually, but the clenching of his jaw says it was anything but. Before I can say anything, he brings his hand up to push the hair back from my face. "When were you planning on telling me about your tattoo?"

His question catches me off guard, my pulse racing. "Wh... What?" How the fuck does he know about my tattoo? It literally just started showing.

A small smile pulls at his lips as he reaches between us to pull my hand up from under the covers. His eyes leave mine, dropping to my hand as he brushes his own tattooed thumb over the two small arrows. "I saw it your first night back…the henna was clever, though." He brings my hand close and kisses the ink, dark eyes meeting mine.

"How the hell did you notice something like that?" It's a whisper, my throat growing tight. I knew I didn't want to have this conversation, but I didn't realize how not ready I was.

"It's my job to notice things Delaney, to look at things from every possible angle so that I can give the best input." Stroking the ink once more, he brings his hand to the nape of my neck, drawing me close, so our foreheads touch. "Why'd you get it, Vita Mia?"

He already knows the answer. I know he does. He has to. But I don't know if I can say it out loud, not to him. We might be okay in this moment, but my heart doesn't forget the hurt so easily. Squeezing my eyes shut, I breathe in the cinnamon on his breath. "Please don't make me say it."

I'm mentally praying he won't push this. Won't make me say what he wants to hear. I'm not ready to tell him the same words he denied me of. I remember being excited to get it, to have something like this to share with him forever. I can thank Remy and Bev for that stupid idea, their matching tattoos my inspiration. To me, they are the epitome of love, and my little impulsive tattoo was my way of emulating that. What a mistake that was. His rings are cool on my heated skin when he moves his hand to my jaw, angling my face to press his lips to mine.

"I'm sorry." His whispered apology confuses me, and I open my eyes to find his already looking into mine.

"For what?"

He doesn't answer right away, trailing his fingertips along my cheek and into my hair. "I knew you weren't ready to talk about it, and I brought it up anyway. I shouldn't have done that."

"Oh." Not sure how to respond, I just shrug, making him smile.

"Do you want to know why I got my tattoo?"

Hesitantly I nod, silently watching his face for any cues of where this might be going. Donatello is a secretive man, to say the least, I actually know very little about him other than what he's let me see. Remy and maybe Andrea are the only ones privy to the full length of Donatello's past. What do I even know about this man besides he drives me crazy? His padre and only family passed when he was in his teens, and much like my brother, his entire life has been dedicated to the Famiglia. He owns three properties, but I've only been to one of them. He never brought the same date to any parties or events.

Him being willing to share this piece of him is slightly nerve wracking. He only has the one tattoo, the one mark on his skin that was intentional and put there with I assume great thought. Those pesky fireflies are buzzing in my belly, but they're almost nauseating instead of sweet this time. What if he's about to tell me it's dedicated to another woman? To a secret child? To the love of his life that died and can never be replaced, least of all by some child like me, who had to make a deal just for a real date? I'm going to puke.

"When I was sixteen, I read somewhere that three arrows represented movement and direction... it sounded incredibly inspiring at the time. So I had it done on my dominant hand, my thumb specifically, so I'd see it every time I shot my gun or threw a knife...a reminder to myself that if I wasn't the first to shoot, first to land my hit, there would be no movement or future for me." He pauses a moment; lopsided grin flashed my way. "Turns out I got the wrong type of arrows done and in the wrong design, so it isn't nearly as cool."

Okay, so no secret lover I need to be worried about but maybe still alarming. "You're really nailing the whole creepy, cute vibe tonight."

He laughs at this, a full belly laugh that shakes the bed and forces a smile of my own. Once he's calmed himself enough, he looks back at me, running his knuckles along my jaw. "Did you know you left the TV on?"

 "I leave it on for noise."

"Oh." He says, mocking my earlier response, and I lightly thump his chest, making him laugh. Wrapping his arm around the back of my head, he tugs my face into his neck, kissing the top of my head when I happily bury deeper into him.

"Take me on a date… in public. That's what I want to do tomorrow." It's mumbled, my lips brushing along his skin with the words.

"Yes, Boss." I smile but say nothing, closing my eyes as he runs his hand over my hair, his fingers sinking to lightly scrape my scalp with each pass. When everything was said and done, it was the little things like this that I missed the most, craved the most. The cuddling, the soft touches, the feel of his heart under my palm.

"I like your hair like this."

"Hmm?"

"Wavy. I like your hair wavy." He repeats, smiling at me when I pull back to look at his face.

"It's a mess... I let it air dry after my shower." He shakes his head at my disbelieving frown, pausing his movements.

"È bellissimo. Sei bello." *It's beautiful. You're beautiful.*

Instead of responding, I palm his cheek and scoot higher to press our lips together. After a moment, he brings his own hand to press against mine, cradling it against his face. His eyes are still closed when I pull back, our noses just brushing. "Who are you?" His brows scrunch at the whispered question, eyes still closed. "You know everything about me... I barely scratch the surface of you."

His fingers lightly pinch against mine as he slowly opens his eyes, a frown still creasing his beautiful features. "Like what? You've known me basically your entire life."

Rolling my eyes, I move a hand between us to smooth my thumb over his frown, smiling when he pulls it to his mouth to kiss my fingers. "I hardly knew you... saw you a lot but didn't know you. You were always running around with Ollie."

There's a moment of silence, making me unsure if he will answer my question or respond at all. "Do you remember when Bianca had a crush on Remy?" He smiles, his lips brushing my fingers.

"Yes! She probably still does." I blow a small laugh through my nose. "She spent months trying to butter me up to get on his good side. It didn't work... I hated her for it and told him I'd never speak to him again if he dated her."

Chuckling, he shifts, so his arm is under the pillow, supporting his head. "You've always had him wrapped around your little finger."

I snort. "I don't know about that anymore." I don't need to say it out loud for Donatello to understand, but our relationship has definitely suffered since Remy found out about mine and Donatello's fling. "He was more my papa than my actual papa for most of my childhood...my mama checked out of her motherly duties when I turned six, and Papa only ever cared about continuing his legacy in the Famiglia; I was an afterthought for them. But I had Ollie. He always made sure I was taken care of, made sure I felt wanted and not like a burden they were obligated to take care of."

After a small pause, a bittersweet smile tips my lips. "I noticed more when I got older that it was weird, that most twenty-five year old guys weren't so invested in their eleven-year old sister's life; they didn't plan birthday parties and attend every riding lesson." I don't remember a time that Donatello wasn't at the house, so he knows most if not all of this, but it feels important to say it anyway. "I wasn't sad when Papa passed, and I honestly won't care much when Mama does either. Ollie is the only real family I have that means anything... and Bev obviously, but that's different."

Donatello doesn't say anything, just runs his knuckles over my cheek once more. "I hate that he doesn't accept us. I don't need his approval. I can make my own decisions, but his disappointment... it fucking hurts." I laugh to try and hide the tightness of my throat. I've been denying how much I'm bothered by Remy's rejection until now. Truthfully, it fucking kills me inside to know that he isn't happy with me.

I swallow so hard it's an audible sound, blinking past the tears wanting to fall. "What do you want to know about my past, Delaney?" Donatello's question helps pull me from my inner meltdown, his hand pushing through my hair, bringing my attention back to him. He's always been good at reading when I need a distraction.

"Um…" I clear my throat, mentally shaking my head to clear away the remaining unease. "How did you meet Ollie? I just remember you showing up one day and never really leaving."

He smirks at me, continuing to run his hand over my hair as he talks. "I was fourteen and thought I was tough shit… just fulfilled my Omerta, a real big man now that I was officially part of the Famiglia. I went out and started shit just because I could, fought with anyone who'd participate to prove how bad I was." He's smiling now, a toothy kind of grin that has me smiling back. "One night, Remy showed up with some other guys I didn't recognize, called me out in front of everyone there, saying I was just some punk made man wannabe who needed to be taught a lesson." He pauses, russet reds finding my own dark eyes. "He beat the fuck out of me, dragged my limp ass across the street to Larry's, and made me apologize for fighting outside of their fine establishment."

He raises his brows with the word 'fine' and I giggle. Larry's is always full of drunks and looks like it's been abandoned for decades.

"Then he took me to the house, made me get cleaned up, and forced me to sit through dinner. It was awkward as shit, me sitting there with my bruised ribs, black eyes, and split lips trying to suck down your mama's spaghetti while making small talk with your papa, the Capo Famiglia…Afterward, he sent me outside and told me to be back at the house by eight A.M. to start my new position with your uncle's men." He cups my face, thumb stroking my cheek. "Your brother was smarter than I'll ever be when he was only seventeen."

He lets out a long exhale, his cinnamon breath hitting my face before I speak. "But he doesn't know everything, Donatello… Ollie isn't always right." He pulls my face towards his, kissing my forehead as I snuggle into him.

He sighs into my hair, his arm wrapping around me. "Ollie usually is… and we both know it." He emphasizes my nickname for Remy, making me huff a laugh against his chest.

"That sounds gross when you say it."

"Remy would probably agree." My eyes start to drift closed, the light thumping of Donatello's heart singing a lullaby made specifically for me. "Your light is still on… I don't know about you, but there's no way I can sleep with it."

I grumble into his chest as he laughs, softly pushing away from me to stand. "I'm going to buy you one of those clappers… like that commercial with the old lady, yea?" He slaps his hands together, loudly yelling, "Clap on!" Slap, slap. "Clap off!" While walking across the room to turn the light off.

Rolling my eyes, I cover my head with the pillow, ignoring his chuckles. He flops onto the bed obnoxiously hard, making me roll sideways and shoves his head under the pillow, so we're nose to nose. "Sleep good, Baby. We got a day date to plan."

Back in Euphoria

My eyes catch on Donatello through the window, and I bite my lip to keep from smiling like an idiot. His eyes barely brush my passing form, his self-control much better than my own. It's hard for me to keep my affections to myself, pretend like my heart doesn't beat a symphony every time I think about being with him. Ever since that kiss in the woods, we've been almost inseparable, sneaking into the shadows for stolen kisses and planning secret get togethers. The last few weeks have been exciting, the thrill of having a secret lover bringing an edge to my otherwise vanilla life that I didn't realize I needed.

"Hey, Ollie." I smile at my brother as I step into the kitchen from outside, setting three peanut butter fudge cupcakes on the counter in front of him.

Without hello, he lifts the cupcake off the counter, eyeing the pretty clear wrapping and bright orange ribbon tying it shut. "Where'd you get this? I'm not eating it if you made it."

Frowning at Andrea chuckling from his spot at the island, I grab a water bottle from the fridge. "That's rude." I spin, resting my hip against the counter, facing the three of them. I have to make a conscious effort not to let my eyes linger on Donatello too long, bringing the bottle to my lips for a drink to distract myself from the fireflies in my belly. "It's from Sienna's party, the one she invited all three of you to." Raising an accusatory brow at Remy to get my point across, I continue. "And I can bake just fine, thank you."

"I have eaten more baked trash from you and your easy bake oven than I could even count." Remy grumbles, unwrapping the cupcake in his hand and smelling it like he thinks I'm lying about its source. Andrea laughs, motioning for me to slide him one as Donatello chuckles, moving to the stool by Remy.

"It's incredibly unfair to judge my baking skill on that easy bake oven." Twisting the cap onto my bottle I set it on the counter, sliding onto the seat opposite of Remy and next to Andrea. Donatello smirks my way, snatching the last cupcake. "Everything came out wrong in that because it was powered by a lightbulb."

"Exactly. It shouldn't have been possible to burn things the way you did." Remy says around a mouthful, the corner of his lips ticking into a smirk when he sees the expression on my face.

"The fruitcake!" Andrea bellows next to me, shifting in his seat so that his mammoth arm can bump into my side in jest. "What was that for? Easter or something?"

His question creates a chorus of mockery on my end, Remy chuckling into his cupcake while Donatello openly laughs. "It wasn't even the right holiday!"

"I honestly don't know how that one went wrong; I followed the recipe exactly." This makes them hoot even louder, and I roll my eyes, standing from the island. "You guys are jerks." Turning in the doorway, I toss my mostly empty plastic bottle at Remy's back. "Last time I do something nice for you!"

Their chuckles follow me out of the door and into the living area. Dropping onto the couch, I use my phone TV remote to turn the TV on, leaving it on whatever channel was watched previously. I mostly want it for background noise. Scrolling through my phone, it isn't too long before I hear the sound of the footsteps coming into the room. The brush of fingertips on my neck draws my attention behind me, and I smile at Donatello as he subtly nods for me to follow him.

Doing a quick scan to make sure Remy or Andrea aren't around, I hop up and follow after him. He steps into one of the back-spare rooms, eyeing me over his shoulder before he disappears into the doorway. He's drawing the blinds when I come into the room, quietly shutting the door behind me. I cross my arms over my chest as he comes closer, brow arched. "If you think you're getting lucky after being rude to me, then you're about to be wildly disappointed."

Smiling, he tugs me to him by my elbows. "Even if I apologize?"

Snorting, I uncross my arms, letting him wrap them around his neck, forcing me to hug him. "Even if you apologize."

He leans in for a kiss, and I tilt my face, his lips meeting my cheek. He chuckles against my skin, moving his lips to my neck instead. "What if it's a really good apology?" He bends slightly, grabbing my legs to lift me up, carrying me to the bed. He sits down, keeping my legs around his waist.

Bringing his lips back to mine, he nips at my bottom lip instead of going for a kiss, tightening his arms behind my back. "Why don't you apologize, and then I'll decide."

He knows he's won, based on the Cheshire grin he's giving me. His fingers dip into the back of my waistband, tickling the skin there as he fans his hands. My heart is thumping its new favorite tune, made specifically for his while I breathe in his cinnamon breath, fanning my lips. I know, right in this moment, in the spare bedroom at my brother's house, that I'm a fool for this man... and I'm positive he knows it, too.

Chapter Eight

"**D**o you sleep this late every day?" Blinking the sleep from my eyes, Donatello's face comes into view, inches from my own.

"I don't know. That depends on what time it is."

He props his head on his hand, sitting up on his elbow as I stretch, reluctant to actually get out of the blankets just yet. I honestly hate getting up, easily the worst part of mornings. "It's just after eight."

At my disgusted face, he laughs, grabbing the edge of the comforter to throw it off. I grip the edge before he's able to, holding it against my chest. "Eight is not sleeping in Donatello. Ten... ten is considered sleeping in." Pulling the blanket from his hands, I tighten my hold on it. "I'm not getting up until at least nine-thirty."

"When you get up at five every morning, eight is sleeping in."

Rolling onto my side to face him, I tuck the blankets around my arms and legs to make sure he doesn't grab them again. "That's disgusting and sounds like a terrible time... good thing I don't do that."

He drops down next to me, shoving his way onto my pillow, and I close my eyes as he chuckles, determined to get another hour of sleep. "You're kind of a grouch when you wake up."

Opening one eye, I peek at him before closing it again. "Shhh. I'm trying to sleep."

He tries to dig his hands under the blankets, but I pin it down, keeping him out. "You have terrible morning breath, by the way." I can smell the toothpaste on his breath, he's so close, but I keep my eyes closed. He probably used my toothbrush too, the sicko.

"Seems like a you problem." I grumble out, smacking the hand away that he managed to wiggle under my guard.

He manages to get the rest of the blankets pulled out enough that he can squeeze under. He presses his big body up against me, shoving one of his legs between mine and wrapping an arm over my waist. "Get up so we can get breakfast, I'm hungry."

I don't respond but nudge my face into his neck, welcoming the warmth he brought with him. His normal spicy scent is mixed with the light smell of coconut, and I take a deep breath, smelling him. "Did you use my body wash?"

His chest shakes with a soundless chuckle as he sneaks a hand up the loose leg of my shorts. "Yea, and that big brown bottle of lotion... took me an hour just to rub it in, though. "

I laugh at that, squeezing his leg tightly between my own in silent warning when his fingers start to wander. "If you're going to be in bed, we're sleeping."

Following a long, drawn out sigh, his hand stops. "I didn't want to say anything to ruin the surprise, but if you don't get up, we'll miss the ferry."

I laugh against his neck. "Nice try. The ferry runs every fifteen minutes."

He chuckles, and it shakes my face against his neck. "That would have worked on Andrea. He never takes the ferry… they freak him out."

"Are you often trying to get Andrea out of bed?" I ask while smiling against his neck.

"More often than I'd care to admit."

My laugh ends on a groan when I sit up and throw my blankets off. "You're obviously not going to let me sleep, so I might as well get up."

He chuckles as I stomp off to the bathroom. It's still warm in the room from his earlier shower and my toothbrush damp. After using the bathroom, I come out to find him propped on the bed, going through his phone.

"Did you figure out what we're doing today?" I ask it as I open my closet.

"No. But we might have to swing by one of the warehouses." He says, eyes still on the phone.

"Fine by me." I grab out a thin strapped white baby doll style sundress that hits mid-thigh and my black gladiator sandals. After I put them on, I pull the top half of my hair away from my face in a bun.

Donatello's eyes are on me when I turn to face him. "What?"

His russet reds are dark when he gets to me, his fingers trailing over my collarbone and up to cup my jaw. "I like this."

I think he's referring to my outfit, but I'm not sure. His fingers tickle along the edge of the hem and tilts down to kiss my lips.

He pulls away, reaching to grab his phone from the bed. "Are you ready?"

After breakfast, Donatello decided we should go to the warehouse first to get it out of the way. I told him it was fine. I don't really care what we do today as long as we're together. Pulling up to the warehouse, he drops his hand on my leg, getting my attention. "Are you coming inside?"

I shrug, looking out the window as he parks. "Sure." I used to come to the warehouses all the time with Remy in the summer, mostly because he didn't like leaving me with babysitters. I haven't been to one in a couple of years, though, there was no need for me to tag along with him.

The one we're at now is just outside of the bay and one of the nicer ones if I remember correctly. It has a fancy sitting area, complete with a receptionist in the front, along with an upper viewing deck for potential clients. It's mostly just a pretty picture to hide what's in all the storage rooms and stacked on the pallets, really.

Donatello holds the back door open for me, and I go in first, welcoming the blast of the AC. There are two large sliding doors open on the farthest wall to my right, letting it all out, though, and the second you step out from under the fan, it's like it's not even there. Donatello starts talking to someone off to the side, so I wander towards the giant boxes stacked nearest me. They're easily ten feet wide and five tall, filled with random things. The one directly in front of me has poster like rolls, and I grab one out, a flawless counterfeit of La Rêve on the other side when I unroll it. I look through them for a while until I find a copy of Nu Couché deciding to keep it for myself. I'm sure Remy will live without the profits.

"I wouldn't touch the goods if I were you…" My head snaps over to see a soldier coming my way, hands in his pockets. I look to where I saw Donatello last; the spot is empty. "Capo Famiglia doesn't tolerate theft. Even if the thief is a pretty little thing like you."

Straightening my shoulders, I raise a brow. He probably doesn't know who I am based on his age. He can't be much older than I am, and it's not like I'm a huge part of the Famiglia, especially this part. "Non gli dispiacerà. Lo prometto." *He won't mind. I promise.* I give him a dimpled smile. When he doesn't smile back, I turn to go find Donatello, but he snatches my wrist.

I try to jerk out of his grip, but he holds on tight, his working muscles making him a hell of a lot stronger than me. Before I can say anything, I hear Donatello.

"Take your hand off of her unless you want to lose it." It's said casually, but there's a blade of steel behind it, a sharp edge ready to slice through flesh.

My arm is released immediately, and I turn to see Donatello walking my way. He's being trailed by a woman I don't recognize but assume is the receptionist. She's dressed in a maxi dress but carrying a binder. When her eyes fall on me, she lightly touches the sides of her mouth like she's trying to check for lipstick smudges, smirking at me like she knows something I don't. It makes my gut clench.

Donatello puts his hand on the back of my neck when he reaches me, his thumb rubbing along my nape as he eyes the man in front of me. "Delaney Luciano can take whatever she wants." He says it loud enough that all the men in the area can hear, some of them even stop what they're doing to look over at me to see what's happening.

The man blanches at my last name, nodding to Donatello. "I didn't realize who she was. Mie scuse." *My apologies.* He lowers his head my way in further apology as he goes by, and I bring my attention back to Donatello.

"Are you done now?" My eyes flick to the woman behind him as she smugly meets my gaze. Who the hell is this?

"I am." He turns to look at the woman behind him. "Send me the call log by tomorrow."

He starts to walk, hand still on my neck, and she stops him with a hand on his arm, her fingers lingering longer than necessary. "Same time as last week?" She smiles sweetly at him, and I have to resist the urge to slap the look off of her face.

He frowns and looks at her a moment like he's thinking about something before answering. "No." I doubt that's the answer she was hoping for because her smile falls, leaving her pouting as we walk away.

I'm more than a little annoyed about the exchange and don't bother to hide it, letting my face show my thoughts when Donatello looks at me as we get into the car. I put my painting on the backseat then rest my elbow on the middle console, chin on my fist as he walks around the front and gets in the driver seat.

"Why do you look like that, Vita Mia?" He turned to face me, frowning.

"Your receptionist was pretty upset that you couldn't make your recurring meeting." I make to emphasize the fact that I noticed they had one last week.

"I don't care." I hum at his response, and he leans down to kiss me, knocking my arm off the console in the process. "She's just the receptionist, nothing more."

I leave it be even though there's doubt prickling at my skin. Some things never change, apparently. Donatello always had women around who meant nothing, always coincidences. I want to believe him, though, I always did.

He sits back and pulls out of the parking spot, eyes flicking over to me as he grins. "Ready for our day date?"

Back in Euphoria

"I'm going to have glitter in my butt crack for weeks." Donatello murmurs into my ear; my back is pressed so closely that I felt his low words rumbling inside his chest as they were said.

Tossing a pile of bubbles from my hand over my shoulder at him, I smile and lean my head back against his chest to see his face. "Same… in retrospect, the mermaid bath bomb was a mistake." I lift more bubbles up and blow them back into the bathwater. "No wonder Beverly said I could keep it."

He shifts under me, bringing his legs up to bend at my sides. Some of the water in the tub slips over the edge, leaving a pool of water and bubbles on the tile. I settle into him, reaching back to hook my hands behind his neck. The water is bordering on too hot; my skin tinted light pink. The air in the room feels nice in contrast, and I lift one of my legs to rest against the lip of the tub, using Donatello's leg to help prop it up. Donatello's fingers are tracing along the backs of my arms as his forearms rest on the tub as well.

I let out a content sigh, letting my eyes close in relaxed bliss. I don't know what we are, Donatello and I, but I know it's nothing like I've ever had before. This feeling of peace... of being wanted as I am. I don't have to pretend around him or hold back my words. I'm... comfortable. One of his hands has moved to rub circles on my exposed knee, and I smile to myself, a warmth blooming in my chest. "What are you thinking about?"

His words are low, lips brushing along my ear. I open my eyes, face turning to look at him as he leans back slightly to look into my face. "Why?"

"You're quiet and smiling." One of his hands comes up to push some damp strands of hair from my face that have escaped my top knot. "That usually means you're up to something."

This makes me laugh, and I let my arms drop back into the water, cupping bubbles just under the surface. "I'm just happy."

He doesn't say anything, so I turn to look at him again. He's still watching me like before, eyes brushing along my face. After a long moment, he smiles back, a lopsided grin that doesn't quite reach his eyes. I want to ask what's wrong, but he wouldn't tell me anyway, so I pretend not to notice, reaching up to tap his nose with some bubbles instead. He catches my hand and uses my fingers to swipe some bubbles onto my nose also, chuckling at his own antics.

Using my arm, I wipe my face off, smiling again when I feel Donatello rub his nose in my hair. "I'm happy too, Vita Mia."

Chapter Nine

I'm nervous. There's an anxious foreboding pressing down on my chest as I get ready, a sick fluttering in my gut that pinches with every movement. "It's just dinner." I remind myself, unplugging my straightener from the wall and leaving it on the counter to cool. The idea of having to face Remy full on, with Donatello as my dinner date, makes me ill. He's been nothing short of horrendous the last few weeks, making his thoughts of mine and Donatello's relationship painfully obvious.

Although I hate seeing the resentment pasted across his face. I'm determined to stand my ground. I want him to see how important this relationship is to me, how much I'm willing to stand up for it. Which is the main reason I'm forcing Donatello to be my date tonight. To say he despises the idea is an understatement. His relationship has been strained just as badly, if not worse with Remy. My brother's hatred of us being a couple is the elephant in the room we've all been poorly ignoring. His distaste a lingering stain on our attempt at happiness.

I hear the footsteps coming my way before I see Donatello in the mirror, the grin on his face looking forced. "Hey."

His eyes sweep over my sundress, his smile softening just a bit. "Hey." He says back in greeting. Leaning against the doorframe, he watches me wrap up my straightener and slide it into the drawer. Russet reds meeting mine when I turn and stand in front of him.

"I'm ready if you are."

He wordlessly nods, running his fingertips along my cheek before letting his arm drop back to his side. A heavy breath slips from his chest as he turns and heads towards the front door. Getting into his car, I can tell he's as nervous as I am, watching his hands grip the steering wheel tighter than necessary. He's only doing this to appease me. I'm glad he's not fighting me moreover it, but I can't help but also be annoyed that this isn't something he'd do for us on his own. Then again, we wouldn't even be a real couple if it were up to him, would we? His love of games making us possible.

The ride is almost solemn despite the sun shining through the windows and the upbeat music quietly playing through the speakers. Neither one of us has said more than a few words; our normal playful banter squelched by the impending drama in store for us. Parking, an audible sigh comes from Donatello's side of the car, drawing my attention his way and off of my hands that I've been anxiously twisting in my lap.

He reaches out, pulling my hands apart and kisses my fingertips. Turning his face into my palm, he briefly closes his eyes. "It's just dinner."

His words echo the same disbelieving anxiety as my earlier ones. I nod, repeating them back to him. "It's just dinner."

The smell of Gretchen's lasagna wafts through the air when we step inside, and I take a deep breath, letting the familiar scent help soothe my nerves. Dylan is sitting just outside of the foyer watching us as we enter, upper lip curling when Donatello puts his hand on my lower back. I smile down at him, reaching to rub his ears in greeting as he grumpily growls at Donatello's passing form. Bev comes down the stairs then, a baby on each hip.

Donatello pulls Carmella from her, and she gives him a thankful smile while holding Amalia out towards me, the baby kicking the air happily. "Take her. My arms are about to fall off." She reaches out, wiping some drool off of Amalia's chin. "They've been demanding to be held all day, and carrying them around is easier than listening to their tantrums."

"Well, I'm more than happy to oblige." I say, tickling the little bit of belly showing under Amalia's scrunched up tank. Carmella starts giggling as Donatello tosses her up into the air, walking towards the kitchen as we trail behind him. "Where's Ollie?" It's asked as we enter the kitchen, Gretchen the only one in the room.

Beverly doesn't answer right away, her eyes on her baby being flung in the air once more. "Upstairs." Gretchen gasps, smacking Donatello with her towel while scolding him for 'abusing' her nipote, making both Beverly and I smile. "He should be down soon. He's being difficult..." Bringing her attention all on me, she sighs. "You should talk to him before dinner, actually."

I scrunch my nose at the idea, my heart sinking into my stomach at the suggestion. She's probably right. I go to hand her Amalia, but she points to a highchair, motioning for me to put her there instead. I do, buckling the wiggly baby in while Bev drops some puff snacks on the tray.

"Remy is probably still in the bedroom." She says as I straighten, heading for the door. The look on my face must belay my inner turmoil because she smiles at me, a softness in her features that usually isn't there. "He's your brother, and he loves you..." Her eyes slide to Donatello across the kitchen before meeting my gaze again. "He'll get over it."

With a slight nod, I exit the room, my feet moving at almost a snail's pace up the stairs. I can hear movement inside Bev's bedroom, and the door is open. I step through before I can chicken out, eyes immediately landing on my brother. He's faced the other way, head turning to look over his shoulder at my entrance. Besides a slight pursing of his lips, he says nothing, turning to look forward once more. He's dressed in a suit still, but he has the jacket off and his sleeves rolled to his elbows. His choice of attire speaks volumes; he's approaching this like a business affair instead of the casual dinner it's supposed to be.

"Hey, Ollie." Gathering my courage, I break the silence, the words hanging between us as he ignores me, looking down at his phone. Swallowing through the tightness of my throat, I creep forward and turn to sit on the bed in front of him in an attempt to draw his gaze. "You can't ignore me forever…"

His dark eyes flick to mine momentarily, a deep hum of disagreement coming from him. His behavior hurts, to say the least, his obvious anger and disappointment digging in my ribs. He's being cruel, and he knows it. "Beverly said I should come talk to you, but I don't see what good it'll do if you're going to just act like this." I wave my hand at him, using my anger at the situation to help hide my hurt.

"We have nothing to talk about." He straightens, tucking his phone into his pocket before crossing his arms over his chest, his cold gaze landing over me.

I blink at him. My fists clenching in my lap. "We have nothing to talk about?" I say it with as much condescending sass I can muster, my lip curling at him.

"No." He shifts, cracking his knuckles objectionably loud. "I've already talked, and you didn't listen. I've no need to repeat myself." He turns in dismissal, walking towards the door. "Besides… you're an adult and can make your own decisions. Right?"

He throws my own words in my face, degrading them and making them seem shallow. "You sit on a mighty high horse for someone who's made their fair share of mistakes and bad decisions."

He pauses at the door, jaw working as he turns to see me standing behind him, fists balled at my sides. "This… charade between you and Donatello is disgusting and disrespectful." I swallow audibly as I wait for him to continue, seeing on his face that he has more venom to spit. "You want to talk? Let's talk, Piccolina." The nickname, little one, isn't said with the same sweetness as always, but with a tone made to slash at my heart.

He steps forward, and I step back, the anger burning under his skin, threatening to lash out and sizzle my own skin if I stand too close. "Part of me was hoping this was all some elaborate farce you two cooked up just to fuck with me. A bad joke gone too far. Never did I actually expect to see the two of you, in my house, at my dinner, together like some happy couple." His face twists into an ugly snarl, his dark eyes looking black with his rage. "But here you are, my baby sister who I raised as my own and my closest confidant stabbing me in the back with your lies and... canoodling." He spits it out, purposefully using the most degrading word for mine and Donatello's relationship to dig his words deeper into my chest.

"I love him." It's said in a feeble attempt to make him understand, see that I'm not doing this to hurt him. Tears are tracking down my cheeks, leaking from my eyes at Remy's onslaught. He never yells when he's angry, but every word, every sentence comes out with a bite that's almost worse than if he were.

He snorts at my whisper, disgust morphing his features as he looms over me. "You are nineteen, and he is a thirty-year-old man... you are foolish if you think he could love you."

I bring my hands up to wipe my face; I know my makeup has already gone to shit, the black of my mascara wiping off onto my palm. "You don't know that... you don't know anything about us."

He laughs a deep, ugly sound that belays no happiness. "There isn't an 'us', Delaney. If he actually cared about you, you wouldn't have been his little secret. You don't hide the people you love." I suck my lips between my teeth in an attempt to keep some of my composure, straightening my shoulders to receive his next blow. "You're nothing but something to pass the time for him."

"REMY." My head snaps towards the door at Beverly's voice, her tone just as dark as Remy's has been. He stares at me a moment longer; his lashings have been ground to a halt, but he knows they've made a lasting mark.

I notice Donatello behind Beverly in the hall, his face blank and devoid of emotion. I don't know how much they've heard, but it was enough to make Beverly level my brother with a glare as she pushes him from in front of me and grabs my hand. "That's enough. Delaney is not one of your men, Remy Oliver Luciano." She keeps her eyes narrowed on him until he gives her a slight nod, his eyes pulling from me to look at her.

She starts to tug me from the room, but Remy stops her, grabbing her free hand to bring her palm to his lips. "You're right, Cuore Mio." The small apology isn't for me; he doesn't regret a single thing he's said, but for upsetting her.

Donatello has come into the room, and his eyes are scanning my face, undoubtedly noting the smudged makeup and tear tracks. He reaches for me, grabbing the back of my head to press my face into his chest, it pulls my fingers from Beverly's, and I clutch his shirt. His action makes me lose all composure, and a cry escapes as more tears squeeze out, the sound muted by his chest. I feel his chin momentarily press against the top of my head before he addresses Remy. "Clearly, it's time we talked."

I hear Beverly's loud sigh but don't bother pulling my face from its hiding place, choosing to use Donatello as a shield.

"Sure..." The bite is back in Remy's voice and I squeeze my eyes tighter. "Stop fucking my sister."

Donatello lightly tugs me from his chest, moving me to the side as he steps forward to stand in front of my brother. "No."

"No?" Remy's hands fist at his sides, the muscles in his jaw ticking as he silently fumes. "You are my Consigliere... your one job is to give me advice. How can I possibly trust anything you say if you can't even make the right ones in your personal life?" His eyes flick to me then back. "You wouldn't be here if it weren't for me. I brought you in from the streets. I gave you a job under one of the best Capo's. I taught you the necessary skills to become a high-ranking member of the Famiglia. You would be nothing but a soldier, if not for me. And this is your thanks? For years of my guidance? Of my friendship? You turn around and snatch up my sister for nothing but your own entertainment." That steel voice of his is still an even tone, never wavering in its vicious attack. "Your disrespect makes me sick with rage. If this were a Famiglia issue, you'd already be dead."

I move to speak, but Remy levels me with a look that cements my feet to the floor. I can see his control slipping, hands trembling with the need to inflict physical pain to relieve some of his own hurt. "Ollie, this isn't about you, no one is trying to hurt you."

He steps forward, not even sparing me a glance and letting me know my plea has reached deaf ears. Donatello stands his ground, letting Remy speak. "Not to mention, she is a child." Remy finally loses to his anger, his fist splitting Donatello's lip and sending his face sideways. The hit is a loud smack in the room, almost echoing around the space.

"Ollie!" It's shouted as I reach for Donatello, but Beverly quickly grabs my arm, pulling me towards the door.

"We don't need to be here for any more of this shit show."

Donatello straightens before I leave the room, his own dark gaze narrowing on Remy. "She's a legal adult, Remy… the pedophile card is getting a little worn, yea?"

Remy grabs him by the shirt as we reach the door, and I pull against Beverly's grip with no success. "You don't deserve her. You'll never be good enough for her."

I'm pulled into the hallway but hear Donatello's reply anyway. "I know."

I'm crying again as Beverly leads me to the back-living space, forcing me to sit down on one of the sofas. She momentarily disappears, coming back with her candy jar and a bottle of wine. Sitting down heavily, she yanks the cork from the pre-opened bottle and takes a long swig of wine. She grabs a handful of candy from the jar in her lap and tosses it into mine while still drinking, making a small laugh sneak out of me. She offers me the bottle, but I shake my head, hiccupping into my arm as I wipe my face. "Candy and wine fix everything." She says, leaning forward to set the bottle on the coffee table in front of us.

"I'm not so sure it can fix this, Bev."

She turns to face me, grabbing a candy bar from my lap that I still haven't opened and forcing it into my hand before digging into her jar for her own candy. "Despite Remy's barbaric delivery, you needed to hear that." She rips open a duo pack of Starburst, whispering a quiet "damn" to herself when it has two reds. "And Donatello needs to hear it, too."

When she looks up and sees I still haven't eaten my candy, she raises her brows, staring me down until I give in and take a bite. Satisfied, she sits back into the cushions while unwrapping hers. "This fight has been a long time coming." As she says it, there's a loud crash from upstairs, and she lets out another big sigh, using Dylan at her feet as a footstool. "I understand why Remy is mad; he wants the best for you and doesn't want to see you get hurt." She reaches forward and grabs my candy bar hand, forcing me to take another bite, which makes me giggle through my sniffles. "Donatello is a grown man with a whole set of problems we have no idea about. Whether you want to realize it or not, he took advantage of you being so young and continues to do so. If you were older, you wouldn't have allowed his bullshit to continue as long as it has." At my frown, she pops more candy in her mouth. "Donatello already told Remy how long this has been going on, and I already knew last summer."

She opens another candy for me when mine is gone, putting it in my hand like she did the last piece. "I can't speak for your brother, but I know he feels betrayed by the both of you, and it's going to take some time for him to get over it... but he will eventually. Although I understand his anger, I think he's being... harsh. He of all people should know we don't choose who we fall for." She smiles then, another sigh slipping from her. "Does he love you?"

Her question catches me off guard, and I frown, looking down at my half-eaten candy instead of her. She's asking if Donatello loves me, and I don't know the answer. I want to say he does, use it as fuel for my side of tonight's argument, but I just don't know. I had to practically beg him to date me in a serious way, constantly play his games. I decide to be honest. "I don't know."

Her hazel eyes shift between my own, but she says nothing, grabbing the wine bottle and handing it to me in a silent order to take a drink. I accept this time. I think we both know what I have with Donatello is nothing but the wishing of a cricket wanting to be a butterfly. Impossible and unrealistic.

"Where are the girls?" I ask in an attempt to change the subject. I'm tired of being forced to see everything I've been denying. Remy was right; You don't hide the ones you love. You don't make them play games. You don't make them question their worth.

"Gretchen took them out to the staff house. She also put dinner into some Tupperware for you... I think she figured no one would be hungry for dinner."

I nod and hand her the wine, scrunching my wrappers in my hand. The sound of footsteps makes both of us turn to look at the doorway. Donatello comes into the room alone, a light bruise blooming over his cheekbone to match his split lip. He holds his hand out to me and I get up, looking to Bev as she speaks. "Make sure you grab that lasagna; you don't want to be on Gretchen's bad side also."

Taking Donatello's hand, I give Bev a small wave, and I let him lead me out of the room and into the kitchen. There are two large Tupperware containers filled with both lasagna and salad, a small bag of breadsticks sitting next to them on the counter. Pulling from Donatello's grip, I grab them all and look at him. He reaches forward and pushes some hair from my face, a low "Let's go." said before he heads outside. We parked on the opposite side of the house, but this way will get us out without having to go through and assumedly, run into my brother.

Sitting in the car, there's a heavy awkwardness clinging to the air. A feeling of uncertainty plaguing the space. Neither one of us says anything until we're outside of the surrounding gates, Donatello the first to break the silence. "Do you want to go home or my place?"

My grip tightens on the food in my lap. The lasagna container is making my legs uncomfortably warm. "I don't know…" I shift my gaze to his profile. My heart is thumping in my chest, playing a tune to match my hesitance. "I don't know what's happening anymore."

He lets out a long breath through his nose, his jaw ticking. After a pause, he pulls off the road and runs his hands roughly over his face. "What do you want, Delaney?" He turns to face me, dropping his hands. "What do you want to do?"

I swallow thickly, forcing air through my tight throat. I know what I want, but I'm not sure we have the same ideas. "I want to be with you."

He nods, facing forward and pulling us back onto the road. "Then we'll go to my place."

The way he says it makes my heart sink into my stomach. That wasn't the answer he wanted, and it's painfully obvious. For my own sanity, I push the growing doubt to the back of my mind, pretending I didn't notice. Because that's what I'm good at, pretending.

Back in Euphoria

Five minutes my ass. Donatello's concept of time is clearly warped because I've spent the last twenty minutes hiding in the upper bathroom, waiting for him to sneak out of a meeting downstairs. If Remy found us, he'd kill Donatello. Well, maybe not kill him, but he'd definitely break his face and probably his hands. Remy has a thing for breaking people, especially with Bev being gone. The thought almost makes me feel guilty for sneaking around… almost.

Fiddling with the strings on my hoodie, I'm about to give up on waiting, hopping off the counter I'm sitting on, to retreat out the back unseen when I hear the slight knock on the door. My skin flushes with nervous excitement as I hurry to crack the door open, showing a sliver of Donatello's lopsided grin. "What's the password?" I whisper, and he quietly chuckles, dark eyes shifting around the hallway before he leans closer.

"Mayonnaise."

Biting my lip to keep my giggles contained, I open the door for him, and he slips in, flipping the lock before turning back to face me. "Mayonnaise? That's the best you could think of?" He shrugs as he gets closer, pulling me to him by my hips and tilting down for a kiss.

"I'll think of a better one next time." His voice is low and gravelly as he tries to stay quiet, whispering against my lips between our kisses. "I have a new joke for you."

"What is it?" It's a breathy, quiet question that's almost swallowed up by his lips. He's backed me up against the counter I was just sitting on, lifting me up to set me back onto the marbled surface.

"How do you make a tissue dance?" His lips are trailing along my neck as he speaks, and I can feel his smile as he waits for my response.

"How?" My fingers dig into his hair with one hand as he nips softly at my skin, the other trailing across his chest, fingers spread wide to feel as much of him as possible. We don't get much time together, and I want to feel as much as him as time allows.

"You put a little boogie in it." I slap my hand over my mouth to keep from laughing too loudly as he muffles his own chuckles against my neck.

"That's so bad…" Pulling his face up for another kiss, I wrap around him as his fingers slide up and under my hoodie, pushing it up my sides. "I love it."

"I knew you would." He mumbles against my lips, tongue reaching out to run over my bottom lip. "E ho circa trenta minuti per fare l'altra cosa che ami." *And I have about thirty minutes to do the other thing you love.*

I smile and nip at his lips, fireflies buzzing happily in my belly as my sweatshirt is tossed onto the tile. "Vai avanti allora...uomo sfacciato." *Go ahead then...cheeky man.*

Chapter Ten

I have two weeks left of my summer break, then I go back to Alabama for school. I've already registered for classes and taking Beverly's advice, I signed up to live in the dorms this year instead of renting off campus. She seems to think I'll need the distraction of meeting new people and decorating a dorm room when I go back; I'm starting to think she might be right.

Things have been on edge between Donatello and I since the confrontation with Remy. Those first few days we, mostly me, tried to pretend we were fine; but like Remy said, it's just a charade. And the more I look at it, I see his words for their truths. The inky black of his venom burning and leaving behind a rot that's done nothing but multiply and infect everything good I thought I had. I don't know what he said to Donatello, but it has had the same effectiveness. His behavior is reminiscent of last summer when he pushed me away and broke my heart. You'd think he'd fight harder for us after our shit show of a dinner, make it worth the fight. But I'm starting to see I'm the only one who sees something to fight for. Beverly sees it too, and I imagine it's a large reason she's been trying to help change my focus.

Shutting my laptop in my lap, I set it on the couch next to me and stretch. Donatello said he'd come by this afternoon, and I hope he does; he's been flaking on our plans the last few days. Despite the feelings of impending doom headed our way, I want us to be okay. I want him to choose me, to want me… to love me. My phone rings from the kitchen island and I move to pick it up, Donatello's number flashing across the screen, his contact still saved under 'Loser' ironically.

I feel nervous picking up; I can almost hear another plan being canceled already. "Hello?"

"Hey…you still home?"

There's a faint sound of traffic in the background, giving me hope that he might be on his way. "Yea. Are you still coming over?"

"Sure."

Holding in the snarky comment that threatens to come out at his passive aggressive answer, I pretend not to notice. "Okay, well, what time are you thinking?"

"I don't know, Delaney." There's a loud exhale into the phone, but I don't respond to him, letting the tension on the line speak for me. "I can be there in fifteen minutes, but I think we need to talk."

I hear him breathe like he's going to say more, and I end the call, cutting whatever he was about to say off. I don't need to hear the words to know what's coming. Everyone knows what those words mean. I toss my phone onto the couch and cross my arms over myself, looking out my windows towards the busy street below. It shouldn't be like this. I'd love to blame Remy for my current turmoil, but I'm not naïve enough to know it wasn't going to happen anyway. It's the main reason I told myself I'd stay away from Donatello this summer… and look at me now. There's a staleness to the air that tightens my throat, an ominous feeling settling like rocks in my gut.

I'm still standing in the same spot when I hear the low rap on my door letting me know Donatello is here. I left the door unlocked earlier and he lets himself in after seeing it's unlocked. I hear him take his boots off and set his keys down but don't turn to look. I stay facing the window even when I feel his heat at my back, little sparks lighting up along my skin at his nearness. I know what's coming, but my stupid heart doesn't. My arms are still crossed, but I lift a hand to pinch my bottom lip between my fingers. My eyes close when I feel the warmth of his lips on the back of my neck, his fingers trailing from my shoulders to my elbows in a slow, soft caress.

I hadn't bothered to change this morning and am still in my sleep clothes, my hair up in a loose messy bun. Normally I wouldn't care what I looked like around him, but with the current state of things, I find myself second guessing my decision to stay comfortably shabby. The feeling of uncertainty burning inside my chest. I hate this. I pinch my lip harder to bring my thoughts under control, opening my eyes in time to see Donatello circle to my front.

He gently pulls my hand from my mouth, bringing it up to palm his cheek. I can feel the burn in my eyes of unshed tears, the heaviness of my heart with every thud against my ribs. He's barely been in the door five minutes, but I already know what's coming, felt it before he even hit my block. I know he sees it on my face, knows I've already predicted how this night would end. "Don't cry, Baby."

I close my eyes again at his words, clenching my teeth for some control. My fingers curl against his cheek as he continues to hold my hand to his face, not letting me pull away. I hate that he's being sweet. I hate that I still want him to touch me knowing he's about to break me.

"Why?" My question echoes what I've already asked him a thousand times before, the question I've never gotten an answer to. Why are you doing this? "Why?" I ask again when he doesn't answer, opening my eyes to let the tears fall that I was hiding. Why don't you love me? "Why, Donatello?" I yank my arm down, taking a step back from him. "Tell me why?" Why am I not good enough?

I already know that he won't answer me. That he is going to give me some generic 'it's not you, it's me' excuse. That he's going to brush off my feelings like troublesome lint. He's already done it before, and that same aching throb is bleeding from my heart now like it never actually went away.

"Delaney..." He reaches for me, but I keep my space. It's the only thing keeping me from breaking completely at this point. He runs a hand through his hair, dropping the hand he had extended towards me. "You knew this was a possibility when you made your deal." He's looking away from me, knowing damn well his words are bullshit and unable to say them straight to my face.

"Don't blame your decision on me, Donatello. You and you alone are making this choice." I say it through my teeth. My limbs trembling with a mixture of rage and sorrow. Fire and ice mixing to burn behind my ribs.

"You're right." His russet reds finally meet mine. "I've made my choice, and I don't want to be together… I think you should move on."

His lame excuse echoes in my head, banging along the walls of my brain. 'I think YOU should move on' of course he wouldn't need to, he never felt anything real for me. I already knew that, but I had hoped it wasn't' true. Hearing it for the truth it is, scorches a path straight to my heart, charring my veins, making it difficult to breathe. I look at my hands, twisting my fingers together and willing my lungs to give me enough air to speak. "Okay."

"Okay?" I don't look, but I can hear the confusion in his question like he didn't expect it to be so easy. We both know it wasn't the last time.

"Okay." I say again with a slight shrug. Untangling my fingers, I wipe the wetness from my face before looking at him. "If that's all you have to say I'd like you to leave." I take a deep breath, forcing myself to calm while ignoring my silent tears. I'm sticking to my earlier promise to myself, the one I made while waiting for Donatello to show up. I told myself that I wouldn't repeat last time, that I wouldn't crumble and beg him to stay and I'll be damned if I break it. If I'm going to be broken, I'll do it standing my ground.

"That's it?" He starts forward, and I move to the side and out of his reach, making him huff with annoyance and scrub at his face with his hand.

Shrugging again, I pretend I'm not on the verge of shattering. That my heart isn't splintering while remaining as strong as I can. "A deal is a deal." I hate those words with all my soul; they feel like acid on my tongue, repeating what he said to me that night we camped.

Shaking his head when I don't say anything more, he starts to put his boots back on. I wait until he stands to speak, when he's just feet from the door. "Donatello?" I'm proud that my voice came out unwavering despite the tears leaking down my cheeks.

He pauses and turns to face me, but I can't see his face properly through the tears blurring my vision. "I thought you were my forever." I hold up my hand, making sure my tattoo is on full display. "You asked me before why I got it…" A sad laugh leaks from me, ending on a half sob as I flip my hand to look at the two little arrows. "I was naïve enough to think that you loved me back…" I slap my hand down at my side, hand curling into a fist while I shake my head at my own stupidity. "You know I thought this time things would be different. That you'd see how perfect we could be, that you'd want me like I want you, that you'd finally choose me." My words are broken as I cry, unable to hold the sobs inside my chest despite my best efforts. "I see how pathetic that was now."

I hear him move as I close my eyes, trying to even out my breathing. He's on me before I can fight it, palms on my cheeks to tilt my face towards his. I should push him away, but my broken heart wouldn't allow it anyway. So, I let myself be weak, sinking my fingers into the thin fabric of his shirt as he rests his forehead on mine. His hands are wet from my flowing tears. I can feel the sticky dampness under his warm palms as he holds me against him. "Vita Mia, I need you to move on. I need you to forget about us… we are not meant to be."

His strained words wrap around my heart, severing the blood flow to the rest of my body. My limbs feel numb, my chest a hollow thudding ache. "Why?" It quietly slips out, an unbidden plea for any kind of truth.

He pulls my face to his neck, holding me to him with a hand at the back of my head. His other hand is pressed under my shirt to pinch my body as close as possible, his fingers digging into the flesh of my lower back. "Ti meriti il mondo." *You deserve the world.*

I frown against his neck, digging my nails into his skin through his shirt. He finally gives me an answer and it's not one I want to hear; I won't accept that. "Non voglio il mondo, ti voglio." *I don't want the world, I want you.*

His hands tighten as he hugs me closer for not nearly long enough before he pulls away, taking small steps backward towards the door. "Move on, Delaney. It's what's best for the both of us."

Wiping my eyes so I can see clearly, I stare hard at his face. "I love you, Donatello... I love your bad jokes and your shitty games and how you always cheat to win. I love how your eyes look red in the sun and how it sounds when you laugh. I love how you smell like cake and taste like cinnamon. I love how I feel when you're with me, and I love how you look at me. I love you with every space in my heart, Donatello Genovese." I swallow thickly, pulling my shoulders back and lifting my chin even as it trembles. "I just thought you should know before you walk out that door, because if you do this, if you leave... that's the last and only time you'll ever hear it. I will NEVER let you hurt me like this again."

I can see the rise and fall of his chest as his hand tightens on the door handle. Can see the indecisiveness behind his eyes. His jaw ticks, but he stays silent, the sound of him pinching his keys the only noise in the space. The creak of the door opening springs a new set of tears to burn behind my eyes, my heart quietly begging him to stay. He keeps eye contact until the last second, my lungs and throat on fire as I force myself to appear stronger than I am. He pauses in the doorway, back facing me like he might turn around, might stay… The sliver of hope I let worm its way in is snapped in two when he disappears behind the door without a single look, the quiet clicking hitting with the force of a sonic boom.

I crumble, slapping my hands over my mouth to help contain the screaming sob so he can't hear it in the hall. This time is worse, a thousand times worse, a million times worse than last time. This time he knew I loved him, I finally said the words out loud, held my heart in my hands and he still left like it was nothing. Like I was nothing.

There's a sharp stabbing in my chest as my heart constricts, every pump feels like there's a shard of glass stabbed into the organ, digging deeper and cutting wider with every hard thud. My hand shakes as I try to rub the pain away, pressing so hard my skin is turning a nasty shade of red. I don't know how long I stand there, feet cemented to the floor, but I eventually move; grabbing my phone from the couch I call the one person I know can help me, the only person who's always been there for me.

Back in Euphoria

Hello?" I open Donatello's door to find every light off, blanketing the large living space in darkness. I let the heavy oak slab door slowly shut on its own, leaning down to take my shoes off. "Donatello, are you home?" I told him I was coming over, and he didn't mention being gone.

Shifting farther into the dark room, I use the waning light from the wall of floor to ceiling windows to guide my way through the space, trailing my fingers along the half wall separating the kitchen from the living room. Now that I'm further into the house, I can hear the low hum of music playing in one of the back rooms. Choosing to continue in the dark, I leave the lights off and continue towards the music; the closer I get, the clearer the sounds gets; it sounds like a sappy old tune, and I smile, knowing one of my own playlists is being used.

One of the doors is open in the hall, a low glow spilling into the hallway. Using the door frame to swing into the open doorway, I announce myself. "Hey! Why are all the lights off..." My voice trails off as I take in the decorated room, Donatello still nowhere to be seen. There are candles lit and placed on every available space in the room, the warm yellow flickering the only light in the room and apparently the entire house. Two bean bags have been thrown in the middle of the floor along with short trays holding my favorite Thai takeout, the music coming from a speaker resting on the bed.

I jump when two large arms wrap around my middle, letting out a relieved sigh when I feel Donatello's smile against my neck. "Ti ho sorpreso, Vita Mia?" *Did I surprise you, My Life?* It's murmured against my skin as he trails kisses from my ear to the top of my shoulder, mouth hot on the skin peeking out of the oversized shirt I'm wearing.

"Yes…" I spin to face him, looping my arms around his waist and smiling up at him. His term of endearment is something new he's started, and I don't hate it; my heart beats a jig in my chest every time it slips past his lips. "What are you planning?" For him to go through so much work, he must be up to something. Donatello isn't one to go out of his way for anything he doesn't deem worthwhile.

He laughs at my insinuation and leans in to kiss the tip of my nose. "This is our date. I can't bring you out, so we are having one here." He gestures towards the food with his chin before dropping his gaze back down to my face. "I even picked up those weird spicy noodles you love."

Choosing to ignore the part about not being able to bring me out, I press a kiss to his clothed chest and back out of his arms, looking towards the food. "Hmm, well come feed me while it's still hot." The low lighting is dancing along his face when I look back at him, his crooked grin causing my pulse to beat in my throat. As Olivia O'Brian's remake of

Complicated buzzes in the speakers, I can't help but feel a certain few sentences are directed right at me and my lost cause of a heart. If I'm not careful, I might just find myself falling for the man who won't even take me on a real date... If I haven't already.

"*...you're trying to be cool, you look like a fool to me...*"

Chapter Eleven

I don't remember the car ride here or even going downstairs to meet the driver, but as the car is parked outside of Remy's house, I do my best to wipe the tears from my cheeks. I jump out as soon as the doors unlock, practically running up the steps to throw the door open. I have tunnel vision as I go up the stairs and straight to Remy's office, where I know he'll be. I'm running on fumes, going straight to who I know can help me; keep my foundation from slipping further into the mud.

Remy looks up from his desk when I come bursting through the door, his honey browns, dark and unreadable from the distance. I didn't tell him what happened on the phone, just told him that I needed to see him. I didn't have to tell him, it probably wasn't hard to guess with my uncontrollable crying. I speak as he starts to stand, my voice rough from the amount of crying I've already done. "I don't need a lecture. I just need my brother; I need my Ollie."

Besides the frown and the ticking of his jaw, he says nothing. Both of us standing silent at opposite ends of the room, him running a tattooed hand over his face while I poorly hold myself together by the doorway. His gaze brushes over my puffy eyes and blotchy cheeks as he opens his arms in a silent command for me to come to him, and my lips tremble at his gesture, my broken heart thumping against my ribs with a sense of relief. A small dark part of me was scared he'd turn me away, too.

I walk right into him, crushing my face into his chest and squeeze his waist as tightly as I can, using him as my anchor. My tears start falling once more when he wraps his arms around me, pressing his cheek to the top of my head when they turn into broken sobs. He's in his house clothes, and I can feel the fabric of his shirt, wet from my tears, sticking to my face as I cling to him. He doesn't say anything, just lets me cry as he holds me.

I know I'm not just crying over Donatello anymore, even though that's what most of my pain is concentrated around. I'm crying for all the time I missed with my brother; for feeling his resentment, his disappointment, for being the reason he is unhappy. I'm crying because I'm angry at myself; for letting myself feel this way, for letting Donatello treat me the way he has. I'm crying with relief. Relief that Remy is still here for me, that he's still my rock despite how strained our relationship has been. After a while, my cries turn into dry hacks and shuddering hiccups. My body, unable to make the tears that still want to fall, the tears my heart says we still have to cry.

Remy softly pulls my face from him as I shake, using his palms to wipe my cheeks. After a moment of hesitation, he looks around the room before grabbing the bottom of his shirt and wiping the snot from my nose. "Shh, take a deep breath and try to calm down now." The frown he had earlier is gone, a kinder expression on his face as he pushes hair behind my ears and holds my head in place as I try to level my breathing.

"It hurts." It's all I can get out, the two words making my lips tremble once more. I take a deep breath to keep from starting up another wave of tears as he continues to push hair from my forehead.

He lets out a long, heavy breath that blows over my face, his lips pursing the slightest bit. "I know." He pulls me to him once more, my arms trapped between him and my own chest as he runs a hand down my back soothingly. "I know it does."

"I told him I loved him, Ollie. I told him I loved him, and he just left... said I needed to move on." I whisper through my fingers; my head turned sideways against Remy's chest.

Remy hums, a deep rumbling against my ear that does nothing to hide his anger. I'm not sure if it's for me confessing my love for Donatello or because of Donatello's actions.

I tilt my head back to look up at his face, a hard sniffle shaking me. "Are you still mad at me?"

After a pause, he gives me a slight shake of his head, pulling his gaze from my face. "Not right now."

I focus on the thumping of his heart against my ear when he says nothing more, letting the steady sound help calm my wired nerves. Besides the random hiccup or sniffle, my breaths have evened out, and I'm feeling less overwhelmed with everything. My heart still aches; this heavyweight threatens to collapse my lungs.

Remy pulls back from me but keeps his hands on my forearms like he can sense that I still need to be touched. "Are you ready?" His words are low, the deep gravel of his voice belaying how angry he is even as his face remains soft. He's asking if I'm going to talk now, tell him everything.

Tangling my fingers, I nod. Even mad, Remy is the only one who I'd even feel comfortable talking to about this right now or even want to. He gestures for me to sit on the couch and I do, sitting crossed legged as he crouches in front of me, so we're eye level. I'm not sure where to start or how to even begin, so I stay quiet, nervously looking between my hands and his face trying to find the words.

He stops my twisting hands with one of his own, drawing my eyes to his as he stays on the floor before me. "Just start talking, Delaney… I promise I won't get angry with you."

It spills out like word vomit, this spew of words that come tumbling out almost too quickly to make sense. I tell him how it started, when it started, all the what's the where's and the why's. I tell him how my heart broke the first time and how I let it break this time. I tell him how badly I felt keeping it from him, how much it hurt to hurt him. I don't let up until everything that can possibly be said is out, because I know if I stop, I won't have the courage to continue. Besides the occasional tightening of his shoulders and the brushing of his thumb over my knuckles, Remy does nothing but listen, his dark honey eyes watching my face the entire time.

There's a radio silence when I'm done, a sense of hollowness filling every space those words were taking. More than my heart feels broken. "I feel weak and unwanted." It's whispered from my lips as I bring my eyes to meet Remy's.

His frown is back in place, as he shakes his head, almost to himself. "You are not weak. You have shown nothing but strength today... watching someone you love leave requires strength. Reaching out for help when you're broken is strength. Speaking your truths and admitting your faults is strength. Don't mistake pain for weakness. Crying doesn't make you weak. Showing emotion doesn't make you weak. You're hurt, you're sad, you're confused... those things aren't weaknesses. It's what makes us human." He reaches and wipes a few stray tears from my cheeks as he continues. "I cried every day that Bev was gone. I sobbed when I thought I'd lost her... I cried even after she was home because just the thought of what would have happened if I hadn't found her when I did, shreds my heart. If you're weak for hurting over a broken heart, then so am I."

"I don't feel like I've been strong. I just feel broken." He sighs at my words, moving to sit next to me. I lean my head on his shoulder, and he takes one of my hands in his own.

"Strength doesn't always feel like strength. It can be little things, like getting out of bed when all you want to do is live in it. Or choosing to ignore a phone call from the one you're healing from. Forcing yourself to continue on with everyday life when you're crumbling on the inside, that takes strength. Being broken doesn't mean you can't be strong; sometimes, it helps prove just how strong you actually are."

He shifts, so I have to sit up and takes my cheeks in each palm. "As for feeling unwanted... that hurts my heart, Piccolina." He hugs me to him, wrapping his arms around the top of my shoulders and pressing his cheek against my own. "You are wanted. You are loved. Not just by me but also by Beverly and the girls. You have always and will always be wanted and loved. I will always."

He holds me in place until I nod, a splintered, "I love you, too." Squeezing past the lump in my throat.

I take a deep breath and wipe my eyes with the back of my hand when I sit back. "Now, I want you to listen to me and really hear me... okay, Delaney?"

He waits until I nod once more to continue. "What you had wasn't love." He stops me with a look when I open my mouth to argue. "You loved... your heartbreak is real, but what you had was not love. I don't care how good the best of times are, you never allow someone to treat you like that. If your self-worth is ever questioned, if you are ever left feeling unwanted, that isn't love. Love shouldn't make you sad. Love shouldn't make you hide. Love shouldn't hurt."

"There are exceptions to everything. Sometimes it does hurt, sometimes it is sad... but it shouldn't. If it hurts more than it doesn't, it's not love." He squeezes the hand he's holding, making sure I'm listening. "Know your worth and expect nothing less than that. You are Delaney Luciano, daughter of the late Giuseppe Luciano, Capo Famiglia of the Italian Mob for almost sixty years and sister to the current Capo Famiglia. You have repeatedly competed and placed at Olympic qualifiers for both Grand Prix and Dressage while maintaining an almost perfect GPA. even with all of the traveling required. Most everything you own or are paying for, you have done by yourself with your winnings alone. You could have chosen to stay home and become some ritzy mob wife like everyone else your age in this business, but you're going to college, out of state, and majoring in Astrophysics... which I honestly have no fucking idea what that is." He smirks when I giggle. "You are not a regular teenage girl. You are smart, funny, and kind. You deserve someone who will see everything you accomplished and are still accomplishing and be in awe because you are nothing short of amazing."

"I think you give me too much credit... I must not be that smart because I let Donatello break my heart twice."

He hums at the mention of Donatello, sitting back on the couch cushions. "He and I will certainly be having a chat soon." His eyes flick back to me, watching as I smooth invisible wrinkles from my tank. "I'm sorry, Piccolina. I'm sorry for belittling your feelings because I was angry. I'm sorry I made it impossible for you to come to me sooner. I realize now what my anger has done." His arms folded over his chest. "That being said, I don't approve of the relationship, even less now than before. I know I can't make you do anything, even if I wish I could, so I only ask that you take everything I've said today into consideration before letting Donatello back in. Remember how you feel right now, remember this pain, if you're going to let that Bastardo in your life again, make him earn the spot. Make him see your worth and respect it." He looks towards the door, sounds of the girls giggling from down the hall floating through the open doorway. "Donatello isn't a bad man, but he's a fucking coglione sometimes... I'd like nothing more than to break his fucking face right now." He cracks his knuckles, and I wince at the sound; more likely than not, Remy will be making good on the statement. "But his and my problems are not yours to worry about."

There's a soft knock on the door, and I look up to see Bev in the doorway, candy jar and wine in hand. "I thought we might need this."

I smile as she comes into the room, the thought of her trying to comfort me, warming my chest. She tries to sit in between Remy and me, but Remy snatches her mid sit, catching her on his lap. She huffs at him, rolling her eyes when she looks at me; I know she's not nearly as annoyed as she pretends to be though. She digs through the jar, pulling out all the pieces she knows are my favorite to drop into my lap.

Remy is frowning over her shoulder, watching her. "Why does she get all the good stuff?" She ignores him, yanking the cork from the wine before offering it to me. "She's nineteen, Cuore Mio."

Rolling her eyes again, she keeps it held out until I take it. "As if you weren't drinking at nineteen." She turns sideways in his lap so she can face me, looking down at his dimpled grin when he pinches at her sides.

"I would never."

"Whatever." She tosses a piece of candy at him, smiling when it bounces off his face.

Their playful banter is comforting to me, a welcome distraction from my aching heart. I take a large drink of the bottle, setting it on the floor by the couch when I'm done. Remy is talking into Bev's neck, mumbling little words I can't, and probably don't want to hear that is making her laugh. I sit like this for a while, eating my candy and listening to them. It feels good to be back in the loop of things, to not have the uncertainty and secrets looming over me.

Bev pulls me from my mental bubble, surprising me when she leans forward from Remy's lap, wrapping her arms around me. "I love you, Laney."

Letting go of the wrappers in my hands, I return her hug, tucking my face into her shoulder. "I love you, too."

She presses her forehead to mine before sitting back, a small smile on her lips. "You know what you need to do now, right? Besides order a case of wine and bulk candy from Costco."

"Party? Have rebound sex?" I toss out, taking a bite of candy as Remy grunts in disgust, and Bev laughs.

"No, boys are stupid." Remy pretends to be insulted, smirking at her when she turns to frown at him. "You get a puppy."

Remy scoffs, and I laugh, shaking my head at her. "Where am I going to put a puppy while I'm at school?"

"Here." She says casually. Her answer is almost immediate, which makes me laugh even more. She's obviously thought about this before now.

"Absolutely fucking not, Cuore Mio. I already said no to another dog."

"The girls need their own dogs! Everyone knows Dylan is my baby. They need that kind of connection."

Remy is shaking his head, looking at me to see if I hear the same nonsense as him. "They're ten months old. They most definitely don't need dogs of their own... No."

Bev huffs in his lap, crossing her arms like he's the one being ridiculous. Settling back against the cushions, I smile at her. "So, what kind of puppies are you getting?" I laugh at Remy's glare. We both know they're getting puppies at some point; Beverly gets whatever Beverly wants.

I spend the next hour listening to Beverly talk dogs, eating candy, laughing at Remy's antics, and feeling as close to peace as I've gotten in the last year. Now, watching Remy play peek-a-boo with the girls I know I made the right choice coming here; These people are the only love I need. I rub over my heart, that sharp ache still there but muted with all the love surrounding me. Bev meets my gaze across the room with a smile and I let my hand drop to my side, remembering my earlier promise; Donatello Genovese will live to regret his choice, and I'll do exactly what he asked of me... move on.

Back in Euphoria

My phone says it's forty minutes past nine and I sigh, looking out at the pier. Donatello is late, again. The sand I'm sitting on is still warm from the summer sun, the beach empty but for me. The pier in the distance is busy though, the sound of the crowds and smell of popcorn drifting my way on the breeze. This is the third time Donatello has been late without letting me know, never giving me a decent explanation.

I stare at my phone, watching the minutes tick by and listening to the waves crash along the shore. Their gentle lapping not helping me feel any more at ease with the situation. When it's fifteen minutes past ten, I finally dial his number.

It rings three times then goes to voicemail, making me frown. He intentionally hung up on me.

I call again, this time it goes straight to voicemail. Frowning, I pinch my lip between my fingers, contemplating what to do. He's obviously ignoring me. Taking a deep breath, I call Luca.

"Pronto."

"Hey, it's Delaney."

"I know, I have caller ID."

I roll my eyes at his response and scrub a hand over my brow. "Whatever, is Donatello there?" I know Luca is playing poker tonight, most of the guys do on Thursday.

"Yea… Why? You want me to get him?"

I can hear him starting to move so I hurry and speak. "No! No, it's fine."

"Oh, okay." He sounds confused but thankfully doesn't question it. "Are you coming down here or something?"

"I'm not. Don't worry about it, that's all I needed to know. Thanks.

"Uh sure. Bye."

"Wait! Luca?" The other end is quiet so I'm not sure if he hung up or not. "Luca?"

"What?"

I let out the breath I was holding, relieved he didn't hang up yet. "Don't tell Donatello I called, okay?"

"Um. Okay?"

"Thanks. Bye." I hang up and tap the phone on my raised knee. Donatello stood me up. He knows I'm here, waiting for him and he's playing poker instead.

There's a small piece of driftwood at my side and I grab it, angrily chucking it across the sand. Fucking Bastardo.

Chapter Twelve

S outh Donahue hall, that's where I'll be staying this year. I had to come to campus a week early to get Grizzle set up at the barns, but all I did was drop my stuff off, putting off setting anything up until now; everything but my laptop under my arm is here and ready to be unpacked. A decision I'm regretting now that two hundred other students are running in and out of the building doing just that. Smiling at a girl who bumps me and raises a hand in apology, I take a deep breath and head into the mess of people.

The hall is only five floors with the rooms set up as suites; I was lucky enough to get a two-bedroom with a private bathroom and kitchenette instead of one of the four-bedroom ones. I could have tried for a single bedroom and not had to deal with a roommate, but I don't want to be alone. I have no idea who my roommate is yet, I'm sure I got an email or something telling me, but I never looked. I figured I'd just meet them when I got here.

Pulling my key from the pocket of my jean shorts once I get to the fourth floor, I work my way through the crowded hall to find my door. It takes me a minute to finesse the key into working, but I finally get it, letting the door swing open on its own. From the silence within I'm guessing my roomie is either out or hasn't gotten in yet. Shutting the door behind me, I scan the area. The kitchenette is on my left, and the rectangular living area acts as a divider between the rooms on each side. I had already picked the room on the left side, so I head there. The room already had a queen bed, desk, dresser, and closet shelving, so I didn't have to bring much, mostly just my bedding, clothes, and toiletries. Each room has its own bathroom, too, something I'm sure I'll be grateful for later on.

Putting my laptop on the desk, I pull a box across the bed to look inside; taking out the clothes on top, I find a note from Remy underneath.

Beverly tried to hide wine in here, but I found it...Be safe piccolina.

I laugh at his note, smoothing the edges as I read it a few times. Folding the note in half, I place it on the dresser next to the bed and keep unpacking boxes. In the bottom of the second to last box, wrapped in towels and covered with a fuzzy blanket that smells like Bev, I find two bottles of some fancy label Moscato and Pinot Grigio with another note.

Don't tell Remy, he's no fun. Love you

Smiling, I fold her note with Remy's and set the bottles on the top shelf of my closet; I imagine having those is breaking some kind of rule. After making my bed with the new bedding I bought last week and fluffing my pillows, I fold Bev's blanket over the top, her familiar scent easing some of the anxiety of moving into a new place. I break all but one of the boxes down and slide them under my bed next, tossing all my shoes into the box I saved and pushing it into the closet. Putting my clothes away seems like a nightmare I'm not willing to live, so I drop it all into the two laundry baskets I brought, hiding those in the closet also. I bring the towels and my bath bag into the bathroom last, setting up everything how I want it before flopping onto the bed.

My room still looks bare and empty, the only difference being the new bedding since all of my stuff is hidden in the closet. I don't know that I really care though, I'll spend most of my free time at the barns any way. I stay like that, lying on the bed staring at the ceiling for a long time, absently rubbing that ache that just won't go away. It's not until I hear the front door opening that I bother to roll over and peak through the crack in my open door across the room; it sounds like several people coming in, but I stay in my spot, lazily hoping they'll walk by and I can see who it is.

"Oh, dolce piccolo Gesù." *Oh, sweet baby Jesus.* I don't mean to say it out loud, but the face that stops to smirk at me through my door is nothing short of dangerous for my libido, much to the chagrin of my sad heart. Baby blues trace over my form as I stay lying on the bed, and I send a silent prayer that this is not my roommate. I do not need this kind of trouble living next door.

"Jessie! What the fuck are you doing? Bring that shit in here so we can go eat. I'm starving."

The voice pulls his attention away, and I quickly sit up while I'm no longer under his scrutiny. That's when I notice the box he's carrying, along with a pair of loose grey joggers (aka every woman's kryptonite), an AU tank, and a backward baseball cap. Jessie, I'm guessing, sends me a wink before disappearing out of sight, and I let out a heavy breath, rubbing my face. I need to figure out who else is out there and probably introduce myself properly.

Standing, I adjust my messy bun before opening my door all the way. The door across the hall is open, and I watch as the guy who spoke earlier drops a stack of boxes next to the desk; Jessie dumps his on the bed as I walk up to the door, lightly tapping the frame. Both guys turn to face me at once, making my palms sweat with the attention. "Hey, I'm Delaney. I've got the other room here." I smile to try and break the awkwardness. "Are one of you, my roommate?"

"No, but I might have to see if Sarah will switch me." Says the speaker from before; he's tall and blonde with a slight twang to his words, making me think he might be from around the area. He has this whole Leo from Titanic vibes going on with his long fade cut and cigarette tucked behind his ear, and Lord knows I'm a sucker for Titanic.

He steps forward, hand extended to shake my hand. "I'm Derek. That's Jessie." He gestures towards Jessie leaning against the bed, and I smile his way, pretending not to notice the way he bites his lip when our eyes meet. "My sister, Sarah, is going to be sharing the suite with you. We're just bringing some of her stuff up since she gets off work late today." Derek continues, bringing my attention back on him, and I politely shake his hand, feeling the heavy stares of the other man in the room when I do. "She'll be in later tonight, and I'm sure she'll come say hi." He finishes as he steps back, putting his hands in his pockets.

"Well, I look forward to meeting her." I run a hand up my arm, feeling awkward, just standing in the doorway. "I guess I'll let you guys finish here… it was nice to meet you."

"Yea, I'm sure we'll be seeing you." Derek says, and I smile politely, backing out of the door to retreat back to my room.

It's only a few minutes when I hear them start to shuffle out of the other room, and I'm sitting on my bed looking at my phone when Jessie lightly pushes my door the rest of the way open, bracing his arms on the door frame. "What were you speaking earlier? When you were perving through the door at me."

Clicking my phone shut, I bring my legs up to sit cross legged, arching a brow. "I was the one perving? You were the one looking into my room."

He smirks at my response, dropping his arms. "Agree to disagree. What were you speaking?"

Propping my chin on my fist, I purse my lips. Jessie is going to be trouble. "Italian."

"Hmm, I liked it… You speak it, fluently?" He's moved farther into the room. Arms crossed over his chest.

"I'm Italian." I say in answer, watching as he nods, bringing his arms up to adjust the hat on his head.

He lifts the hat up, brushing his hair back before setting the cap back in place; his hair is dyed a light silver on top, faded into his dark roots. The color is not something I'm normally attracted to in men, but his might change my mind on the matter. "Say something else."

I laugh at him, not sure if he's being serious. "What?"

He walks the rest of the way to the bed to stand in front of me, hands in his pockets. "Say something else." He smirks in challenge like he thinks I can't or won't do it.

Sitting up straight, I arch a brow at him and lift my chin. "I tuoi capelli dovrebbero sembrare stupidi, ma sono stranamente attratto da esso." *Your hair should look stupid, but I am strangely attracted to it.* I deliberately run my gaze over him as I say it, flashing some dimple when I'm done. If he wants to play games, I'll play.

"Sembrare stupidi? You're not talking trash, are you Laney girl?" He's full on smiling now, his pronunciation of the Italian words almost perfect, which makes my eyes narrow.

"Wouldn't you like to know?" Picking my phone back up, I click it on, dismissing him and his nickname. This ladies and gentlemen is a fuck boy in his natural state of fuckery, and I am not in a place to fall into that trap. Flicking my eyes up to him and his silence, my eyes catch on a sliver of skin that peeks out as he digs his phone from his pocket, lightly pulling the top of his joggers down in the process. Maybe rebound sex could be on the table, though.

If he sees me looking, he doesn't say anything, just holds his phone out to me until I take it. "What am I supposed to do with this?" I ask, eyeing the German Shepherd he has on his lock screen; Beverly would love this. "Is this your dog?"

He nods, tongue coming out to lick his bottom lip. "That's Duke... and put your number in there. It's unlocked."

"You're very forward." I say, more to myself than him, but it makes him laugh anyway. I text myself, noting that there aren't nearly as many messages or notifications showing as I would have originally guessed. I hand his phone back to him, tilting my head towards my phone on the bed when it pings with a text alert. "There. I texted myself. Now you have my number."

"Cool." He smiles at me, and I can't help but return it. He reaches forward and brushes his thumb over my dimple almost absentmindedly, and I internally cringe; the simple touch all too familiar. Thankfully he pulls back almost immediately, not noticing my discomfort. "It was nice meeting you, Laney girl."

"Bye Jessie," I say, picking up my phone once more. I don't watch him leave the room.

My heart suddenly hurts, the never-ending ache more of a throb. I don't notice I'm crying until a wet drop splatters on my phone screen. A dark reminder from my heart that we're still taken, even if I don't want to be.

I'm towel drying my hair when I hear the door opening to the suite, followed by a loud "Hello?"

Finishing my hair, I set the towel down. "Uh... Hello?" I say in response, hanging my towel in the bathroom. My door is still open, and I almost run into the little blonde coming around the corner as I'm about to step into the living space.

"Oh! Hi." She says, her voice carrying the same twang as Derek's. I'm going to assume this is Sarah. Going off of looks alone, she seems like someone who is genuinely nice, like they spend their free afternoons cleaning trash off the roads and making food for the homeless kind of nice. She has long, bright blonde hair, that pretty buttery blonde only true blondes have, dark green eyes and a cute button nose; I shit you not on the nose. She's maybe five foot and standing next to her I look like a goliath, towering over her at five foot seven. She also seems like she's older than me, mid-twenties maybe.

"I'm Sarah. You must be Delaney." She holds her hand out, just like her brother had, and I smile, shaking it. I must look somewhat confused because she shrugs and drops my hand. "Derek told me he met you earlier."

"Oh, right… him and Jessie."

Taking her purse off, she gestures for me to follow her and walks to her room. "I hope they weren't too much…" She smiles at me, standing near the door. "They tend to turn stupid around pretty girls."

I laugh at her comment, crossing my arms. "Oh no, they were fine."

"Good." She smiles again, and I find myself smiling back; she's easy to be around, and it's nice. I was kind of worried I'd hate my roommate. "Have you eaten yet? I was planning on walking over to Panera. They're open twenty-four hours over there."

"I did, but that sounds good, I'll come with…" I look down at my sleep clothes and back. "Just let me change really fast."

She waves her hand at me, digging through one of the boxes on her bed. "No worries, hun, don't rush."

Smiling, I head back to my room and change my sleep shorts out for the denim I wore earlier, leaving my loose sleep tank on. Grabbing my phone and card, I slip them into my back pocket and look over myself in the mirror. It's around ten PM, and I doubt it matters much what I look like. Running my fingers from one hand through my damp waves to remove some of the tangles, I use the other to grab my sneakers, putting them on at Sarah's door. "Okay, I'm good."

"I reckon those curls of yours are hell in this humidity." She says, gesturing towards my hair as she ties her own in a ponytail.

"You'd reckon right." I say, moving so she can step out of the door. "They're usually waves, but the humidity turns them into this."

"I'd shave my head bald." She says, making me laugh as I follow her out the door. "Then again, my hair isn't nearly as nice as yours even with the humidity."

"Well thank you, it doesn't always feel nice, though." Holding the door open for her, we head outside. "Derek said you had to work late and that's why they dropped your stuff off, where do you work? If you don't mind me asking."

"Oh, you're fine." Her ponytail swings as she flashes me another big smile. "I work over at the nursing home. I do the later shifts so I can have a more open schedule for classes."

Why am I not surprised? "That's cool. Are you doing pre-med?"

"I am. I'm in my last year though...then off to medical school for another four years." Another little smile. "I'm hoping to be an OBGYN when I grow up." I laugh with her, and she continues. "I started school a few years later than most of the other students, so sometimes I feel old."

She scrunches her nose, and I smile and lightly bump her shoulder as we walk. "Well, you look great for being in your fifties."

This makes her laugh, and I smile. We're almost to the Wellness Kitchen, where Panera is. "What are you majoring in?"

"Astrophysics, it's my second year." I smile and shrug at the look she gives me. "I like the stars, and I'm more likely to get a good job in that field than I am in just astrology." She opens the door for me to go inside, and I continue. "I also have my horse here, and we're on the equestrian team."

"You have a horse! I love riding." We get behind another late-night student in line. "We have some horses on the ranch, but I can guarantee I don't do anything fancy like you."

I laugh. "You should come to the stables sometime. The team is fine, but it would be nice to ride with someone who isn't so routine focused."

"I'd love that." She smiles once more, a genuine kind of smile like she would actually love that.

I smile to myself as she orders. I like Sarah. I'm glad Bev pushed me into getting a dorm this year; it'll be nice having someone to come home to every day, and

Sarah seems easy to get along with. Just the kind of distraction I need right now. My phone vibrates in my pocket, and I pull it out. It takes me a second to realize the unknown number is Jessie's; guess I didn't save his number earlier.

You still up, Laney girl?

Hard pass. I tuck the phone away without a response and step to order. That can be an issue for another day.

Back in Euphoria

"**H**oney, I'm home!" I yell it in sing song as I come into Donatello's house, taking my shoes off and dropping my purse on the floor. I can hear talking but can't make out the voices, which makes me frown. There weren't any other cars parked out front, but I wouldn't have seen them if they'd been in the garage. I pause in the living room, unsure what to do; Donatello knew I was coming over.

Still unsure, I head towards his bedroom, figuring that's the safest place to wait for him since I don't know who else is here. I'm only alone for a few minutes before Donatello comes through the door. I smile at him, standing from where I was sitting on the bed. "Hey." He frowns at me, looking over his shoulder before he shuts the door; his behavior is making me uneasy, pulling down the corners of my lips.

"What are you doing here?" His harsh tone catches me off guard, and I take a step back, confused with his reaction.

"You told me to come by earlier?" I say it as a question. Him making me unsure.

"Right." He rubs his face roughly, letting out a loud sigh. "Now isn't a good time, Delaney."

"Okay?" I twist my hands in front of me. "I don't know what you want me to do."

He scowls at me like I'm an idiot. "Leave. I want you to leave." He shakes his head at me. "I thought that was clear when I said now wasn't a good time."

I swallow at his words, his unfair anger fueling mine. "You don't have to be cruel, Donatello. I'm not the one who made a scheduling mistake. You did."

I go to stomp past him, and he catches my arm. At first, I think he's going to apologize. "Wait. I need to make sure no one is out there that will see you."

Jerking my arm from his grasp I give him a scowl of my own. "That seems like your problem, not mine."

I yank the door open and get one foot out the door before I'm jerked back, the door shutting with my back as Donatello holds my upper arms. "Don't test me today. I'm not in the mood for games."

Clenching my jaw, I speak through my teeth at him. "Get your hands off of me, Donatello, or I'll scream, and everyone in the house will know you have someone up here."

He brings a hand up to grip my jaw, tilting my face like he's going to kiss me. "Wait in here for five minutes, then leave." He pinches his fingers ever so slightly. "This is for your benefit, not mine. Just do as you're told."

I slap his hand from my face, narrowing my eyes on him. "Vaffanculo." *Fuck off.*

His lips pinch, and he looks like he might grab me again, so I move around him and away from the door. I gesture for him to get along as he clenches his fists in annoyance. "Hurry the fuck up so I can get out of here, Donatello."

He pauses before heading out of the door. "I'll call you later."

I huff at his weak attempt to seem apologetic. "Whatever. Just go."

Chapter Thirteen

"Monkeys or ducks?" Bev asks through the phone, and I pause my writing to think about it.

"Ducks. Definitely do ducks."

"Okay cool because I already bought the duck costumes for them last week."

I laugh at her response, putting the phone on speaker and setting it on the bed so I can write easier. "Why did you ask then?"

"Validation that I made the right choice." I roll my eyes at my paper as she continues. "Remy won't dress up for the Halloween party, and I don't want to do it alone, so I want the girls to look cute for us."

"Ollie never dresses fun for anything." I confirm, propping my chin on my hand. "Why don't you just get all dolled-up Jessica Rabbit style and say he's Bond and you're a Bond girl? He'll already be wearing the suit and have the guns."

"That's actually a really good idea… I'd kiss you if you weren't a million miles away."

I laugh. "It's most definitely not a million miles."

Sarah pokes her head into the room, and I lightly cover the phone with my hand, so Bev doesn't think we're talking to her. "I'm going to the Wellness Kitchen, you want anything?"

I shake my head. "No, I'm good, thanks."

"Okay, I'll be right back." She smiles and disappears behind the door as I hear Beverly mumbling on the phone.

I quickly pick it up and take it off speaker before she can say something rude Sarah might hear. "Was that goody two shoes?" She asks, and I can practically see her rolling her eyes on the other end.

"Yes, that was Sarah… you might like her once you meet her in person. She's really nice."

She huffs. "Doubt it."

I laugh even though she's being a jealous brat. "You're not very nice, Beverly Marie."

"I don't care… and you know that's not my middle name."

I smile to myself, she's right, I do know that's not. But I like how she always responds to it anyway. "Okay, well, if you're done being jelly, I have to finish my schoolwork."

"Whatever, Smarty Pants. I'll send you pictures of the girls' costumes later… love you."

"Love you, too… Oh, send me pictures of you also if you get dressed up."

"Will do. Bye, Laney."

"Bye."

I hang up the phone and stare at the paperwork in front of me. Sarah and I have become friends since meeting. She's even participated in some of the video chats I've had with Bev. Beverly hates her, of course. She says that Sarah is far too chipper to be a real human. I can think of five people Bev likes off the top of my head, though, and she doesn't shy away from saying how she feels most of the time, so I wasn't surprised when she loudly voiced her opinions of Sarah. I love her cynical butt anyway.

Being in the dorms has been good for me. Last year I didn't have the same kind of friendships I've been able to develop in the short amount of time I've been here. Living alone off campus was lonely, and probably one of the main reasons I sought out parties and alcohol so often, using my heartache as another excuse to be wild. Here I haven't felt as alone, even on the rougher nights. Derek and Jessie are almost always at the suite or meeting Sarah and me for meals. I haven't had the time to wallow, and I'm grateful for it.

There's only so much that friendship can do, though, and I've fallen back on my old habit of using others to help comfort my ache. Last time it was random frat boys. This time I have Jessie. He's filling a space for intimacy and comfort that feeling unwanted created. On particularly bad days, where I can't seem to hide from my tears, and I feel lost, he's always here without question, never making me say more than I'm ready to say. He stays in the suite with me when Sarah works night shifts, so I don't have to be alone.

I'm using him to create a sense of false happiness, and I don't care how selfish it is. I need something to keep me from going down my angry path like before, to stop me from dropping into the abyss. It'd be easier if I was home and surrounded by my family, but I'm not. So, I have Jessie. Just over two months, that's how long it's been since Donatello left and broke my heart. Sometimes I tell myself I'm feeling better, that the ache has faded, that my days and nights don't rotate around the pain. And sometimes I can't will myself to pretend hard enough.

I'm still lying on my bed, belly down, doing homework when my door opens, and Jessie flops onto the bed, sending my pen bouncing onto the floor. Speak of the devil. "Who let you in?" I ask, leaning over the edge of the bed to grab my pen.

"Sarah... new shorts, Laney girl?"

He's eyeing my legs when I sit back up, and I roll my eyes at him. "I told her to stop letting the brush weed in."

He palms his chest in mock hurt, rolling onto his back to look at the ceiling. "This is the treatment I get for comforting a friend in troubling times?" He rolls his face in my direction, his silver hair flopping over his forehead, hiding one of his baby blues from me. "And, I think you mean tumbleweed."

"What are you talking about?" I start putting all of my papers in their binder and stacking my books up. I'm not going to get anything done while he's here.

"Tumbleweed blows around, not brush weed."

I frown at him, setting my stuff on my dresser. "What? No, not the weed thing. The troubling times..." I sit cross legged next to him. "What troubling times?"

"Oh." He shuffles and drops his head in my lap, smiling up at me. Cheeky Bastardo. "Homework… that shit sucks."

I laugh, and he chuckles with me, bringing his arms up to tuck his hands under my thighs. I let him, taking advantage of his touch to soothe my need for intimacy. "Don't you have some sorority girls to badger for a date to the party tonight?" I ask it as I push the silver strands from his face, finally losing to the battle of keeping my hands off of him. Sarah is going to a Halloween party tonight, but I'd planned on staying in to finish some schoolwork, so I'd have the weekend free.

He pretends to bite at my fingers as I pull away, and I narrow my eyes at his smirk. "No. I already have a date." I squeeze his face with my legs, and his smirk grows as he holds my legs up, not letting me put them back down. "I could get used to this."

"That's sleazy, Jessie." I flick his nose, and he laughs, letting my legs drop. "I'm not sure your date would like you being in my lap right now."

"I think she's fine with it." He says, pulling his hands out from under me and purposefully dragging his fingers along my skin.

"How would you know?" I stretch my arms and legs out, cracking my back with the motion. I've spent the better of an hour in here doing work already.

He sits up and shakes his hair with his hand, his bicep flexing earning most of my attention. He's wearing a tee today and another pair of joggers; it seems like that's all he wears, not that I'm really complaining. He spins on the bed to face me, smiling as he grabs my legs and pulls me flush with him. I don't fight it, letting him run his palms up the outside of my thighs. "Were you fine with it?"

I scoff past my smile, pushing back from his chest to put some space between our faces. "Is that your attempt at asking me to be your date? How very corny of you."

"Is that a yes? Because I know you watch all of those nineties rom coms and love the corny shit."

I laugh, he's got me there. "That's true. But we have a problem with your plan."

His hands slide even further up my legs to cup the sides of my butt. "What's that?"

"I wasn't planning on going to the party and don't have a costume." He pulls me farther up his legs, forcing me to bend mine behind his back.

"That's not a problem." His breath brushes along my lips when he speaks, and I feel mine catching in my lungs.

"How is going to a Halloween party without a costume, not a problem?" I have to lean back to speak or risk brushing his lips with mine. He's taking advantage of me being lenient with his touching today, but it feels good to be touched like this, so I don't mind it.

"Just wear some lingerie and draw some whiskers on your face… that's what all the other girls do anyway." His palms are on my back now, the fabric of my sweater bunching under his hands. My own hands have found their way to his chest, one hand pinching the cotton of his tee while the other runs up and over his shoulder.

I chuckle at his ridiculous solution. "That's a stupid costume."

His crystalline eyes drop to my lips as he smirks, using his arms to push my back straighter and bring my face closer to his. "I definitely don't think you'd look stupid." He says it lowly, pupils dilated when his gaze comes back to mine.

"What are you going as?" I don't even know why we are still having this conversation; it definitely doesn't match the same intensity of our body language.

"Phil Collins." I must frown because he closes his eyes and shakes his head, smiling when his eyes meet mine again, a slight pink tinting his cheeks. "I didn't mean to say that. You're distracting me… A zombie."

I laugh, making his smile grow. "Sembri adorabile quando arrossisci." *You look adorable when you blush.*

He leans his head back with a groan, his hands dropping to squeeze my ass. He's biting his lip when he brings his face back to mine. "I love when you talk like that."

I laugh again, both of my arms going to loop behind his neck. "You don't even know what I'm saying. I could be calling you a toad for all you know."

"It drives me crazy." He ignores my toad comment and leans forward, his lips just skimming mine when he speaks. "Say something else."

I let out a slow breath, my skin prickling with the need to feel raw and wanted; my heart is thumping loudly against my ribs, that sad ache pushed to the background. Voglio che mi baci." *I want you to kiss me.* I say it honestly even though I know Jessie won't understand.

His lips just brush the corner of my lips in a light kiss as he trails them over my cheek and jaw. "Say more... keep talking." It's a soft command, not a request, as his nose skims the skin behind my ear.

"Mi piace quando mi dici cosa fare, voglio fari piacere." *I like when you tell me what to do, I want to please you.* He groans against my neck, and I press into him, pretend he can understand me, pretend he's playing the same game that I want to. Donatello and I always used to play this game; this one, I was actually fond of. "Voglio essere cattivo per te." *I want to be bad for you.* I whisper it into his ear, shifting in his lap as his joggers do nothing to hide how excited he is. The knowledge that nothing but my secret words have that effect on him is... empowering.

In response, his tongue swipes along my pulse point in a hot wet kiss followed by another low groan, like the taste of my skin alone drives him wild. The sound pebbles my nipples against my bra. I bend my knees at his waist, squeezing him tight as I tilt to give him better access to my neck.

"Non voglio andara alla festa, voglio invece che tu mi scopa." *I don't want to go to the party, I want you to fuck me instead.* My admissions are getting bolder, knowing he can't understand what I'm actually saying. "Voglio usarti per riparare il dolore nel mio cuore. *I want to use you to fix the pain in my heart.*

His hands have made their way under my sweater, the warmth of his palms sliding over my skin and pressing me against his chest. His lips haven't left my neck, pressing soft, barely there kisses in between the pass of his tongue.

Grabbing his head with my hands in his hair, I bring his face to mine, whispering my last confession against his lips. "Voglio usarti per dimenticare completamente." *I want to use you to forget completely.*

One of his hands leaves my back to cradle the back of my head, his nose brushing against mine. "Don't worry, Laney girl... Vi posso aiutare." *I can help you.*

I'm almost sinking into him; my lips almost sealed to his when his words register, confusion making me pull back from him. "Wait. What?"

He smirks at my confusion, using the hand on the back of my head to keep me close. "My mom is from Sicily and only speaks in her native language."

"You understood me this entire time?" I ask, needing to clarify. I can feel my cheeks heating, my secret confessions apparently not so secret.

"I did. I understand more than I can speak, though." He tilts back slightly, baby blues scanning my face. "I ruined the mood, didn't I?" It's said like he already thinks it's done, and I can't help but smile at him.

"No, I just... why didn't you tell me? It's literally been weeks."

"I liked how freely you talked when you thought no one could actually understand you. I liked knowing your thoughts when no one besides me could. Made me feel special, and I like feeling like that with you." I can feel my cheeks warming once more with his admission, feel my pulse fluttering in my throat. "I think I like you, Laney girl."

I'm not even sure how to respond, my lips parting as I let out a deep breath that was hiding in my chest. Of course, I'd find the one Italian at this school to mess around with. His fingers are lazily tracing patterns along my skin, the hand on my head now tickling up my side with the other. After a moment's hesitation, I finally speak. "I think you're pretty okay, too."

He smiles at my admission, fingers sinking just a little deeper into my skin. "Can I kiss you now?"

My only response is a shallow nod, my chest rising and falling with quick breaths. Now that I'm not lost in the moment, it's harder to push that ache back, but I'm determined to lose it. His tongue comes out to run across his lower lip as he moves his face closer, eyes staying locked with mine until our noses brush. The first press of his lips is just a butterfly kiss, brief and petal soft. His next few are just slightly deeper, barely there kisses, teasing me with the hint of taste. He kisses the corners of my lips next, and it's not until then that I realize he's waiting for me to set the pace, letting me decide what happens next. His sweetness tightens my throat with emotion, his concern for someone he barely knows, touching my sad heart in ways it hasn't felt in a while.

Palming his cheeks, I pull his lips to mine more fully, giving us both what we want. I can feel him smiling against my lips, and it hits me right in the chest. I've always been the one being devoured, the one being dominated, but he's letting me take the lead this time, and I like it.

Adjusting so I'm straddling his waist instead of wrapped around it; I sit back. I watch his face as I grip the bottom of my sweater, watch as his pupils dilate further with every inch of skin exposed, watch him watching me. Tossing my sweater onto the floor, I feel high off his lust, the quick rise and fall of his chest spurring me to unclasp the hook of my bra, to toss it onto the floor with my top. Even with his hands already on me, he looks to me for permission to touch me, his hands sliding slowly up my sides to scrape against the outside of my breasts, his thumbs scraping over my nipples. My head drops back with his touch, and he leans forward, trailing wet kisses down the column of my throat and over my collarbone as his hands explore my sensitive flesh.

The need to feel his skin on mine has me tugging at the bottom of his shirt, my hands greedily running over the hard ridges of his toned stomach as the muscles flex with his movements. He turns and throws his shirt at the door hard enough to push it the rest of the way shut, and I suppress a smile at not even realizing it was still open; hopefully, Sarah didn't get an eyeful. He's hard and lean, not quite as big or wide as Donatello, but filled out in all the right places. I should feel guilty about comparing them, but I can't help it.

He's been patiently waiting for me to finish my perusal of him, letting me run my hands and lips over him at my leisure, but I can see his patience waning, the blue of his eyes a shade darker, his touch sinking deeper into my skin. When my face meets his once more, he doesn't wait for me this time, he grabs my face and kisses me without the previous tenderness. Jessie's kisses are bittersweet, lighting up my insides while burning away at my heart. I can't help but miss the taste of cinnamon on my tongue when his passes over mine or wish the peppery scent coming off his skin was sweeter, closer to that of spice cake.

Throwing an arm behind his neck, I pull us backward, so he lands on top of me, his body crushing me in the best kind of way against the mattress. He groans against my skin when I arch into his touch, wiggling my hips against the hardness in his joggers. Sitting up on my elbows, I watch as he moves down my body, only breaking eye contact to unbutton my denim shorts. I lift my hips to help him get them off, pulling my underwear with them. I watch with hooded eyes as he drops his own bottoms, squeeze my thighs together as he kneels before me, pumping his hand over his own erection while crystal eyes eat up my form.

I lean back against the bedspread with closed eyes as he crawls over me, running his hands along my skin as he works his way up my body. His teeth graze my chin, then catch on my bottom lip as he settles over me. I hook my leg over his waist, pulling his hips closer and working my hips so that his shaft rubs along the length of my core. He groans at the contact, and I eat it up, needing his unfamiliar touch to burn away the memory of a familiar one. Pulling from his lips, I gesture towards the dresser, and he reaches over me, opening the top drawer to pull out the box of condoms I have there. They're unopened because I haven't used these yet, and it takes him a minute to get the plastic wrapping off. I smile at his awkwardness, leaning up to kiss the line of his chest as he pulls a condom from the box.

His lips are on mine as he tears it open, blindly rolling it on his bobbing erection. His eyes meet mine just before he pushes into me, kneeling before me, a hand on each thigh, spreading me for him. He bites his lip as he slides into me, a crease in his brow as he hums his pleasure. My body instinctively arches up to meet him, and I moan at his entrance, my fingers digging into his forearms as he grips my hips, setting our pace.

Unexpectedly, he shifts us, pulling me up into a sitting position to hug me to him. His arms wrap around my back as I take over, my hips straddling his kneeling form. His lips lock on mine, my arms cradling his head as they wrap around his shoulders, holding him to me in an almost too intimate gesture for two people who are basically strangers, but I need it.

Trying to be courteous of Sarah in the suite, I try to keep my sounds quiet, using Jessie's lips and neck to mute them. I can feel my release just out of reach. The sound of his heavy breathing in my ear, the feel of his lips grazing along my neck and cheeks, the soft press of his lips on my own, all working to help deliver that delicious warmth pooling in my gut. Crystal eyes lock me in their gaze as he holds me impossibly closer and his lips brush along mine before locking them in place with his. I orgasm with the sweet kiss, the extreme high banging into me with such force I cry against his mouth and hug his neck tighter. His answering groan tells me he's found his own release, and I sink into him, laying my head on his shoulder.

Brushing the hair from my face and over my shoulder, he uses his palm to wipe the tears I didn't realize I was crying away. I sit up, suddenly embarrassed, and try to shift off of him, but he keeps me in place with the arm around my back, drawing my gaze to his. "Stay with me, Laney girl, I like to cuddle." He says, brushing the rest of my tears away, using his joke to help me feel less vulnerable.

I can't help but smile at his sweetness, and I oblige, resting my face back into the crook of his neck. "Thank you." I whisper it into his skin, and he pulls my face towards his again, pressing a kiss against my lips.

"Let me help you forget."

Back in Euphoria

I wish I had stayed home instead of coming to this bogus terrace party. Donatello told me not to come, that I wouldn't want to be here; I should have listened. He and his date are currently sitting across the table from me, and I'm seconds from flipping the whole damn table. Remy looks about as pleased as I am to be here, leaning back in his seat, scowling at everyone who dares to come within an eight-foot radius. I don't blame him, though; it has to get annoying having everyone ask where Beverly is. He's only here to be respectful. His presence is the only thing required for that, not idle chit chat.

Donatello's date, Raelene I think it is, giggles into her glass, reaching over to touch Donatello's arm, and I have to grip the table to keep myself from throwing my plate at her head. From what I've seen, he's barely acknowledged her outside of being polite, but that doesn't make me any less annoyed. "I'm going to find the bathroom." I say to Remy, tossing my napkin onto the table as I stand.

He slides his gaze over to me, mumbling into his drink just loud enough for me to hear. "Bring back a bottle for me."

I give him a little fake salute, and he rolls his eyes as I walk away. Raelene is cackling again, but I don't look their way, it'll just irritate me more. I swipe a mimosa off of a tray passing by, downing the whole thing to set on an empty table. I walk past the server tables and behind the bar station, winking at a server who pauses to watch me. I bend and grab a bottle of whiskey off the shelf as he stares, unsure if he should say something or not. Taking the top off, I take a big swig, grimacing with the burn as I turn to hold it out to him. He shakes his head, and I shrug, walking out of the space and right back to my table. I drop it in front of Remy, who raises a brow but says nothing, grabbing it to fill his empty glass past the appropriate line.

My eyes find their way across the table, and I notice Donatello is gone, his date typing away on her phone. I turn to leave, but Remy stops me. "Where are you going now?"

"I never went to the bathroom." I say it over my shoulder, starting back into the crowd at his answering hum. I'm really looking for Donatello, obviously. I'm annoyed that he has a date and didn't tell me; all he said is I wouldn't want to be here. He could have said why.

I'm about to give up when I spot him in one of the walkways that branch off the main terrace. He's looking down at his phone until he sees me coming, sliding it in his pocket as I get to him. "You have a date?"

He looks around us, probably to make sure no one can hear before he bothers to respond to me. "Not willingly. I'm doing it as a favor to Andrea."

I cross my arms over my chest. "How?"

"He was supposed to come with her and couldn't. He didn't want her to come alone."

I snort. "And she was just fine coming with a completely different person."

He shrugs, taking a slight step away from me when he notices how close we're standing. "I guess."

I take a deep breath, turning my face to look at the people mingling. "Are you lying?"

"Why would I lie, Delaney?" He pulls his phone out, silencing the ring on it without looking to see who is calling. "Why do you even care? I couldn't have brought you as my date."

"Do you seriously not see how you being with her might upset me?" I frown when his phone pings again, and I grab it before he can stop me. There isn't a name on the number, but several texts are asking where he is and when he's coming back to the table. It's not hard to guess who that might be. "Really?" I chuck his phone down the walkway, feeling somewhat vindicated when it bounces and shatters on the marble tile.

"Fuck! Delaney!" He must be pretty angry for him to be yelling my name loud enough for someone to hear. He grabs my arm and stops me from going back to the party. "Listen to me." I yank my arm from his hold but stay, waiting for him to speak. "She has my number because Andrea gave it to her. I can't help if she's texting me. If you hadn't broken my phone, you would have seen I haven't responded to any of them."

"The problem isn't her texting you. It's you seeing nothing wrong with it and thinking it was okay to even bring her, to begin with Donatello."

"We aren't even dating. You shouldn't care." I don't respond, just drop my face to hide the hurt his words have caused. "Come on, Delaney, you know that's not what I meant."

I sidestep his hand, spinning on my heel and disappearing into the crowd before Donatello can say anything else. I know that's exactly what he meant, and it hurts because he's right.

Chapter Fourteen

The campus is almost vacant, most students have left for Thanksgiving break already. I chose not to go home, much to the annoyance of Beverly. She's only mad because now she will be left alone to deal with both her nightmare parents and my mother. I'm not envious of her but looking forward to the dramatic retelling she'll have for me later. Needless to say, it's a holiday none of us really enjoy anyway, so I didn't see the need to travel back for it.

Jessie is staying with me even though I told him it wasn't necessary. He reassured me that the holiday wasn't all that big of a deal in his house so he wouldn't be missed. I can't help but feel bad for keeping him from seeing his family, though. From what he's told me, they seem nice. Derek and Sarah went home yesterday, but they only had to drive a few hours to get home. It's sometimes hard for me to wrap my head around the fact that not everyone lives under the Famiglia and that there are people out there that just live normal, happy mundane lives. Must be nice.

I don't know what Jessie and I are. We haven't necessarily said we're officially dating, but we're happy and, most importantly, not a secret. He's sweet, kind and doesn't care that I have emotional baggage. He doesn't know all the details of Donatello or my family for that matter, but he knows enough to have an idea of why I'm so broken; why I crave a sense of validation. To say I'm completely over Donatello would be a blatant lie, to say that I'm even marginally over Donatello would also be a lie.

I spent the morning at the stables, utilizing the empty arena while everyone is gone. I like competing but riding for pleasure is so much more enjoyable. Being able to stretch out in the arena without an audience is calming. The smell of horse and hay clings to my hoodie as I pull it on, deciding to walk back to the Hall from the shuttle instead of having Jessie pick me up. It's hardly cold considering it's Fall, but there's a slight bite to the breeze making it feel chillier than usual.

There's something peaceful about walking the empty campus. I take the long way back, choosing to go through the garden before heading back to the Hall. Jessie said he was going to be at the library and would meet me at the suite, so I don't feel the need to rush, knowing he will still be there for a while. It only takes me a few minutes longer than normal to get back to the Hall, even with my detour; the chilly air apparently making me walk quicker than I had planned.

"Delaney." My spine goes rigid at the smoky caress of my name, all the hairs on my body standing on end as my head screams at me to run. What. The. Fuck.

I slowly spin, willing my ears to be wrong, that the person who owns that voice is not the one behind me.

I know that's just wishful thinking though, every cell in my body knows who this is.

My eyes land on him immediately, drawn to him like a beacon. Thump thump. Thump thump. Thump thump. That's all I can hear. All I can feel. The pounding in my chest trying to reach the very one who broke it in two. "No." That's the only word I can get out, my throat suddenly too tight to breathe.

"I just want to talk." His honey voice drenches me in its sticky residue, rooting me to the spot.

"We already had the talk, Donatello. Or did you forget already?" I might be stuck under his current trance, but I'm not stuck in his web like before.

"I don't want to do this outside..." Russet reds flash around the parking lot, scanning the grounds. It's empty, so if his argument is that he doesn't want people to hear, then it's null. "Just give me a few minutes to explain myself."

"No." I lift my chin, standing my ground and crossing my arms over my chest. My interior isn't nearly as strong as I'm pretending to be on the outside. I feel like I'm about to be sick, nauseous with the fireflies that have been vacant until he showed up.

He sighs, the scent of his cinnamon breath washing over me with enough force to make my knees threaten to buckle. As if that weren't enough, he steps closer to me as I press against the railing, standing so close I can feel the brick biting into the thin fabric of my riding pants. "Just give me a chance to make things right, Baby."

I close my eyes, trying to pretend I can't smell the spice coming off of his skin or that I'm not on the brink of giving in. "Leave me alone, Donatello."

I feel his knuckles brush my cheek and tighten my hands into fists, refusing to open my eyes. "I should have never left you."

His whisper is reminiscent of a gut punch, leaving me ill and out of breath. "How dare you." It's a pained whisper as I force my eyes to look into his. "How dare you do this to me."

Before he can respond, another voice yanks our attention from each other. Pulling me from the quicksand I'm about to be swallowed in.

"You good, Laney girl?" Jessie. My eyes snap over to find him walking up the path, hands in his joggers as he takes in the scene before him. I know he's smart enough to know who this is or at least guess.

I use the distraction to move out of Donatello's reach, shifting to stand closer to Jessie. Donatello notices immediately, his dark eyes narrowing on who he now sees as a threat. "Yea, I'm fine…" I smile at him as he eyes me warily trying to read me and understand the situation. "Donatello was just leaving."

Jessie pulls his hand from his pocket, doing the exact opposite of what I was hoping he'd do. He doesn't realize the kind of monster he's poking. "This your dad Laney girl?" He asks as his eyes are still one me, deliberately mocking Donatello's age. He knows that Donatello isn't anywhere near old enough to be my Padre; neither does he look it.

"Don't." I whisper to him, widening my eyes in silent warning to quit. But like every man with a working dick, he feels the need to pull out the ruler.

"Nice to meet you. I'm Jessie." He holds his hand out to Donatello, and I watch in silent horror as Donatello takes his hand, squeezing hard enough that Jessie's jaw ticks with pain.

"Donatello Genovese." Donatello's dark gaze meets mine just before he lets go, and I know it's taking all of his self-control not to act on the disrespect in front of him. The dark tone of his voice warning alone.

I grab Jessie's arm when he steps back, turning to use my own body as a physical divider between the two. Jessie doesn't see the potential target he's just painted on his back, but I do. "Can you go inside? I'll follow you up."

I can feel Donatello burning at my back, so I drop my hands, removing them from Jessie. He smiles down at me, eyes flicking to Donatello. "Sure." He leans and kisses my forehead, crystal eyes never leaving Donatello's over my head.

I watch him walk past Donatello, wait until he's inside the Hall doors before I bring my eyes back to the steaming man in front of me.

"Laney girl." It's all Donatello says, face twisted with disgust.

I scrub my hands over my face, the distraction of Jessie and my false bravery starting to slip away now that I'm back to being face to face with Donatello alone. "It's none of your concern Donatello… go home. We have nothing to talk about." I move past him, staying just out of reach and avoiding eye contact.

"Don't do this, Delaney." His words stop me in my tracks, cracking the stale air around us like the snap of a whip. Those words are rich coming from him.

"Don't do what Donatello? Don't leave? Don't move on? Don't do the one thing you demanded I do?" Turning, I force my gaze to his, ignoring the way my heart squeezes at the pain slicing through his dark eyes. "Jessie is good to me. He's kind and sweet. He doesn't make me play games or cry or feel unwanted." I take a deep breath, gathering the courage to say what I need to. "You had your chance, and you threw me away. I let you pull me back in over the summer and foolishly thought maybe you'd finally fucking want me as much I want you. Love me as much as I love you, but what'd you do, Donatello? You broke my fucking heart for the second time, turned your back on me... on us. AGAIN." His jaw flexes, and I can almost hear his teeth grinding at my confession. His eyes are so dark they're almost black. I've invaded his space, letting my anger get the best of me. "I refuse to let you break me, Donatello. Not again. Never again."

The jokes on me because I'm already broken. Spitting my play, pretend lies to appear stronger than I am. The air feels heavy as I wait for him to speak. I start to angrily move away after a long pause of his silence, assuming he's going to stay quiet, but he reaches out and snatches my wrist, stopping me. "I don't want to break you, Vita Mia." He palms my cheek as he says it, pulling my face towards his, so I'm forced to look at him. Thump thump. Thump thump. Thump thump. My heart is banging to reach him, making my resolve waiver just the slightest bit. "I love you."

It's almost an audible crack, the sound of my heart breaking for the third time at his quiet confession. A loud humorless laugh bursts from my chest, a manic, harsh sound squeezing past my tight throat to hide the burning ache that's been rekindled like wildfire. What I would have given to hear those three little words months ago. "Now you'll know how I felt for so long… how it feels to love someone who doesn't love you back." It's a bitter confession, lashing out at him like a snake.

"You don't mean that." His voice is low, brows pulled into a confused frown. Russet eyes shifting between mine in an attempt to read past the look of cruel indifference I'm giving him. Every dark word I spit at him is a knife in my own heart, the pain in his voice a punch to the already bruised and battered surface.

"I don't love you… not anymore." The words are hard to say, but I force them past my lips while my heart beats loudly in my ears, hissing and spitting like a cat over the lie. I tell myself that it's only a white lie, though; the fact that I'm able to even say it speaking volumes. My dry cheeks and unwavering voice solidifying the statement in ways any other reassurances would fail. I throw his hand away from my face and start towards the door once again, pausing a few steps away to see him standing in the same spot, lips twisted into a nasty scowl. "Go home, Donatello. I'm not yours to play games with anymore."

Looking away sharply, he scrubs a hand over his face, his shoulders uncharacteristically hunched for a fraction of a second before he straightens once more. Pensive russet eyes snap back to mine, a steely resolve covering a flicker of desperation that was gone so fast I almost missed it. His lips part like he's going to speak, but he must decide against it because they close without a word as he turns his back to me and walks to his car.

My chest feels hollow as I watch him leave without a single glance my way. I tuck my hands in my pocket, suddenly feeling more cold than I had before. I don't know why I stopped to begin with, why I stayed outside to watch him go; maybe a small part of me thought he'd fight a little harder for us after his admission. But this time is no different than all those times he left me to cry over him before, except this time I'm not crying.

Pulling my door card out, a slip of paper falls to the ground, and I bend to grab it, my fingers unfolding it as I straighten.

What do you call a broken can opener? A can't opener.

My fingers curl around the small piece of paper, Donatello's chicken scratch breaking the dam that was keeping everything in place, letting loose the tears I was so proud I hadn't shed just moments before. My tears plop on the paper, blurring the ink and smearing the joke. I don't know when he slipped it into my pocket, but I hate him for doing this to me, for breaking me down so easily after I was strong for so long. I stomp over to the garbage can just outside the doors, intent on throwing the paper away, but my fingers refuse to let it go, my own body betraying me.

I lose it. Tilting my face back to the sky, I scream. Scream as loudly as I can for so long that my lungs burn and ache with the strain. When I run out of air, I do it again. And again. And again. I scream until my throat feels raw, and my voice hoarse. My fingertips are white from clenching my fists so hard, the blood cut off to them for so long they feel numb. After all of my screaming, only one thing becomes painfully clear over everything else. I hate Donatello Genevese no more than I hate the stars.

Back in Euphoria

Donatello's palm slides up my back, fingers pressing into the skin under my shirt as he pulls me into a tight hug. My eyes are closed, but I'd know it was him even if my blankets didn't smell like spice cake. "Good morning." It's a low murmur whispered against the top of my head as his other hand brushes the hair from my face using his fingertips.

Smiling into his chest, I keep my eyes closed, savoring my last few moments of sleepy bliss. Pressing a kiss onto his clothed chest, I peel my eyes open and tilt my face back to look up at him. "Morning." Becoming more alert, I realize it's still mostly dark in the room, a bluish glow coming through the edges of the curtains. "Is it actually morning?"

Chuckling, he tugs me up, so we're face to face and pulls me close for a soft, lingering kiss. "Technically." Cupping my face in his palms, he peppers little kisses along my cheeks and jaw, pausing to whisper against my lips. "This is the only time I was able to come see you today."

His soft words pang in my chest, clamping down like a vice on my heart. I hear what he doesn't say. This was the only time he could see me without people seeing us together. At some point, I started caring more than I should. I'm not sure when it happened, but it's become progressively harder to pretend I'm okay with how things are between us. I try to hide the flash of hurt that crosses my face by pressing my lips to his, but I must not have been quick enough.

He pulls his face back so I can't reach his lips when I dive in for another one, dark eyes scanning my face as I try and fail to plaster a small smile on my lips. "Delaney, don't do that. You know how I feel about you… you know why we can't do this." He brushes a few stray pieces of hair from my cheek as he speaks, and I fight the frown trying to tug at my brows.

My throat is tight as I shake my head and flash a watery smile. "No, I know… I'm just tired." Pushing my face into his neck to avoid his gaze, I grip his shirt in my hands tightly in an effort to keep my unwanted tears at bay. I'm lying, of course; I don't know. I don't understand why we can't be a real thing. Why we have to hide in our shadows, pretend we are nothing more than casual acquaintances when people look our way. Why he refuses to talk about it when it's brought up. Despite my fake nonchalance, my heart earns a new crack with every step that brings us deeper into the fog.

Sighing, Donatello pulls my face from his skin, and my eyes drop to the damp spots, speckling the top of his shirt collar. Seeing the marks of my tears, I grit my teeth, fighting back more tears, not because I'm ashamed of crying, but because I know he will leave me now. He always does when I cry… which always just makes me cry more. I've been crying a lot lately.

"Look at me." I can feel my heart beating an uneven rhythm against my ribs as I try to keep a passive look on my face, taking shallow breaths through my tight throat as I meet his gaze. He doesn't speak right away, and it gets increasingly harder to maintain my resolve as the seconds tick by. "I need to go. I didn't have much time… try to go back to sleep." He places a kiss on my forehead and scoots off the bed. I sit up as he gets to my door, sight blurry with the tears I'm keeping trapped. "I'll call you later."

I know he won't leave without a response, so I nod my head, unable to speak past the lump in my throat; those pesky tears finally breaking free to streak down my cheeks. His gaze tracks their path as I'm unable to look away, a new crack splintering my aching heart as he disappears through the door without another word.

Chapter Fifteen

We are all watching a movie in the Hall's main living space, some of the other students who live in the building mixed in with our group. I haven't been paying attention to the movie though, my mind has been muddled since Donatello showed up. I haven't seen or heard from him since, unsurprisingly, but I've been on edge.

Jessie isn't sitting by me, not intentionally, he just showed up later than the others and all the spots were taken. My eyes find him on the other side of the room; his face resting in his hand and his leg thrown over the side of the chair's armrest. He hasn't said a single word about Donatello. I expected some kind of questioning when I came inside after the whole ordeal, but there was nothing but conversation over what I wanted for dinner. I don't know if he's waiting for me to say something or he just doesn't care, and I don't know which I'd prefer.

He must feel my eyes on him because his flick over to me, a smile peeking out from behind his fingers. I stand and go to leave the room, Sarah who's next to me doesn't even look up, her eyes glued to the TV. I'm not watching it and I'd rather be in my sleep clothes if I'm just going to be lounging around. I look over my shoulder at the sound of footsteps following mine on the stairs and find Jessie behind me, his eyes raising to mine.

"You didn't have to follow me out." I slow so he can catch up, walking again when he reaches my side.

"I was only in there because you were."

I smile at his words, unlocking my suite and letting us in. He follows me into my room and shuts the door, falling onto my bed as I grab a pair of sleep shorts and a tee. "Are you staying the night?"

He has his arms crossed over his forehead but drops one to look over at me at my question. "Do you want me to?" I nod, dropping my clothes onto the bed so I can sit and take my shoes off. "Then, I will."

I smile even though he can't see it, standing to unbutton and pull my jeans off. I'm still facing away, tossing them into the laundry basket by the bathroom door before pulling my sweater and shirt off in one go. I toss my bra next, turning around in just my underwear to slip into my fresh tee. Before I can grab my shorts, Jessie tugs me down onto the bed, making me laugh.

He grabs one of my legs, pulling it over his waist while smirking at me. "You're a tease, Laney girl."

I shrug, and he raises a brow. "It's nothing you haven't seen before."

He hums, biting his lip as he looks at me. "Damn."

"What?" I'm still smiling, watching as he sits up on one elbow.

"I was just thinking…" He quickly rolls me onto my back, keeping a thigh between my legs as I squeal in surprise and giggle when he props up on his forearms to smile down at me. "How'd I get so damn lucky."

I roll my eyes at him. "You're ridiculous."

Instead of responding, he just leans down to kiss me, his lips on mine for only a second when someone knocks on my door. He drops his face into my neck with a loud sigh. "Maybe if we're quiet, they'll go away." It's whispered into my neck, and I can't help but laugh. "That's not being quiet."

"Delaney? You in there?" It's Sarah. I almost ignore her but decide against it, smiling at Jessie, who groans when I shift out from under him and walk to the door.

"Hey…?" I ask it as a question, not sure what she needs. Usually, she leaves me to myself when the door is closed.

"Hey, sorry, Hon." Her eyes come back to me after spying Jessie on the bed, and she smiles in apology. "Someone from the stables called and said they have a horse at the stable that was unloaded under your name. No one there had your number, so they called the front desk, and Cheryl found me downstairs."

I frown in confusion, that makes zero sense. "A horse? You're sure that's what she said?"

Sarah just shrugs. "That's what Cheryl told me."

I nod, shaking my head to myself. "Okay, thanks." Leaving the door open, I grab a pair of joggers from off the floor and sit on the bed to put my sneakers back on. Jessie is sitting up watching me. "I'm going to go check the stables out, are you going to stay here or go back to your place?"

"Do you want me to come with you?"

I grab my hoodie from earlier out of the basket, considering his question. "No, it's probably just a mix up of names or something simple."

He nods, pulling his phone out of his pocket to look at the time. "I'll probably go by my place then. Just let me know when you're on your way back, and I'll come over."

Grabbing a scrunchie off my dresser, I stare at him as I throw my hair up into a bun. "Okay."

He scoots over to where I'm standing, pulling me between his legs. "I drove here; I can drop you off if you want." I nod, and he smiles, taking my face in his hands. "You seem nervous."

He's right, I am. I do think this is just a mix up like I told him, but there's a small part of me that's a little more concerned. "I'm sure it's nothing like I said."

"Okay." He smiles again, probably to help put me at ease, and I lean forward to kiss him, my lips lingering.

"Let's go."

"I'll text you later." I say just before shutting the door, smiling and pushing it shut when he nods. The sun is on the cusps of disappearing in the sky, yellows, and pinks mixing with the clouds as I walk into the main resident barn. I'm not sure who called, but they'll probably have someone in here who can at least point me in the right direction. I stop at Grizzle's stall on my way by, doing a quick stall check before continuing on my way.

Knocking on the open door to the back office, I'm greeted by one of the barn supervisors that I don't know the name of. He smiles at my entrance, putting down the cup he had in his hand. "Hi, I'm not sure if you can help me, but someone called and said a horse was unloaded for me."

"Oh, yes! I didn't call, but I was there when the call was made. I can take you to Clarrisa. She's in charge of intake." He stands, and I move aside to let him go out the door ahead of me. "They put him in one of the vet pens to hold him until you were able to get here." He glances my way. "They just need some signatures before they can get him checked and given a stall."

I just nod. I don't want to waste time explaining to him that this isn't my horse if he's not the one in charge. We go out back and walk across the road to one of the other buildings; I hadn't even realized there were more stalls back here. As soon as we walk through the door, my eyes land on a very familiar

Paint in the pen to my immediate right; what the hell is Pete doing here? Frowning, I follow my guide into a little office where a lady, I'm assuming Clarrisa, is going through some papers.

"Oh, good, you got my message, I wasn't sure." She looks at my guide. "Thanks, John."

He nods and I smile at him in thanks as he leaves. Turning my attention back to Clarissa, I step up to her desk. "Do you know who was in charge of this transfer? I know the horse, but he isn't mine."

She frowns in confusion, moving to grab a file off the desk. "Are you Delaney Luciano?" I nod, and she looks over the paper quickly before handing it over to me. "I have a transfer of ownership for you here, but I'm not sure who set up the actual transfer to get him to the school. He's been issued a student boarding pass under your name, and all his living fees have been paid for the remainder of the year." She continues as I flip through the papers. "We only need your signature for consent to get his checkup before we can allow him with the other horses."

"Um, okay, yea. I'll sign whatever you need." I look up from the papers to answer, rubbing my face with my free hand. Maybe Remy did this? "Do you think he could be put by my other horse? It'd make it easier to take care of them both."

She nods, biting her lip as she pulls something up on her computer. "Do you already have stall B74?" She looks at me, and I nod. "Okay, we already have him assigned at B73." She slides me the vet paperwork, and I sign it, even more, confused than when I first showed up.

"I'm sorry, but I'm just really confused here because I didn't know this was happening, is there no way to see who might have made the arrangements for him to be sent here?" The papers are crinkled in my hands, my fingers pinching the edges.

"Well… let me look at something really quick, and maybe I can find an electronic signature for you." She smiles, and I return it as she turns to her computer. It seems like forever before she startles me with an "Aha!" smiling over at me from her seat. She waves me over, and I come around her desk to look at the screen. "It looks like a Mr. Genovese signed for his transfer to the university."

What. The. Fuck. I just blink at the screen for a solid thirty seconds before I remember I'm not alone. I force a smile. "I know who that is. Thank you for looking that up for me."

She nods, probably confused with my response, then stands to walk me out to Pete. His ears perk up when he sees me, a familiar face after what I can only assume has been a long, confusing trip for him. I stroke his face as Clarissa talks. "I'll go call the vet now and have them come do the exam so you guys can get out of here and get him settled into his stall."

I just smile at her instead of actually responding, waiting until she is in her office to pull out my phone. My hands are shaking, but I need to get answers. I dial Donatello's number, which is no longer saved in my phone but ingrained in my memory. My heart is pounding in my throat as the phone rings, and I hold my wrist with my other hand to keep the phone from trembling with my hand.

"Pronto."

"Why did you send Pete here?" I say it quickly, willing myself to have a steady voice.

"Delaney? Your number didn't come up." I changed it when I left, but he wouldn't know that.

"Just answer the question, Donatello."

"The stables were going to auction him off because his owner died, and none of the relatives wanted him. That didn't seem like something you'd want to happen, so I bought him and had him transferred to your name." He says it all so casually, like buying a horse for the ex who says they hate you isn't that big of a deal.

"You just bought me a horse?" Before he can answer, I'm already asking another question. "How did you even know that was happening?"

"Meagan called me."

My teeth grit at his answer. I don't know why but it irritates the shit out of me that she even had his number to call. I shouldn't even care. "Why would Meagan call you?"

"I'm assuming it's because she was concerned about Pete?" He says it as a question like he's not even sure why she called him about it.

"Why the fuck did she even have your number to call?" It slips out unintentionally, it's not even what I should be worried about in the whole scheme of things, but I don't try to take it back. It's easier to let my anger give me bravery than be a nervous wreck.

"Why are you fucking hipster Ken doll?"

I almost throw my phone, stopping my arm mid throw. Breaking my phone isn't going to help anything, even if watching it break would be somewhat satisfying. Bringing the phone back to my ear, I see the vet coming in, and I wave in acknowledgment, pasting a fake smile on my face. I shift the phone away from my mouth. "Go ahead. I just need to finish this call." He nods, and I turn away from him.

"Ti odio, cazzo." *I fucking hate you.* I say it into the phone, switching to Italian, so no one but Donatello will understand what I'm saying.

Donatello laughs, and I have to resist throwing my phone once again. "No, you don't... even if you've convinced yourself you do, I've decided I'm not letting you go." My fingers squeeze around my phone almost painfully as I swallow past the lump in my throat. "I love you, Vita Mia, and you will love me."

I end the phone call before anything else can be said, walking outside the building as quickly as I can. As soon as the door shuts, I scream into my arm. Thankfully no one is outside, or I'm sure I'd scare the hell out of them. I know I look like a crazy person; I feel crazy. I take a few long breaths, forcing myself to calm down; I still have a horse to take care of, my horse apparently.

I had Jessie pick me up. I need his presence to help calm me. It feels wrong turning to him for comfort over another man, but I'm too selfish to stop. We are in his room because I didn't want to worry Sarah and then feel obligated to explain anything to her. I'm just in my joggers and tee, having taken my hoodie off almost as soon as we got here, but I feel uncomfortable, my skin hot with my annoyance.

"You're mad that your ex bought a horse?" Jessie asks, then laughs, holding his hands up at the expression on my face when I look at him. "I'm just trying to understand why you're so mad, Laney girl."

"He bought the horse so it wouldn't be auctioned off." I stop stomping around to yank my joggers off, grabbing one of Jessie's shirts off the floor when I drop them. "Because the owner died, and no one wanted it." I rip my shirt off, switching for Jessie's larger one. I climb onto his bed when I'm finished, yanking the blankets out from under him to wrap up in.

"You're saying it like he did it for the wrong reason, but that sounds like a good reason."

I pull my head out from under the blankets to stare at him. How is he not getting this? "He did!"

Instead of getting mad at me for yelling at him, Jessie just smiles and takes his shirt off, sliding under the blankets with me. He palms my face once he's directly in front of me. "I'm going to need you to explain better because I can't help you when I'm confused with the details."

I close my eyes and put my hand on top of his, weaving my fingers through his. "Donatello said he loved me last week." I open my eyes, trying to read Jessie.

"Is that what you want?" His thumb rubs along my cheekbone when he asks, and I lightly squeeze his hand.

"It was before, but I don't think so now... I don't really know what I want." I answer honestly.

"Do you still love him?"

I swallow hard at his question. I don't want to say yes and have him leave me, but I also don't want to lie and say I feel nothing for Donatello. Jessie waits quietly for me to answer, letting me pull him closer to me so that our noses brush. He moves the hand from my face, to rest on my hip as I tangle our legs. The extra touch helps to ground me. "I don't want to, but I do." I finally manage to get out, nervous with how he's going to respond.

"Where am I in this? Where are we?" His fingers stroke along my skin as he asks, his demeanor so much calmer than what I expected, than what I feel.

"I don't know." I reach down, pulling his hand back up to my face. "Is it selfish to want you to stay with me while I figure it out?"

He smiles, a silent chuckle shaking the bed. "It is Laney girl." He sits up on an elbow, forcing me to roll onto my back to look into his face. "Lucky for you, I'm not ready to leave, though." His lips land on mine, and I greedily pull him to me. I don't know what's going to happen between us. I don't know what's going to happen with Donatello. But I know that for tonight, Jessie is going to help me forget about it all.

Back in Euphoria

"Love the camaro out front." I'm being incredibly sarcastic. I'm one thousand percent positive that bubble gum pink monstrosity does not belong to Donatello.

His face jerks in my direction at my entrance. I smile at the slight widening of his eyes, the tick of his jaw. He didn't know I was coming because I didn't tell him. I didn't think he'd have 'company' over, though. "You didn't call."

"What? Is someone here?" Ahh, so now we have a voice to go with the car. I can't see who it is, but the voice sounds familiar, tightening my gut with a burning rage.

I kick my shoes off as he watches, toss my keys, and phone onto the console table; I want him to see that I plan on staying. I walk right past the half wall to see none other than Sienna fucking Dall'oca all dolled up in her favorite apron and whisking something in a bowl.

"Delaney! I didn't know you'd be stopping by!" She says it in typical Sienna style, all sweet and happy.

Normally I don't have a problem with her but seeing her here makes me sick.

My eyes flick to Donatello and back before I paste a sugar sweet smile on my face, dimple and all. "That's quite the ride you got out there," I say, feigning excitement when she pauses her whisking with a delighted gasp.

"Isn't it cute! Papa got it for me as a late graduation gift."

"So cute." I scrunch my nose at her giggle before bringing all my attention to Donatello. "You don't mind if I borrow Donatello, do you?"

"Oh, sure! He won't get to lick the spoon, though." She giggles again, and I can't stop my eyes from rolling.

I walk forward, grabbing Donatello's arm to pull him out of the room with me. "I'm sure he'll live."

I drop his arm once we're out of view, knowing he'll follow me. I walk to the back of the house and out the double french doors to where the pool is. I hear Donatello shut the doors behind us, and I pull my crop top off, my swimsuit already on under my clothes. "Why the fuck is she here, Donatello?" I ask it as I take my shorts off, turning to face him once I'm in just my black string bikini.

"She's baking."

I scoff at his nonanswer, crossing my arms under my chest in a way that I know makes my boobs like fantastic. "You often lend your house to the locals?"

"Her padre is trying to set us up. I imagine he thinks he'll have greater pull in the Famiglia if his daughter marries me." His eyes drop from my face to run over my length, lingering a little longer than what's considered appropriate.

What he says makes sense. People are always trying to weed their way into the ranks through marriage in the Famiglia; most of the old school Capo's were outraged when my own papa allowed Remy to marry outside of who they considered to be the best match for him. BUT Donatello always has seemingly coincidental reasons for things. Always. Which makes me think they aren't so coincidental.

"Kind of funny how you always have an explanation for everything, Donatello." I turn and drop into the pool, coming up out of the water to rest my arms on the edge.

"You don't believe me?" He's frowning, looking down at me in the water.

"No, I don't."

He shakes his head, dropping down on his heels to grab my chin. "What do you think then?"

"I think you're seeing other people."

He lets out a loud exhale, closing his eyes like what I'm saying is an annoyance. "Would you even believe me if I said I wasn't? That I haven't been with anyone but you since we started messing around?"

My neck is starting to hurt at the angle it's being held, but I stay in the water anyway. "No, I wouldn't."

He lifts my face higher, forcing me to use my arms to lift myself partially from the water. "Then what's the point in trying to convince you."

I finally jerk my face away, letting myself sink into the water and away from his touch. I come up in the middle of the pool where my toes just barely touch, far away from where he could grab me again. "Guess there isn't one."

He scrunches his face up at me, wiping a hand over his jaw. "Fuck." Shaking his head, he turns and opens one of the doors, yelling inside. "Go home Sienna, tell your papa I was busy today." He turns, slapping the door shut and ripping his shirt off with one arm over his back.

I watch as he removes his jeans, yanking them off his feet and coming to the edge of the pool in his boxers, dropping to the edge as he climbs into the water. "You think she'll actually go home?" My heart is thumping as he swims towards me, surprised not even a big enough word for his actions.

"Don't know." He jerks me to him, my body slamming into his as he grabs the back of my head. "Don't fucking care either."

Chapter Sixteen

What does A **nosy pepper do? Gets Jalapeno business.** I scrunch the paper joke in my fist and throw it in the garbage on my way by. It's just one of many I've received since Donatello declared war on my heart. That's what it feels like anyway. He's just waiting for me to wave the white flag so he can bang his chest and carry me away like some cheap prize. My head and my heart are in a constant battle, I don't want to find his determination endearing or his tenacity sweet, and I resent him for making me feel this way.

Jessie wordlessly watches everything. My silent sweet man who is somehow okay watching another man try and woo me. As much as I'm grateful and in need of his support and comfort, I don't understand it. I don't understand how he can just stand by and not feel the need to assert himself to Donatello. Every man in my life has always been that way with stubborn, dominant personalities. I've been morphed to find the brasher and somewhat barbaric qualities of an alpha male appealing. I crave a little fight, the rush that comes with a good argument.

Jessie doesn't argue. He doesn't yell or get angry. He doesn't question my decisions or make me question his loyalty. He dotes on me; does everything I ask and more. He's the perfect man, and I feel wrong for wanting anything different. His perfection makes me question myself and my dirty secrets. I've never shed blood or ended a life but how would he feel knowing my family deals in nothing but blood and sex? That our fortunes started and lasts with the fall of others?

I can never leave the protection of the Famiglia, I may have never taken the Omerta, but my birth name made the decision for me on the matter. Remy has allowed me to play adult, but I was always meant to come back. Jessie is half Italian, Sicilian even; Remy would at least allow him soldier status if he took the Omerta. But could I ask him to do that? I tend to be selfish with most things, but that's a line I'm not willing to cross for my own desires. There's a reason people marry inside the Famiglia, among other things, it's easier.

I'm not ready to give Donatello my forgiveness and end things with Jessie either. Donatello denouncing my hatred of him has done nothing but spurred me into proving just how much I can; teased my stubborn beast into an angry, broken hearted tirade.

"No smile for me today, Vita Mia?" I don't look his way. I don't need to look to know that he's leaning against his car, a stupid grin on his face as he waits for me to get out of classes for the day. Every Monday and Friday, like clockwork, he's been waiting for me. Trying to wear down my resilience with all the things he knows I love. How he's even managed to stay away from the Famiglia this long is beyond me. My only guess is that he's somehow wrangled Andrea into helping him with his bullshit.

Eyes forward and not on his form, crossing the street to get to me, I answer. "Forse se sono fortunato, verrai investito da un autobus uno di questi giorni." *Maybe if I'm lucky, you'll get hit by a bus one of these days.*

He laughs, a genuine loud guffaw that warms my gut even as I grit my teeth with annoyance. "Sempre la mia ragazza cattiva... dimmi tutti I modi in cui voui che paghi, Piccolo." *Always my naughty girl... tell me all the ways you want me to pay, Baby.*

A sick part of me loves these games we play. Loves that I can still make him talk to me like that when, for all he knows, all I'm saying, is that I want nothing to do with him. What a fucking farce.

"Leave me alone, Donatello. Don't you have someone else you could be bothering?" I look over at him, finally allowing myself to actually see him. "I'm sure Meagan would love hearing from you... if she hasn't already this week." Just saying it leaves a bitter aftertaste.

He chuckles, tongue swiping along his lower lip as he meets my gaze. "She probably would. You should get that pup of yours, and we can plan a double date."

Huffing in annoyance, I shift the book in my arms. "Stop fucking calling Jessie that."

He clucks his tongue, putting his hands in his jacket pockets. "I call it as I see it."

I'd like nothing more than to bash his head with the book in my hands. "He's not even that much younger than you. You guys are like the same height. He's not a pup."

He taps two fingers to his forehead, a mocking salute. "You're right. I forgot those were the main qualifiers for manhood."

"You're a dick."

He pushes me then, jostling me sideways into a small walkway between the Science and Math buildings. My book falls from my arms, and my back is pressed flush to the brick wall, Donatello's hand wrapped around my jaw. "Tell me that's not what you want. Tell me that's not what you need me to be. I'm playing your game, your rules." He moves his face lower, running his nose along my neck. "Tell me that your pretty boy knows you like to be fucked in the ass. Tell me he knows how to make you wet with just his words."

He stands, and I can see what his angry tone is hiding in those russet reds. Apprehension. He's nervous that I might not want him anymore. I wish that were the case.

His words have already done what he wants me to admit Jessie can do, knowing he can't. "Not everything is a game."

He smiles at my words, bringing his thumb up to run across my lower lip. "You've always been a sore loser."

I smack his hand away, pushing him aside to pick up the book that landed in the dirt. "I hate you... how many times do I need to say it before you take the hint?"

"When you say it and mean it, I'll consider it."

"I don't want to go out, Sarah… and you know why."
I'm curling her hair for her as she does her makeup.
She and some of the other girls from the building are
all going out tonight. She's been nagging me to go all
week, and I would love to if I didn't have a stalker.

"What can your ex possibly do in a crowded club?" I
roll my eyes behind her head. I hate how they use 'ex'
to describe Donatello. I mean, he is, but I still don't
like how it sounds. "You can get all gussied up and
show him what he's missing. A little jealousy could
do a relationship good."

"He's a grown-ass man that's been spending weeks
following me around, leaving his equivalent to love
notes and bashing Jessie. I don't think we need to add
jealousy to that." I put the curling iron down,
unplugging it from the wall. "You're done."

She spins on the stool, facing me. "Just come out with
us. You need a break. How will he even know you're
going out anyway?"

He always knows. I want to say it, but I don't, it'd be
pointless. I stare at her as she continues to babble on
excuses for why everything will be fine. I'm tempted
to go just to see what kind of reaction it causes, even
though that was my main argument for not wanting
to go originally. God, my mind is so fucking muddled.

"Fine. I'll go." I may have interrupted her because her mouth is still half open when I bother to turn my attention back to her. Poor Sarah, I don't think I've been the greatest friend lately. "Sorry, I was lost in my mind there for a minute and didn't mean to interrupt you… but I'll go."

She bounces in her seat, glossy pink lips in a wide smile. I grab one of the bottles of wine that Bev sent, that I still haven't opened, and hold it up for Sarah to see. "Let's pregame this shit."

Thirty minutes later, I'm the only girl here not regretting my outfit choice. While they all opted for the typical open back, strapless, sleeveless, booty showing options, I went a little warmer. I have a snug mauve long sleeve that dips below my breasts tucked into a black suede tube skirt that I paired with my black thigh high boots; only an inch or two of leg shows, so I'm mostly covered. It's December, so I'm not sure what they were expecting weather wise. We might not have snow, but fifty degrees feels cold when you're used to eighty.

It's another live band night, so the floor is already packed with both fans and party goers like my group. I head to the bar first, my usual club routine, and order a few tequila shots, splitting two with Sarah. I make a conscious effort not to constantly eye the crowd looking for Donatello. For all I know he isn't even in town, I actually have no idea where he's staying or if he's even staying around here.

Sarah apparently is a fan of the band, because she's been belting tunes, very off-key tunes, in my ear the past hour. I'm feeling decently buzzed, but I think she's sliding into drunk territory, a cute giggling southern mess demanding I dance with her. Handing her off to one of the other girls, I head back to the bar for water. Sliding cash across the counter, I catch sight of Jessie and Derek coming through the doors, watching as they easily find Sarah. Someone probably messaged them that we were out, tattletales.

Water in hand, I take the cap off of one and hand it to Sarah. I put the second in her shoulder bag for later, encouraging her to drink most of the bottle before I recap it and stick it in the bag also. We've moved back towards one of the booths directly next to the dance floor, and I slide into the booth, smiling when Jessie scoots next to me.

"Who told on Sarah?" I have to lean into him to ask, so he can hear me over the music.

"I think Cassidy texted Derek. I'm pretty sure she just wanted an excuse to get him down here, though." He smiles when I laugh, biting his lip when his eyes drop to my outfit. "New outfit, Laney girl?"

I bump him with my shoulder, flashing some dimple in answer. "Dance with me." We've been here a while, and Donatello hasn't shown up, I'm sure dancing with Jessie is safe at this point.

"Anything for you." He stands and holds his hand to me, making me smile with his mock chivalry. He's wearing his staple joggers and a long sleeve, if I had to guess, he wasn't planning on going dancing tonight.

The band is either done or on break, so they have a DJ playing now, the atmosphere switching from randy honky tonk to high end club with a flip a switch. I prefer the change, only because I recognize the songs and know the lyrics to sing when I dance. I turn my back to Jessie, letting him hold my hips as he dances. My fingers run along his nape when he bends to press his lips to my neck, closing my eyes and swinging to the tune of whatever is playing. We stay like that for a while, dancing in our own little bubble. It's not until someone announces that Sarah was headed to the bathroom alone that we stop.

"I'll be back. I just want to make sure she gets there in one piece." I say to Jessie, who just laughs and points into the crowd.

"You better hurry, she's practically running."

Following the direction of his finger, I see her weaving through the crowd and hurry to follow, not wanting to lose her when I know she's drunk. Jessie was right; she is running. I'm breathing hard when I get to her, laughing as I hold the bathroom door open for her. "Damn, you're fast for a drunk."

She laughs, but it quickly turns into a gag as she rushes to a stall. Explains the running then. I wait until she's done, then point to her bag, reminding her she has water in there. She waves me off, saying something about not needing a babysitter, and I smile at her sass. "I'll wait outside then, but I'm not leaving you." She waves again, and I step outside into the hall.

"Delaney!" I frown at my name being called, unsure who called me until I see Derek jogging into the hall.

"You need to go outside, that big guy is fighting Jessie out back."

"Big guy?" Fucking Donatello. I start towards the door but stop Derek when he starts coming with me. "Wait for Sarah. She's in there. I'll handle it."

He just nods, and I hustle to the back of the building, a door is propped open, and I can hear someone yelling they don't allow fights on the property. Pushing the door open, I see Donatello, pulling his arm back for another hit while Jessie scowls at him from the pavement, his nose bloody, and his lip already split. "Donatello!"

Donatello doesn't look at me but drops his arm and releases the front of Jessie's shirt, letting him flop back onto the asphalt. He's already standing when I get to them, and I kneel by Jessie as he starts to sit up, "Are you okay?" Before he can answer, I scowl up at Donatello. "What the fuck is wrong with you?"

Donatello doesn't say anything, just crosses his arms over his chest, watching as Jessie stands and spits blood from his mouth.

"I started it." My head whips to Jessie's confession. "I deliberately egged him on." He brushes some blood from his lip with his palm, a small smile directed towards me. "Maybe I wouldn't have if I'd known he'd kick my ass for it."

I don't return his smile, shaking my head in disbelief. He just got beat up, and he's taking the blame. "No, Jessie I don't care what you said to provoke him, Donatello knows better. He's just been waiting for a chance to hit you."

Jessie just shrugs, like it doesn't make a difference. "I'm fine, Laney girl."

Donatello scoffs, and I turn my attention on him, shoving his chest. "What the fuck is wrong with you? He's twenty-three, Donatello."

He reaches forward to brush some hair from my face, but I smack his hand down before he can touch me. "Sounds like a legal adult to me." He replies, purposefully avoiding the real problem here.

He's well aware he just beat up someone who didn't' have a chance in hell of fighting back. "You could have killed him, Donatello."

Donatello frowns and shakes his head like that's the most ridiculous thing I could have said. "One or two more hits, and I would have been done." He looks over my head and at Jessie. "He just needed to learn his place, now he has. Right, Jessie?"

I don't look, but he must nod, because I don't hear any response, just see Donatello's smirk. "We're good now."

I huff and step away from Donatello. "Well, we…" I gesture between him and me with my hand, "definitely aren't."

"Perche? Il Bastardo annacquato va bene." *Why? The watered-down bastard is fine.* He gestures vaguely in Jessie's direction, frowning at me. How he even knows Jessie is half Italian is beyond me, but I'm annoyed with his insult. Jessie probably doesn't understand it anyway, because he has no reason to know that the Mafia values full blooded Italians over lesser amounts.

"Jessie speaks Italian, Donatello. Stop being a dick."

He just shrugs his shoulders, looking at me with an expression that says he doesn't give a shit.

Jessie grabs my arm, stopping my forward progression towards Donatello. I had full intentions to slap the look off his face. "Come on, Laney girl, it's probably time we go home."

Frowning, I let Jessie pull me to him, wrapping his arm around my shoulders as he leads me away from Donatello. "Ti odio, Donatello!" *I hate you, Donatello!* I yell it back at him before fully turning away.

He just laughs, yelling back to me. "Ti amo, Vita Mia." *I love you, My Life.*

Back in Euphoria

Dropping the last of my boxes inside my loft for the summer, I pull my phone from my pocket and see a missed call from Donatello. I didn't tell him I was leaving for school early; I didn't want to see him after he ended our relationship… if you could even call it that. Donatello didn't. I look at the tattoo on my finger and resist the urge to throw my phone across the room. Last week I did nothing but cry, this week I'm angry. And sad. But mostly angry.

My phone pings, and I swipe it open, snorting when I see it's from Donatello.

Call me.

I leave it on read, clicking my phone shut. As if. My throat goes dry as I stomp to my room, ripping through the duffel bag of clothes I brought in here earlier. My heart is pounding in my chest, demanding tears, but I keep them back, refusing to let myself spiral. Getting annoyed that I can't find what I'm looking for, I tip the bag out onto the bed, throwing it away from me once it's empty. My hands are shaking, so I close my eyes and force a deep breath through my lungs to try and calm. Once they're open, I see the dress I was looking for right on top, my anger hiding it from me before.

I change quickly, sliding the dress over my head before digging in a box by my closet for a pair of heels. Slipping them on in front of the full-length mirror on the back of my door, I appraise my outfit. The top is a high neck long sleeve made of see through black mesh that shows off my black lacy bra underneath, the bottom a tight black pencil skirt with a slit in the back of my legs. The shoes I grabbed are chunky black four-inch heels with an ankle strap and silver studs running along the edges. Running my hands through my waves, I decide to braid one side flat, pinning it behind my ear.

Leaving the room, I snatch my flat black wallet and phone, making sure I have both my fake ID and enough cash for the night. It's pushing nine P.M., which is still early for most of the clubs around here, but I'll make it work.

Getting into my Uber, I smile at the driver, "Know of any good parties tonight?"

It's Friday night in a college town; I'm sure there's something going on. The driver turns to look at me over his seat, smiling in return after accessing my outfit. "I know a place."

I flash my dimples, sitting back in my seat. "Let's go."

Fifteen minutes later, I'm standing outside of a place called 1716. You can hear the live band through the open doors and see the large crowd bumping around through the large windows spread across the front of the building. I smile to myself; this will work. After paying the cover charge my first stop is the bar where I down four shots of tequila, earning a few lingering stares from a handful of guys waiting around the bar for their own drinks. Picking a cute blond boy in the group nearest me, I convince him to dance with me.

My only plan for tonight is to get completely shitfaced and make questionable life decisions in the process. Blondie here being questionable decision number one. Even under my current state of inebriation, I make sure to get as many videos and photos of me and my 'date' to post on my Snap story. Adding a couple of racy images for my Instagram. I know Donatello will see every single one, know it'll make him angry. I can only hope it hurts him as much as it hurts me.

Chapter Seventeen

"Hold on Laney girl." Jessie grabs my hand before I swipe my card to unlock the Hall doors to my suite, and I frown in confusion. "I don't think I should go up there with you."

"What? Why not?" He's smiling at me, but he doesn't look happy. "Is this because of Donatello? He won't do that again, I promise."

I go to tug his hand, but he holds me in place. "I think you know we can't keep doing this." I start to shake my head, open my mouth to say something, but he grabs my face in his palms to silence me. "We both know who you want, and it's not me."

I'm getting dumped. By my boyfriend, who isn't really my boyfriend. Why the fuck does this keep happening to me. "That's not true. If you want me to choose right now, then I choose you." I say it quickly, swallowing through the tears clogging my throat. My heart doesn't know if we agree, loudly thumping its displeasure in my ears.

Jessie smiles, his tongue swiping across the cracked seam where it's split. "I'm flattered, but we know that's not true." He drops his hands to run one through his silver hair. "I need to leave before I fall for the girl who doesn't have a heart to give; it's my turn to be selfish."

I'm trying to blink back my tears, but I feel my lip trembling, and I know I'm about to lose the battle. I don't have anything to say, no arguments to make. Everything he says is true, and there's no point in me making this worse for the both of us.

He looks back at my face, groaning when he sees my tears. "No, don't cry, Laney girl." He cups my face again, using his thumbs to wipe my tears. "It's not me. It's you." He smiles as he says it, trying to make me smile with the sad little joke. It doesn't work.

"I don't want you to leave." It's true. I don't. I don't want to be left alone to deal with my own shit show.

"I need to leave… and not just because your ex hits like a fucking Mack truck."

This time I do laugh, a sad sound that ends with more tears.

"I'm still going to be here for you, Delaney, but it needs to be as your friend…" He wipes more tears, "best friend." He emphasizes best, and I laugh again, which makes him smile. "You could never be mine because you always belonged to someone else. And you knew that already."

He wraps me in a hug, pressing a soft kiss to my neck, then my cheek, before cupping my jaw to place a lingering kiss on my lips. He steps away from me, tucking his hands into his pockets. "Goodnight. Laney girl."

"Goodnight, Jessie." I say it more to be polite than I believe either of us is actually going to have one. I'm sad and broken in a different kind of way than when Donatello left. Jessie says we can still be friends, but this feels a lot like losing my best friend.

I watch him turn and walk down the path, stare at his back until he disappears from view. I don't know how long I stand there, staring at the spot I saw him last, my fingertips starting to burn with the cold. I'm so fucking tired of being the one getting left behind.

"You want to get drunk?"

I drop my head back with an audible groan, resisting the urge to scream. "Are you fucking kidding me? Can I not get a single fucking break tonight?"

Donatello shrugs, coming to stand next to me while looking towards the same spot I've been staring. "You just got dumped, seemed like a logical question."

I scrub my hands over my face, this time screaming into my hands. I don't even care at this point if Donatello sees me lose my shit. He's seen me at my worst already; he's the one who made me this mess. "I didn't get dumped. We were never officially dating."

"That a thing of yours?"

I turn my whole body to face him. He's smirking like he thinks he's the funniest fuck in the land. "Fuck. You."

I go to storm into my building, but Donatello grabs me around the waist. The sound of his smile behind his words. "No, Delaney, I'm sorry. You're right, that wasn't funny." He's lifted me off my feet to keep me from climbing the steps, and I start kicking in his arms. "Just come get drunk with me. We could both fucking use it, and neither one of us wants to be alone."

He holds me up like that until I get tired of kicking, letting my head fall back onto his shoulder. "Put me down... I won't run away." I'm not lying either. I'm over everything right now.

He sets me down, and I turn to face him, rubbing at my already ruined eye makeup. "What's so wrong with you that you need to get drunk?"

"Vita Mia, you are the reason I need to get drunk."

I drop my hand and look at him with pursed lips. Fair enough. "Fine, let's go get this shit show started, shall we?"

I messaged Sarah that I found someone to stay with for the night so she wouldn't worry when I never came home. I didn't tell her who, because even I know saying I'm staying the night with my ex who broke my heart three times, is now stalking me, and beat Jessie up less than two hours ago sounds asinine.

"What do you want?" Donatello asks from across the car, parking in front Kroger Grocery.

I'm trying to wipe the makeup from my eyes when he asks, using the visor mirror to see. "Besides a noose to hang myself?" I flip it shut, giving up and look at him. "Makeup remover wipes and tequila."

He nods and gets from the car; he ducks down before closing it. "You want limes or anything?"

"Nope." I purse my lips as he smirks, straightening, and shutting the door.

My eyes track him to the door, then close. This is probably a mistake, but honestly? Who gives a fuck anymore. I keep my eyes closed until I hear the driver door opening, and Donatello leans over the console to drop a few bags between my feet. I have to spread my legs wider, so they fit, and he smiles at me, eyes trailing up my boots and parted thighs before he meets my gaze.

"I like these." His finger trails along the top of the leg closest to him, and I smack it off.

"Then get a pair." He laughs, and the sound digs its way into my gut, trying to force a smile of my own. I win the fight, though, crossing my arms to frown out of the window as he pulls out onto the empty road. It is pushing three AM. "Where are we going?" I never asked before I realize.

"My hotel. It's just up the road."

"Have you been staying in a hotel this whole time?"

He shakes his head, glancing my way. "No. I go back home after I see you."

I frown over at him. We're definitely in Donatello's personal car. "You drive?" I ask it like he's crazy.

Because he is, he nods, and I stare at his profile. "That's a fifteen-hour drive, Donatello."

He chuckles, looking over at me as he parks at the Marriott. "It's only a day's drive if you leave early."

He gets out before I say anything else, walking around the front of the car to my side. I watch as he opens it, leaning in to grab the bags from between my feet. "Ready to get smashed?"

I snort at his wording, correcting him. "I'm ready to get drunk, yes."

He shuts the door when I'm out, and I wait for him to lead the way. He takes us to a back entrance that's empty but for a trashcan, a large fake bamboo plant, and an elevator. I cross my arms in the elevator, ticking my fingers along my arm as I watch the floor number change. Surprisingly, Donatello isn't in my space, leaning against the opposite side instead. I let him exit first, taking a bag that he holds out to me so he can dig a room key from his pocket and unlock the door.

He's in one of the nicer rooms that have a small kitchenette and seating area, not large like the normal penthouse suites, but larger than the normal rooms. I set my phone and wallet on the kitchenette counter, pulling the smallest bag from Krogers to me in search of the makeup wipes. I should just shower, but that feels like too much work. Finding what I need, I rip the pack open and start washing my face. It takes me a few wipes, but I finally get it all off, feeling slightly better.

Donatello already has his own whiskey bottle out, pouring himself a glass. "Do you have extra clothes? I don't want to sleep in this." He glances my way, downing his glass and setting it down before walking to the other side of the bed to grab a shirt from a duffel on the floor, tossing it to me. "No pants?"

He smirks over his shoulder, already pouring another glass. "Not unless you want me without pants."

I roll my eyes, sitting on the bed to unzip my boots and drop them on the floor. "Just the shirt is fine." I stand and face the wall, so my back is to him. "Don't look."

I hear his mumbled, "Okay." As I untuck my shirt and pull it over my head, letting it drop to the floor. I'm not wearing a bra since the shirt was cut too low for one, so I slip the tee over my head, making sure it's covering my butt before I push my skirt off my legs. When I turn around, I'm unsurprised to find Donatello leaning against the counter, watching me. I knew he'd look anyway.

"You were looking." I grab the tequila from off the counter, not bothering to find a cup and just tipping it back. I drink at least three shots worth before I put the bottle back on the counter, wincing at the aftertaste. It tastes like shit, but it gets the job done.

"You can watch me change if you want." I ignore Donatello, deciding to bring the bottle to the bed with me.

"Where are you sleeping? Because it won't be with me." I rip the blankets from the edges of the bed before I get in; I hate when they're tight around my feet.

He flicks off all the lights, but the dimmers above the bed before dropping onto the bed with me, setting his bottle on the nightstand. "Fine. But I'm sleeping on the bed, so where are you sleeping?"

Instead of answering, I just down another two shots worth of tequila, setting the bottle on the nightstand on my side of the bed. I'm already starting to feel hot from the liquor, so I throw my blankets off, staring up at the ceiling. "I shouldn't be here."

Donatello snorts into his glass, the sound loud and echoey. "Probably not."

I roll my face over to look at him; his bottle is already half empty. "This is all your fault."

He hums, polishing the rest of his glass and setting it by the bottle before looking down at me. "You'll have to be more specific."

"Did you sleep with Meagan?" It's off topic, but I suddenly have to know the answer.

He reaches out and brushes his fingertips over my forehead, trailing them down my cheek as far as his hand can reach. "No." He pulls his hand from me, sitting forward to pull his shirt off. "But I was going to." He throws his shirt off the end of the bed, standing to drop his jeans and pull on a pair of sweats from his bag. He lays back on the bed before he speaks again. "I couldn't, though. It didn't matter how angry that fucking pup of yours made me. I couldn't do it."

"His name is Jessie, stop calling him pup." I sit up and take another drink before flopping down on my side, facing Donatello. "JESSIE dumped me tonight because of you. The least you can do is call him by his fucking name."

"I have a lot of things to be sorry for, but I'm not sorry he's gone." Is his answer, crossing his arms over his chest as he frowns down at me.

"You should be sorry!" I sit up, twisting to sit on my knees and face him. "He was the only thing keeping me from breaking completely. He was the only one making sure I was even okay. Jessie is good to me… he's good to fucking everyone because he's just fucking good! He's not tainted like the rest of us." I clench the bottom of my shirt in my hands, needing something to help stay grounded. "I wouldn't have even needed him if you hadn't broken me to begin with."

"I thought I was doing what was best for you and for the Famiglia." He says it quietly, dark eyes flicking between my own.

"Oh, of course, it all makes sense now, what could possibly be a better reason for tearing my fucking heart out." I make sure to lay on the sarcasm, trying to keep from yelling too loudly. "Tell me, if you thought you made the best choice, why have you been here, destroying any chance I have at healing?"

"I was wrong." I scoff, and he narrows his eyes in a silent command to stay quiet. "I didn't just break your heart, Delaney…" He reaches over and grabs the whiskey, taking a long swig before he drops it back down. "I broke my own fucking heart. Nothing has ever been more painful than leaving you like that. It's a pain that keeps on fucking giving, too." His eyes aren't on me anymore but staring forward vacantly. "Even after I pulled my head out of my own ass and decided to acknowledge the fact that I fucked up, I find that you're so shattered you can't even have a normal conversation with me without looking like you're about to fall apart. That you, Vita Mia are finding comfort from some douche with a girl's name because I broke you." He wipes his palm over his lips, russet reds dropping to find mine. "I found that my

Vita Mia isn't mine anymore. I let the best fucking thing to ever exist in my life go."

I'm crying at his admission, silent fat drops hitting the tops of my thighs.

"That wasn't the worst of it, though, was it?" He shifts on the bed, so he's facing me, peels my fingers from where they're clenched so he can kiss my wrist, hold my hand against his face. "Mi dispiace tanto, Piccola." *I'm so sorry, Baby.* His fingers curl against the hand he's holding. "Every time I left you, every time I let you think I wasn't faithful, every time I made you think I didn't want you… I fucking wanted you. I still want you. I never didn't want you. I swear to you that I never touched anyone else while we were together, I never should have let you think that. I will forever regret the decisions I've made."

"Me, too." He closes his eyes when I say it, frowning into my palm. He turns his face, kissing my palm, then sits up, letting my hand drop from him. "I'm here because I can't stand not being with you. I tried the first time you left, and I was fucking miserable. I tried to stay away when you came back last summer, told myself I'd be cured of you if I just saw you one more time, but I was wrong." He lets out a deep breath, dropping back against the bed. "I was so fucking wrong. Every fucking day I'd convince myself I just needed one more day. One more minute and then I'd be done. Then I could let you go. But I couldn't, and I let us become something too much for me to handle, so I ran." He props up on his elbows to look at me. "I had myself convinced there for a while that you were better off this way; you could experience school without having to worry about me. You wouldn't have the pressure to quit and become a casalinga *housewife*. I told myself I'd work more efficiently; I wouldn't be distracted. My relationship with Remy wouldn't be strained. In my mind, those pointless, ridiculous reasons seemed logical, seemed right." He looks away, down at the hands twisted in my lap. "I was a coward. From the beginning, I've been a coward."

"I don't forgive you. My heart still fucking hurts, and hearing this doesn't fix that. This doesn't make anything feel better. My heart still aches, and I can't trust that you won't do something to hurt me again."

"I'm not letting you go again, Vita Mia; I definitely don't plan on hurting you again."

"I've heard prettier words turn to lies. You don't have me to keep, Donatello. My heart might be broken, but it won't heal for you if I have a say."

He laughs, but it's a sad sound. "You don't cry when you see me anymore. You've been talking to me, actually talking, for the last two weeks. I know you've memorized every single note I've given you, every single joke since I've come back. I know you walk out of your building on the side I park instead of using the front. I know you deliberately provoke me every day just to get me worked up because you like it when I grab you. You want me to touch you just as badly as I want to touch you. You can lie to me, but you can't lie to your heart, you still love me, and that means I have you. And I plan on keeping you, Baby."

"I hate you." Thump. Thump. LIE.

He smiles. That lopsided grin of his waking up the fireflies. "I missed you."

"I hate you." Thump. Thump. LIE.

Still smiling, he kneels in front of me, gripping the hair on the sides of my head. His lips hovering over mine, his shoulders hunched as he holds my face. "I missed how you taste." He pulls my lips to his, and I let him, my hands splaying over his chest and abs. He groans against my mouth when his tongue passes over mine; my hair tugged lightly at the roots.

"I hate you." Thump. Thump. LIE.

"I missed how you smell." He rolls my head back, running his nose and tongue up the arch of my neck, his teeth scraping across my chin.

"I hate you." Thump. Thump. LIE.

His lips are back on mine; my face jerked back to his. "I missed how you feel." It's said against my lips, his teeth biting into them as he speaks. One of his hands grabs one of my own, forcing it to move over his skin, forcing me to feel his heart beating against his ribs.

 I can feel myself spiraling, losing myself to his touch like always. He flips himself on top of me, his fingers grabbing my thighs hard enough I can already feel the bruises his fingers are making. I can't hear anything past the thumping of my heart, smell past his spicy skin, taste anything but the whiskey and cinnamon on his tongue.

"I hate you." Thump. Thump. LIE. It's a broken whisper as I sit up to help him remove my shirt, my teeth biting into the skin of chest as he jerks my panties off.

"I don't love you." Thump. Thump. LIE. I'm arching into his mouth, his tongue sweeping over my nipples as he squeezes my breasts together with his palms.

"I'm just drunk, and you're a good fuck." Thump. Thump. LIE. I moan against the sheets when he flips me, yanking my ass into the air so he can sink to the hilt into my wet, throbbing core. He grabs my hips, jerking them back with each thrust, forcing himself deeper. My fingers and toes curl when my orgasm hits, my back arching against his hands as I cry out against the mattress, my tears leaving blotchy stains on the sheets.

Donatello drops over my back, his breath hot against my neck as he groans his release against my skin, his lips trailing a wet path to the top of my butt. Breaths still choppy, he pulls himself off of me, dropping down beside me to pull me face to face with him, pressing my lips to his with a hand on the back of my head. "I love you, Vita Mia."

Chapter Eighteen

I feel like I'm crumbling. My castle loses another pebble every day. I constantly feel overwhelmed or tired. I don't know how much longer I can keep up the charade that I'm fine, hold the illusion that my castle is made of steel instead of stones. I'm tired of feeling tired. I'm tired of feeling sad. I'm tired of feeling broken. I'm tired of everything all the time. And it makes me angry. I can feel myself turning into this angry, sad, broken thing. I'm done holding onto memories. I'm swimming in the deep end, and the sun is starting to set, the shore starting to drift out of sight.

Donatello's confessions have done nothing but pierce the flesh of my already marred heart. Instead of creating the stitches it desperately needs, his words hacked and cleaved the holes even wider. It was almost better, not knowing, then I could create my own elaborate reasons for why he wrecked me. Rationalize his actions in a way that doesn't make him out to be the beast of our story. But now I can't. Now I know Donatello broke my heart twice for no other reason than he was scared. A coward, he said.

If that wasn't enough, if living with a broken heart wasn't enough, I've now lost my greatest emotional support at school. Sure, I have Sarah, but Sarah is no Jessie. Jessie filled my need for intimacy, both physical and mental. He was my grasp into the real world, the untarnished side. He's nothing more to me than another Sarah now.

I'm going home now, for winter break, but I almost wish I could have stayed at school. Buried myself in my room until I was forgotten, and the world passed me by. Christmas is usually one of my favorite times of the year; the gift giving, music, and parties. I don't think I've listened to a single Christmas song yet, and Christmas is next week. I haven't been in the mood to be merry.

I have no idea what is in store for me when I get back, the unknown making my skin itch. Donatello and I are worse off than before, and I may have left on good terms with Remy, but what now that Donatello is now claiming ownership? The only one I can count on to be normal is Beverly. Waiting to get off the plane, I grab my duffel from the top bin, waiting till I'm walking through the terminal to pull my phone out of my pocket and take it off airplane mode. There are a few messages from Jessie, asking about my flight and other bullshit. I don't want to deal with his pity texts, so I swipe them off my screen and pull up Beverly's, pressing call.

"Are you here? I don't see you."

I close my eyes in silent prayer, thank fuck something is going my way. "Uh, just a second, and I'll be outside." Walking through the exit, I stop while Bev yells into my ear.

"I see you! Look over here."

Smiling, I click the phone off, having heard her both on the phone and outside; it's not needed. She's not driving but in the back of a Famiglia car waving out the window at me. She opens the door from the inside, scooting over so I can come in, hugging me the second the door is shut, and my duffel is on the floor. "I fucking missed you. It's awful being alone with these people."

I laugh, rolling my eyes at her. "Who's all at the house?" I'm staying at her and Remy's place instead of having to deal with groceries and junk at my apartment.

"If you're asking if Donatello is there, then yes, he is." I groan, but she ignores it, speaking over me. "And yes, I've already heard all the latest tea. But I've only heard Donatello's version so…"

I can tell she's annoyed I hadn't told her anything yet. "Stop looking at me like that. You're going to give me an ulcer." She purses her lips, and I smile at her. "Just so you know, I haven't talked to anyone about any of this, so stop whatever Sarah hate you're doing in that head of yours."

"Should I have brought wine?" I laugh, the fact that it's a serious question making it even better.

"No." I run my hands over my face, rubbing almost too roughly. "I don't even know what to say to you. I'm so lost in everything right now. Sometimes I don't even feel like myself. I feel like I'm somebody's puppet…" Leaning against the headrest, I roll my head sideways to look at her. "And whoever has my strings is fucking drunk." She snorts at my description, waiting for me to continue. "I feel like I'm turning into this angry, miserable person, and I don't know how to stop."

"Well, considering I'm an angry, miserable person, I can confirm it's not so bad." I laugh while she smiles, tucking her leg up under her butt as she shifts to face me fully. "You're only nineteen, and you've had to deal with more grownup problems than most grownups, that's bound to start taking its toll at some point... Just if it ever gets to be too much, call me. Call Remy. We'll be here."

I reach and grab her hand. "I know." She scoots to the middle of the seat, and I link our fingers, feeling marginally less lost.

"I got the room above the garage set up for you." Room is kind of a stretch for the suite she's referring to.

"You did, or you had someone do it?"

She rolls her eyes at me, squeezing my hand almost painfully. "Shut up, and just say thank you."

Donatello is outside when we get there, grabbing something from his car. He probably planned it that way, trying to catch me off guard. I've been avoiding him, and up until now, it's been relatively easy to do. "I'm going to put my stuff away before I deal with... everyone." I say to Bev as we park.

"I figured you'd want to shower after your flight anyway." I open my door, dragging the duffel out with me. I can already feel Donatello's stare on my back.

"Okay, I won't be too long." I tell her, after she circles around to my side of the car, putting herself as a buffer between Donatello and me.

Smiling in thanks, I walk to the stairs leading to the garage, hearing her intercept Donatello as I get to the top. Going through the door, I toss my duffel onto the loveseat and take a deep breath. I don't really need to freshen up. I just needed a minute to mentally prepare myself. Grabbing my face wash, I go into the bathroom and wash, drying my face with one of the towels on the rack. I let my hair out of the scrunchie it's in, running my fingers through it to get out the tangles. Grabbing a pair of leggings from my bag, I swap out my skinnies for them, leaving my hoodie on, then grab my slippers. I stand and stare at the door for way longer than necessary before I walk out the door.

Chaos. That's the only word that comes to mind when I finally get down into the house. Beverly is standing in front of a fuming Remy, her back pressed to his chest and her arms out like she can use her body as a barricade as he yells over the top of her. Andrea has Donatello in a full nelson, his arms locked above his head as he jerks his upper body in an attempt to get free, yelling back to whatever Remy is saying. Dylan is even on the madness, barking and snarling from Beverly's side, ready to take out anyone who gets too close. There's a brief moment where I almost turn around and go back to the garage, almost pretend I didn't see any of their bullshit. But I don't, mostly because I know there's a ninety-nine percent chance this is about me.

"What the fuck is going on?!" I yell, but they don't even look over, so engrossed in their nonsense that my voice is swallowed up with the rest of the screaming. Grabbing a flower vase off the side table closest to me, I launch it in-between them, the loud crash bringing their attention to me. Dylan stops barking as soon as the yelling stops, a slight wag in his tail when I make eye contact with him. "What the fuck is happening?"

Beverly looks like she's about to lose it, her face red as she looks at me. "Why don't you ask your stupid fucking boyfriend and your stupid fucking brother?"

Okay? "Remy, what is happening?"

"Go back to the garage, Delaney. This isn't your concern." Remy spits, his dark gaze never leaving Donatello's.

Before I can speak up, Beverly is already yelling. "No! This is her concern. Tell her what you fuckhats are fighting about." Remy says something to her that I can't hear, and she spins to face him, looking angry as ever. "I don't fucking care anymore. Andrea, let him go." She walks towards me, leaving Remy unblocked, who immediately starts forward for Donatello.

Andrea sends a somewhat worried look towards Bev, but lets go of Donatello, dropping his arms just in time for him to dodge Remy's punch by dropping his shoulder and tackling him onto the floor. They hit the ground hard, both grunting with the impact. Donatello lands one punch to Remy's face before he's tipped. Remy sits up with a forearm punch, slamming into the side of Donatello's face twice before he's able to block it.

I watch in horror as they both land their next hit, Remy's lips splitting as Donatello's side folds sideways. "Why is no one stopping this?!" My question is mostly aimed at Andrea because there's no way Bev or I could safely jump in there.

Andrea looks over at me and shrugs, a slight shake to his head. "I'm not getting in on that. This shit isn't my problem."

Looking back at them on the floor, Remy somehow has Donatello in a chokehold, squeezing his throat with a clenched jaw. "He's going to kill him!"

Bev grabs my arm as I launch forward, stopping me while Andrea pipes up from his spot on the other side of them. "He won't kill him… probably."

When I'm positive Donatello is about to pass out, he somehow manages to get an elbow into Remy's ribs, making his arms loosen enough for him to break out of his hold.

"See, he'll be fine." Andrea says, gesturing to the two idiots on the floor. Bev slaps a hand over her mouth to hide her laugh at Andrea's comment, and I scowl at her. What's wrong with these people?

"Are we seriously just going to stand around and watch them? How long will they do this?" I wince hearing an audible crack coming from the pile of stupid on the floor.

"They look like they're getting tired." Andrea says, nodding towards them. He's right, they're both standing again attempting to put each other in a headlock, but it looks more like a weird bloody hug with how slow they're moving. "Didn't you have Christmas photos being done Saturday?" He asks Bev as he attempts to hide a smile that the question provoked, already knowing the answer.

"Fuck!" I jump at Beverly's yell, and Dylan jumps up from his spot by her feet, equally startled. "Remy Oliver Luciano, if you ruin my pictures, I will never forgive you!"

I'm not sure how she expects them to look fine, considering I can see at least one of Remy's eyes swollen shut, and his lips busted from here, but I'm not about to say anything about it. Remy knees Donatello in the side as Beverly yells, looking over at her before shoving him back and stepping out of reach. Donatello stays back only because Andrea steps forward and grabs the back of his shirt.

Donatello wipes his arm across his face, spreading blood from his nose and whatever else all over. "Fuck you, Remy."

Remy laughs, using the collar of his shirt to wipe off his mouth. "How's your nose feel you fucking piece of shit?"

Andrea lets go of Donatello's shirt, and I step forward to get their attention. Neither one of them acknowledges me as Donatello curses at Remy. "I'm pretty sure it's broken, you fucking bastard... and it fucking hurts."

Both of them snort in amusement, and I look around the room, confused as hell. "Why can't anyone in this house be normal?" I'm not asking anyone in particular, mainly because I know that no one is listening to me anyway. "Can someone please tell me what the fuck is going on now?"

Donatello looks over at me like he's just now noticing me even though I've been in the room the entire time while Remy uses his fingers to touch the side of his face that's swollen.

"This figlio di puttana came in here spouting his love for you. As if he even has the right to fucking look at you after what he did." Remy says, smiling at Bev when she throws a wet hand towel at his face like she isn't fuming.

"You're fighting because Donatello said he loves me?" I ask as Donatello catches his own cloth.

"More or less." Donatello says, trying and failing to clean his face.

"You're stupid." I point between them. "Both of you. I'm going to the garage." I spin, stomping towards the doors, yelling to Bev over my shoulder. "Tell me when dinner's done please."

I hear footsteps behind me but ignore it. "Remember, you're in my house, Donatello." Remy says as I'm walking out the door, purposefully shutting it on Donatello, who's following me.

Still stomping, I make it to the garage before Donatello, shutting the door on him once again. He pushes it open as I get to the loveseat, not looking his way.

"You've been avoiding me."

I roll my eyes, toeing off my sneakers. He just fought my brother, but he wants to talk about this. "Correct." I pull my hoodie over my head, tossing it onto the couch.

"Why?"

Frowning with annoyance, I finally turn to face him. "What the fuck do you mean why? I told you that I don't want to be with you. I don't care how sorry you are. I'm not over it. I'm still mad." I pull my hair into a top knot, using the length to wrap it tight. "I shouldn't have slept with you. That was a mistake. But it doesn't change the fact that I don't want to see you. And then to top it all off, I come home to find you and Ollie fighting in the fucking living room less than an hour after being here." He takes a few steps towards me, and I stop him with a hand in front of his chest. "Please stay away from me. I'm mad, and you're covered in blood."

He nods, looking down at his shirt. "I should shower."

"You should. At your place, leave."

He ignores me, walking into the bathroom and turning on the water. I stand in the doorway and watch him strip, getting in the shower without looking my way.

"Are you going to tell me what really happened down there?" I pinch my lip between my fingers, watching his form through the curtain.

"Remy and I have come to an agreement."

I huff, crossing my arms. "That's not what it looked like." He just hums. "About?"

He turns the water off and steps out, grabbing a towel from the rack. "You. I told him I loved you. We fought, now we're good."

I fail to see how that makes any kind of sense. "Okay, whatever. This was all unnecessary because we aren't even together, and I don't want to be."

He tries to take my hand, and I pull away. "I know you love me, Vita Mia." He says it like it's supposed to mean something. Like I should just forget everything else because of his huge revelation.

"So? Loving you has never made me anything but broken. Just because you've decided you're ready to love me doesn't mean I have to suddenly accept everything, Donatello. If you really want us to work, to be a real happy couple, I need you to give me time. I need space. I need to figure out what I want. All I wanted was you for so long, and you denied me, now I need to figure out if I think you're still worth it." I angrily wipe tears from my face. "You had your time. We played by your rules already and look where that got us. Now it's my turn."

"Fine." The way he says it makes it seem anything but fine. But I don't care.

"Fine. Let's start now." I'm walking towards my bag, my eyes off of him as he puts his pants on, keeping his bloody shirt off.

He reaches out, running his fingers over my cheek, and I close my eyes. Pretending I'm fine for the three seconds, his fingers are on my skin, giving my heart one last chance to say it's goodbye. "I'll give you your space, Vita Mia, but I won't wait forever."

My eyes open to watch him leave. "Donatello?" He looks over his shoulder at me, russet reds finding mine. "Thank you." I'm not sure what I'm thanking him for, but for once, it feels like we might actually be on the same page, that he's taking me and my wants seriously.

"Qualsiasi cosa per te, Piccola." *Anything for you, Baby.*

I sit on the couch as soon as he's out of sight, grabbing the pillow beside me to scream into. I know this is what I need, so why does it hurt so fucking much. I throw the pillow back onto the couch, watching as it bounces onto the floor. With a loud sigh, I lay back on the cushions. I have a feeling this will be my most miserable Christmas yet.

Chapter Nineteen

At what point do we stop looking into the past for answers? Stop relying on those treasured moments to hide the current pain. Stop using the sweet memories as fuel to keep going, to stop from breaking further. When do we stop using our past as a way to survive the present?

At what point do we just admit we're lost.

When do we look at those memories and see all the things we've chosen to forget, see the mold that was woven into the threads. Notice that the glowing haze isn't our fondness seeping through the seams, but the spread of fungi infecting our brains. When do we see that it's morphed what we once knew to be true with our wishful wants, making those memories we cherish nothing but intricate fabrications?

When do I acknowledge that it's more than just my heart's that broken?

Knowing and acknowledging are two completely different things. I know I've been weaving my threads of truths with the threads of want. I know I've been living in my pretend land where I'm doing better than I actually am. I know I've been crawling deeper into unknown territories on the inside of my mind, putting up a stronger face than I actually have to give.

I've been clinging to all my moments, reliving them inside my head, pretending I see Donatello in the same light. I've held on to all of the good memories, but some of the more painful ones started to slip in, reminding me that what Donatello and I had wasn't the fairytale kind of love I was pretending it was. Every good memory is shadowed by one a little darker, more sinister. My castle has been raided, my knight in shining armor nothing but a beast holding a sword, a sword that he used on me. Cutting and slashing at me until I was weak, my will bending to his.

I believe that he believes he loves me. I believe he believes that he won't hurt me again. I believe he believes he's remorseful. But I don't know that I believe those things, no matter how hard I pretend I do.

But my knight has already weakened my resolve, already made me forget how to stand on my own, making sure I've lost my ability to decipher what I truly want, what I truly need. My knight has broken more than just my heart. He's broken my mind. I can't think through the fog that clouds my mind anymore. My feet are stuck in the mud, and I'm too tired to pull them out. I'm living in a constant rotation of being sad and unsure.

Donatello is the only thing that stays clear in my mind, the only thing I know to cling to, to see my way out of the fog. Even though his touch burns and bubbles up my skin, the venom of his previous transgressions eating away at my flesh, he's all my sad, stupid heart wants. I've spent countless hours crying and pleading for someone else, but my pleas fall upon deaf ears. I'm being held prisoner by my own heart, forced to love someone I don't know if I can ever trust again. Forced to love someone I don't want. I love him in my heart, but not in my head.

It's become hard for me to find the pleasure in things I used to; I find myself wishing to be with the stars, wanting to dance across the moon. My grades are slipping. I've taken leave from the equestrian team. Sometimes I forget to eat. Spending hours upon hours daydreaming about those stars.

"Laney girl, did you hear me?" Jessie comes back into focus, and I stare at his beautiful blue eyes and force a smile I don't feel. By the look on his face, he knows I wasn't listening. "What time do you need to be at practice? I can drop you off."

Practice? He must mean at the stables. I may have forgotten to tell him I extended my leave. I'm still riding a few times a week, but just to make sure the horses get exercise. "I don't have practice. I'm still on leave."

He's frowning now. It's something he's done a lot around me lately. My sweet Jessie can probably see through the mask I've been wearing. "I thought you were going back this week?"

"I was." I pick my pencil back up, noticing that I put it down at some point and start drawing on my paper. "Now, I'm not." I give him a closed mouth smile, the only one I can muster right now.

He's looking at me in a way that always makes my heart squeeze. I know he's concerned for me. I'm concerned for me. It makes me sad that I'm sad. It makes me sad that I'm making him sad. Logically I know I'm destroying our friendship. I know I could potentially ruin my college and competition career if I keep this up. Logically I know I shouldn't feel this way. Knowing that doesn't make it any better, it makes it worse. Because even knowing, I can't stop. I can't stop my downward spiral.

"Have you talked to Donatello lately?"

I drop my eyes to my paper, continuing my doodles. He's fishing. "Yes."

"Has he seen you recently?"

I pause my drawing at his phrasing. He wants to know if Donatello sees what he sees. "We aren't together, Jessie. He has no reason to come see me." I raise my eyes to him before he can speak. "And it was my choice."

"How about Beverly? I haven't seen you video chat in a while." He's being kind, trying to find the best way to help, trying to figure out what's wrong with me. I appreciate his efforts, but I don't want help. I don't want to have to need it. I'm tired of not being what I need on my own. I'm tired of everything.

"We talked yesterday." I go back to shading in my moon, smudging the lead with my finger. I'm lying. A little white lie, really. Beverly texted me, and I didn't respond.

His hand is suddenly on mine, drawing my gaze. "You'd tell me if you needed help right, Laney girl?" Silver hair falls over his brow as he looks at my face, and I watch the strands as they lift in the slight breeze. "You know you can come to me for anything. I'm your best friend... remember?"

My eyes catch on his smile, unable to look at his baby blues. "Of course."

I failed my midterms and not just for one, but all four of my classes. I've never failed at anything. I held over a 3.8 GPA in all of them, so I'm still technically passing the classes themselves, and that's all that matters, right? Passing a trash can, I drop my entire binder into it without pause, continuing even after someone shouts that I've dropped something. Jessie said he'd give me a ride back to the Hall, but I want to walk, want to feel the spring sun warming up the back of my hoodie. I should text him not to wait, but I'm not going to. He'll either figure it out or he won't.

Spring break is next week, and I had originally planned on going home, but now I'm not sure. I'm not ready to address why I've been distant. I'm not ready to jump headfirst into the drama that comes with all of them. Seeing them all feels like a chore, I want to put off as long as possible. Jessie is leaving, probably because he doesn't know I'm not. I'm both grateful and sad over that. I want him to stay, to keep me company, but I also just want to be alone. If I'm alone, no one can force me to pretend. I can drown in peace.

Sarah is packing a bag when I get to the suite, smiling like always. She's on the phone, and thankfully, her attention is not on me so that I can slip into my room unbothered. I'm sure she'll come say bye later since she and Derek are going home tonight, leaving a day early, if I'm not sleeping or pretending to be. I'm also sure she'll ask if Jessie is coming to stay, and I'll tell her yes, so she doesn't worry even though he's not.

I change into a loose tee and sweats, closing my blackout curtains and turning on my star projector I lay on the bed, staring up at the constellations painted across the ceiling and walls. I've found that counting them, telling myself random facts and stories about them helps me gather myself. These stars are the only thing I haven't lost a grasp on, the only constant. They may shift in location, but they always stay the same.

I know he's here before I see him. It's always been like that with him. I can feel him, see him even with my eyes closed. I feel the brush of his fingers over my face, feel his fingers sticking in my messy hair. I can smell his cinnamon breath, feel it hitting my face. I don't know how he got in the building, knew what suite I'd be in, I just know that this is without a doubt, my knight.

I finally open my eyes, blink through the haze of just waking up. I'm lying on my stomach; face turned towards where he is kneeling by the bed. He's not smiling when my eyes focus enough to see him. "Why are you here?"

He rests his chin on the bed, his hand still splayed over the side of my face and head. "You didn't come home. Remy was worried when you weren't answering your phone."

My chest feels heavy, and I close my eyes again, attempting to banish the feeling. I should have told Remy. I shouldn't have made him worry, not after what happened to Beverly. There's always something I should've done differently. I don't say any of that to Donatello though, just keep my eyes closed.

"Delaney." His voice is loud in the room. I've gotten used to the quiet. I open my eyes to acknowledge him, shifting my face under his palm. "How long have you been in bed, Baby?"

I shrug, biting at my lower lip while I try to think of what day it is. Sarah left Thursday night, and I've pretty much been in my room since. I don't even know where my phone is. "Friday?" I can tell that's not the answer he was hoping for, based on the way his gaze shifts around my dark room and back. His long exhale hitting me in the face. "Maybe it wasn't then… maybe it's only been since Sunday." I say, trying to redeem myself, erase the concern from his features. I don't want to see it on his; I don't want him to know how far I've fallen down the rabbit hole.

"It's Tuesday, Vita Mia."

I shut my eyes on his words, shutting out his face along with them. Embarrassed and ashamed. I know that I can't help it, that I'm not being like this on purpose. But that doesn't make me feel any less pathetic. I feel more. Because I know and can't fix it. Everything. It's the same for everything all the time now. Feeling bad for feeling the way I'm feeling because I know I shouldn't. An endless loop.

My eyes open when I feel Donatello pulling away. A moment of panic smacking me in the chest. I don't want him here, but I also don't want him to leave. "Where are you going?"

"You need to shower, and you need to eat. It's time to get out of bed." He's right. I know he is. But I don't want to do that.

"I'm fine." I sit up, pushing the blankets from my legs as he watches. "No need to be worried."

His eyes don't leave my face. "I'm going to turn the shower on, and you're going to get in it."

I look down at my hands at his response. Nodding because I know he'll stand there until I respond. Turning so, my legs are dangling off the end of the bed, watch as he turns the shower on and adjusts the temperature through the attached bathroom door. I get up when I see he's done, walk myself in there before he tries to take it upon himself to do so. His eyes are brushing along my skin as I undress, but they hold a look of concern, not lust. He stays in the bathroom while I shower, watching me through the frosted curtain. I can't see his expression, just his outline, but I don't have to see it to know he's worried. If I were him, I probably would be, too.

I'm struggling to get a knot from the back of my head, my waves tangled from laying on them for so long. He must sense that I need help, because he opens the curtain, eyes going to my hands in my hair. "Can I help you?"

I just nod again, dropping my arms. I see his form opening drawers, watch as he comes back to the curtain with a comb. He motions for me to turn around, so I do. He points at my conditioner, and I hand it to him. He tells me to rinse, and I turn into the spray, washing the soap out. He watches me as I finish, his shirt wet and splotched from the shower. He doesn't leave the room to change, just pulls it over his head, and drops it onto the floor by my clothes. When I turn the shower off, he holds a towel out for me, wrapping me up in it.

He picks me up, cradle style, and brings me back into the room, setting me on the bed while he goes through my dresser and closet, pulling out underwear, a tee, and cotton shorts. He waits until I'm dressed before he grabs my towel and sits on the edge of the bed, settling me between his legs. He uses the towel to dry my hair, finger combing the strands he pulls it into a loose braid, wrapping a band from my dresser around the end. Once he's finished, he scoots farther back on the bed, so he's leaning against the headboard, and I'm in his lap. I feel the soft press of his lips on my shoulder where the wide collar of my tee has pulled down and I run my fingers into his hair, holding his face against me.

"No more time, Baby." He kisses my shoulder again; his lips brushing my skin when he speaks. "No more space." Another kiss. "Just as friends, I won't ask for anything more... but let me stay. Let me help you."

I don't use words to answer, just keep my fingers in his hair, rest my cheek against his head. I don't want his help, but I need it. I don't want him, but I need him.

Besides getting me food, we stay like that. He doesn't make me talk, doesn't ask me questions when I turn on my star projector, just quietly listens to my ramblings, offering me comfort with his presence and touch. The wolf in sheep's clothing, comforting his lamb.

Donatello gave me to the end of spring break to stay in my cocoon. He stayed with me every night, made me develop a routine of sorts to keep me from saying in bed too long. At the end of spring break, he unofficially moved me out of the dorms and into an apartment he rented where he could essentially babysit me; make sure I didn't drown.

The first night I broke down and lost it. I broke things. I screamed. I cried. I poured out everything I'd been keeping to myself, letting all of my hurt dump onto Donatello like a landslide. He let me hit him. He let me scream. He let me cry... but he didn't leave. He rocked me through my sobs and wiped the tears from my skin. The next morning, he continued on like it never happened, made sure I got up, made sure I ate, made sure I went to class.

He held me to my routine, made me spend time with my friends, including Jessie. He made me grovel to get back onto the equestrian team and attended every practice with me. After weeks that felt like years, I slowly started to feel myself coming back together. Slowly felt my mind coming back to me. I'd let myself get so lost in the deep that I'd forgotten which way to go for air, but I can see the light of the sky shining beams below the surface now. Can almost graze my fingertips along the surface.

Confident I can float on my own now, I'm moving back into my room with Sarah for the last two weeks before summer break, and Donatello is going home. As I watch him throw his duffel into the back of his car, I can't help but feel anxious. I know he needs to go back; Andrea and Remy have been doing his share of the work so he could be here with me, but part of me wishes he could stay.

He comes up to where I'm standing on the sidewalk, grinning in a way that I can't help but smile back at. "Why are you smiling like that?"

He frowns in jest, standing down on the street, so my eyes are level with his. "Is this better?"

I roll my eyes. "Yes."

He chuckles, tucking his hands in his pockets, and I almost wish he would have touched me instead. "You're coming home in two weeks, yea?"

I let out a loud breath and nod, biting my lip. I wish I were going home now.

"You'll call me?"

I smile, nodding again. "Yes. And yes, to whatever else you're going to ask."

"Good." His lopsided grin tugs at my heart as he backs towards his car, quickly looking at the vacant street to make sure it's clear. "Bye, Delaney."

I can't do it. He stops when I start his way, pulls his hands from his pockets just in time to catch me. I wrap around him, burying my face in his neck. He has an arm across my back, the other holding the back of my head, his thumb rubbing the back of my nape. "I don't want you to go." I tighten my arms even more. Close my eyes and let my heart soak him in.

"Two weeks, that's nothing." He kisses the side of my head, speaking against my hair. "Two weeks, Baby. Focus on finals, then come home."

"Yours or mine?"

"Yours, I'll help you unpack… because I'm a great best friend."

I smile against his neck. "Jessie says he's my best friend."

"Jessie can fuck off." I laugh and sit back so I can look into his face. "Now quit stalling, I really do need to leave."

He lets me drop, and I step back so he can open his car door. He turns and kisses my forehead before sitting in the driver's seat and starting the car. "I… I'll miss you." It's the closest to what I want to say, but I'm not ready to say.

He smiles, shutting his door and speaking through the open window. "I love you too, Vita Mia."

Epilogue

It's always when you're looking forward to something that time seems to drag on. That's how the last two weeks have felt, endless. I passed my finals and my classes, but I'll probably end up retaking most of them because I barely passed. I'm nervous to see Bev and Remy, but also excited. I missed them; I just don't want it to be awkward. I don't want them to think I purposefully chose not to reach out to them when I was sinking. But that's a problem for tomorrow.

I knock once on Donatello's door before walking inside, leaving my things by the door and walking through the house to the back where I know he'll be. The french doors are open to outside, and I stand in the doorway, smiling when I see Donatello shirtless and bent over an upside-down lawnmower. I whistle when he doesn't notice me, fireflies tickling my gut when he looks my way.

He drops whatever he was holding and stands, brushing his pants off as I walk over to him. "I didn't know you were a handyman."

He laughs. "I'm not. I have no fucking idea what I'm doing."

Snorting, I meet him in the grass, smiling up at him. "I'm back."

His fingers brush along my cheek, and I live in the touch, tilting my face to feel more of his skin. "You're back."

"Did you miss me?" I know he did, I could hear it in every phone call, hear how much he wanted to be with me in every word, but I like hearing him say it out loud.

"Mi sei mancato più di quanto alla luna mancheresti le stelle." *I missed you more than the moon would miss the stars.*

I hug him, resting my ear over his heart. "I want to stay here…" I pull my face back, kissing his chest before looking into his face. "Permanently. I want to move in with you." He grins, and I trace his bottom lip with my fingertip. "I want to transfer to a university here so that I can see everyone more often." I wrap my arms around his neck, and he picks me up, immediately plopping into the grass with me on his lap. "I want to be with you. For real this time… I want what I didn't get before. I want all of you." I need all of him. Because he already owns all of me.

"You already have me, Vita Mia, you always did. I was just too stupid to admit it." He kisses the corner of my lips, fingers in my hair. "You're my moon, my stars, my sun. You're Vita Mia, my life. I'm obsessed with everything that is you. I'll do whatever you want to do, give whatever you need me to." He kisses the other corner, his thumbs brushing along my temples. "I love you, Delaney Luciano, and I won't ever keep that a secret again. I want everyone to see. Everyone to know." He kisses me, holding my face almost too hard like he's afraid I'll pull away. "Marry me."

I don't know what to say, so I just kiss him instead, my own hands framing his cheeks as I savor the kind of touch I've craved for weeks. Melt into the taste of Big Red on his tongue and the spice of his skin. I pull back, out of breath and lips wet from his kisses. "I love you." It's the first time I can say it without it hurting, and I smile, repeating the words. "I love you." I press another closed mouth kiss to his lips. "But I'm not going to marry you."

He frowns and I laugh, kissing his cheeks.

"I love you, but we are not there yet. I'm not there yet." He's still frowning but it's less deep. "I'm not even twenty, Donatello. I'm still in school, I can't marry you."

His frown turns into a slow grin. "Rock, paper, scissors..." He pauses to laugh when my head starts shaking no. "Thumb war?" He tickles my sides when I mouth no, and I laugh. "What about Candyland?"

"No to all of that, but especially to Candyland. I can't even look at that stupid game without getting mad."

"Fine, Vita Mia. Your rules this time." He leans back on his elbows, looking up at me with his lopsided grin. "What did the fish say when he swam into a wall?"

"What?"

"Dam."

Author Note

We get one shot at living this life, don't waste it by letting someone love you the wrong way. And let's be honest here, Donatello loved Delaney the wrong way for a while. This was not the ending I wanted for these two; I wanted Delaney to tell Donatello to shove it and let him live out his days wishing he would have done things differently. If I were Delaney that's what I would have done. But I'm not Delaney and for reasons I still fail to understand, she was adamant that she got her shot at a happily ever after with Donatello. So, I gave them a fairly happy ending, right? They're together and happy. BUT who else loved Jessie? He's still whispering in my ear for some time with Delaney and I couldn't resist; He is coming back IN A BIG WAY. Just saying.

Besides all that...I truly hope you enjoyed this part of their story. Even with all of my qualms with their relationship, I am happy with how things concluded in the book. Thank you all for the likes, comments, shares, follows and reads. Your support is beyond amazing and there could never be enough words to express my gratitude. So seriously, thank you – AJ

Sneak Peek Blurb

MY GIRL

-JESSIE-

Delaney Luciano thinks her heart only sings for that Bastardo Donatello, but I've heard its sweet whispers. Every tired confession. Every desperate plea.

My Laney Girl doesn't know it yet, but I'm what her poor bandaged heart really wants. What it really needs.

I'm coming to take back what I never should have let walk away. I'm coming for my girl.

Stay updated on all things AJ by following
her social accounts:

:camera: AJWOLF_AUTHOR

:pinterest: AJWOLFAUTHOR

g AJWOLF_AUTHOR

FACEBOOK READER GROUP:
AJ WOLF'S PACK